Saros Cowa...
Regina. Bef...
years an A...
Bombay. Ed...
several critical studies, novels and short stories.

For
Hedy Miller
with all good wishes

Saros

24 June '97

By the same author

Fiction

Stories and Sketches
Goodbye to Elsa
Nude Therapy
The Last of the Maharajas (screenplay)
Suffer Little Children
Stories from the Raj (ed.)
Modern Indian Short Stories (ed.)
More Stories from the Raj and After (ed.)

Criticism

Sean O'Casey: The Man Behind the Plays
O'Casey
So Many Freedoms: A Study of the Major Fiction of Mulk Raj Anand
'Coolie': An Assessment
Author to Critic: The Letters of Mulk Raj Anand (ed.)

Women Writers of the Raj

Short Fiction from Kipling to Independence

Selected and Introduced by Saros Cowasjee

GRAFTON BOOKS
A Division of the Collins Publishing Group

LONDON GLASGOW
TORONTO SYDNEY AUCKLAND

Grafton Books
A Division of the Collins Publishing Group
8 Grafton Street, London W1X 3LA

A Grafton Paperback Original 1990

This selection and introduction copyright © Saros Cowasjee 1990

ISBN 0-586-20563-2

Printed and bound in Great Britain by
Collins, Glasgow

Set in Plantin

All rights reserved. No part of this publication may
be reproduced, stored in a retrieval system, or
transmitted, in any form, or by any means, electronic,
mechanical, photocopying, recording or otherwise,
without the prior permission of the publishers.

This book is sold subject to the condition that it
shall not, by way of trade or otherwise, be lent,
re-sold, hired out or otherwise circulated
without the publisher's prior consent in any
form of binding or cover other than that in
which it is published and without a similar
condition including this condition being imposed
on the subsequent purchaser.

CONTENTS

Acknowledgements, 7
Introduction by Saros Cowasjee, 9

FLORA ANNIE STEEL:
   The Doll-Maker, 22
   At the Great Durbar, 33
   The Gift of Battle, 51
   The Shâhbâsh Wallah, 64
   Surâbhi, 80
   'London', 91
   The Squaring of the Gods, 105

BITHIA MARY CROKER:
   Jack Straw's Castle, 120

SARA JEANNETTE DUNCAN:
   The Pool in the Desert, 125

ETHEL WINIFRED SAVI:
   The Interloper, 157

ALICE PERRIN:
   Mary Jones, 172
   Caulfield's Crime, 181
   Ann White, 191
   The Fakirs' Island, 205

MAUD DIVER:
   Sunia: A Himalayan Idyll, 215

KATHERINE MAYO:
   The Old Grey Cow, 233

CHRISTINE WESTON:
  The Mud Horse, 240
  The Mangoes Are Gone, 247
  Mimosa, 254

Biographical Notes, 260

Glossary of Indian Words and Phrases, 263

Fiction by women writers in
  Stories from the Raj (1983) and
  More Stories from the Raj and After (1986), 266

ACKNOWLEDGEMENTS

Thanks are due to the following copyright holders for permission to reprint the stories listed:

'The Old Grey Cow' by Katherine Mayo (Jonathan Cape Ltd and Harcourt Brace Jovanovich Inc.); 'The Mud Horse', 'The Mangoes Are Gone' and 'Mimosa' by Christine Weston (the author).

Every effort has been made to trace the owners of copyright material but in some cases we have not been successful. We apologize to those our enquiries did not reach and invite them to apply to Grafton Books for proper acknowledgement, if it is due.

EDITOR'S NOTE

The Editor wishes to thank the Associate Vice-President (Research) of the University of Regina, Regina, and the Indian Institute of the Bodleian Library, Oxford, for help received.

The spellings of Indian place names and Indian words have not been changed or modernised but retained as they appeared in the stories when they were first published.

To the memory of 'Baby Darling'

INTRODUCTION
Saros Cowasjee

It is one of the ironies of the Raj that while Anglo-Indian*
women have been repeatedly censured by male writers for
their lack of sympathy and understanding of India, a gifted
few of these very women have provided us with the best
insight into the Indian mind and family. The attack on the
Anglo-Indian woman ('memsahib' as she is known in India)
pre-dates Kipling, who gave us the notorious Mrs Reiver
and Mrs Hauksbee. But Kipling was not wholly critical of
Anglo-Indian women, as can be seen from stories like
'William the Conqueror' – a song of praise for those women
who helped administer the Raj. It was the poet and publicist
Wilfred Scawen Blunt who in 1885 made the first significant
attack on Anglo-Indian women in his *Ideas About India*:

The Englishwoman in India during the last thirty years has been
the cause of half the bitter feelings there between race and race. It
was her presence at Cawnpore and Lucknow that pointed the
sword of revenge after the Mutiny, and it is her constantly
increasing influence now that widens the gulf of ill-feeling and
makes amalgamation daily more impossible. I have over and over
noticed this. The English collector, or the English doctor, or the
English judge may have the best will in the world to meet their
Indian neighbours . . . on equal terms. Their wives will hear of
nothing of the sort, and the result is a meaningless interchange of
cold civilities.

* The term 'Anglo-Indian' was applied originally to the British in
India, and only later to people of mixed British and Indian descent. Here
it is used in its original meaning.

Add to this some of the lesser charges brought against Anglo-Indian women – their life of idleness and frivolity, their scandal-mongering and flirtations, their insensitivity and their rudeness towards Indians – and you have the conventional portrait of the memsahib with all her traits. And it was with one or more of these traits that she was portrayed by E. M. Forster, George Orwell, Dennis Kincaid, J. R. Ackerley and Edmund Candler.

Taken piecemeal, what the men writers say about Anglo-Indian women is true, and even women writers such as Ethel Winifred Savi and Flora Annie Steel admit to the shortcomings of their fictional counterparts. What is false is the overall picture that ignores the resolution and fortitude with which many Anglo-Indian women faced an emotionally difficult life in India. Equally false is the notion that the majority of these women hindered their men from establishing a cordial relationship with Indians. Maud Diver, as early as in 1909, pleaded in *The Englishwoman in India* for sympathy and understanding, and reminded a questioning public in England that 'India's heroines and martyrs far outnumber her social sinners'. In recent years several well-documented studies have striven to set the record straight; among these are Pat Barr's *The Memsahibs: The Women of Victorian India* (1976), Marian Fowler's *Below the Peacock Fan: First Ladies of the Raj* (1987), Margaret MacMillan's *Women of the Raj* (1988) and Mary Ann Lind's *The Compassionate Memsahibs* (1988).

That the stereotyped portrait of the memsahib should still persist in the popular imagination is, of course, a tribute to the fictional artistry of Kipling, Forster and Orwell. The present anthology of short stories by women writers cannot wholly correct this imbalance, but it does go to show that their achievements have not always been fully acknowledged. For let it be said outright that the contribution of Anglo-Indian women in the field of short fiction outstrips that of the men. No doubt the women writers have had the advantage that, except for Kipling, none of the major men writers of the Raj wrote short stories about India. Forster did not write any, nor did Ackerley, Dennis Kincaid or Edward Thompson. The stories of Orwell and Leonard Woolf do not add up to even half a dozen and they are not strictly about India. Philip Mason's collection *Whatever Dies* was published a year after the end of the Raj. This leaves only Kipling, formidable story-teller that he is, to contend with.

A factor which gave the women writers an edge over their male counterparts was their access to the Indian domestic life – to the women behind the *purdah*. The tragedy of the mute and suppressed Indian women touched them deeply, and some, like Katherine Mayo, gave expression to that tragedy with a wholesale attack on Indian religions and customs. Others, like Maud Diver, Bithia Mary Croker and Flora Annie Steel, offered a more subdued though none the less stringent criticism. Steel, who learned the Indian languages and dialects which came her way, is easily the most perceptive observer among Anglo-Indian writers. Her admission that India 'is a hard country for a Westerner to grasp' leads her to examine the Indian psyche closely and not to pass judgement based on European mores.

The women writers did not, however, confine themselves to portraying Indian domestic life. A good few of them wrote on subjects which male writers had marked as their own. Among these subjects were hunting, soldiering, administration of justice, and blood feuds on the Frontier. Alice Perrin's 'Caulfield's Crime' and Flora Annie Steel's

'The Gift of Battle' are the two stories in the present volume which show the female writer poaching, as it were, on a male preserve – two stories among many that might have been selected. Flora Annie Steel travelled widely with her husband, who was a district officer in the Punjab, and came to know the Pathans intimately. Her 'Faizullah', set in the northwest province of Baluchistan, is something Kipling himself might have written with its blood-letting, jealousy, intrigues and primitive passions.

I shall allow myself one more general observation on the women writers. Almost without exception they remained the staunchest adherents of the Raj. Except for Christine Weston, none of them shared Forster's view that Indians should be treated as equals, or Orwell's ambivalence on the question of Indians governing themselves. They believed in upholding British 'prestige' and could never have agreed with Orwell that the Raj was a gigantic confidence trick. Their conservatism can be gauged from the fact that many of them approved of General Reginald Dyer's massacre of unarmed Indians at Jallianwalla Bagh in 1919, and a few even contributed to the Dyer Appreciation Fund which raised £26,000 for the dismissed general. This conservatism, the most serious shortcoming of the Anglo-Indian women, emanated from the horrors that had befallen them during the Mutiny, and every political agitation on the part of the Indians seemed to raise in them the fears of another mutiny. But their attitude towards India can be attributed in large part to an innate sense of racial superiority from which even Flora Annie Steel was not free. Pat Barr tells us that Steel 'was a natural-born autocrat of a not entirely benevolent type'. In *The Complete Indian Homekeeper and Cook* (1888), Steel recommended a 'system of rewards and punishments' to be adopted towards servants – the truly incorrigible to be dosed with castor oil. It is no surprise that in most of her stories, as well as in the stories of other Anglo-Indian writers, the good Indian is the obedient Indian, and the best Indian has a childlike dependence on the English rulers.

The stories in this collection are a sampling of the best written by women during the Raj. Others equally good, and perhaps one or two even better than some of the stories found here, are included in my two companion volumes, *Stories from the Raj* (1983) and *More Stories from the Raj and After* (1986).* One among these deserves special mention: Sara Jeannette Duncan's 'A Mother in India'. It deals with the estrangement of parents and children – a painful concomitant of the British presence in India. (Most Anglo-Indian parents were forced to send their children to England at an early age for reasons of health and schooling, while they stayed back to nurse a wound which, as one mother puts it, 'never heals at all'.) Helena, on a visit to England to see her daughter Cecily after a separation of five years, is led to her child sleeping in a crib. 'Won't you kiss her?' the child's well-meaning guardian asks the visiting mother. 'I don't think I could take such an advantage of her,' replies the mother. A few moments later she drops the ironic mask and admits her loss without a trace of sentimentality: 'I may have been Cecily's mother in theory, but I was John's wife in fact.' To choose between husband and child was the tragic lot of these women, and they knew that they would have to fail either as wife or mother.

Among the women writers, Flora Annie Steel, Alice Perrin and Christine Weston deserve a high place. Steel's pre-eminence rests on a sympathetic understanding of those Indian ways and attitudes which most Europeans find

---

* The titles of the stories are listed at the end of this book for quick reference.

frustrating. For example, speaking of the Indian irreverence for time in her autobiography, *The Garden of Fidelity* (1929), she observes that

> . . . one of the first lessons to learn in India is that 'Time is nought'. At first it is exasperating; but when one comes to realize the philosophic truth which underlies the crude statement one is forced to respect it.

The same grasp of philosophic truth underlies one of her best short stories, 'The Doll-Maker'. An old servant, who has outlived his usefulness, makes a rag doll and gives it to his master and mistress as a Christmas gift for their children:

> 'It is for the child-people,' he said, in his cracked old voice. 'This dust-like one has nothing else, but a doll is always a doll to them, as a child is a child to the man and the woman.'

The children have been packed off to England, and the husband and wife, their lives now empty, are drifting apart. But the rag doll kindles memories of the past and the couple make an attempt at being together. In the simple observation of the doll-maker – 'a child is a child to the man and the woman' – there is the wisdom of the ages.

In her portrayal of the Indian peasantry, Steel reveals her power of observation, her narrative skill, and her sense of humour. Her humour is, in fact, one of the distinguishing features of her story-telling style. She has a singular way of portraying the ridiculous without ridiculing it. 'London' is the story of an illiterate farmer who goes to London to implore the great Queen herself to settle his land claim. The story brings out those qualities of the Indian farmer (his simplicity, his courage, his perseverance and his reliance on British justice) that have endeared him to generations of Anglo-Indians. It also throws light on the hard-working district officer, a familiar figure in Anglo-Indian fiction, and the rules and the red-tape that forever hampers even the most efficient of bureaucracies.

There are few stories funnier than 'At the Great Durbar'. Nânuk, an old Sikh farmer whose crops have been destroyed by rats, sets out to seek the *Lât-sahib* – 'the vice-regent of God upon earth' – to tell him why he cannot afford to pay the taxes. To make his case fool-proof, he takes along a captured rat from his field, for the law requires the presence of both plaintiff and defendant. Instead of the *Lât-sahib*, he stumbles on the intoxicated Private Smith on guard duty who beckons him to partake of the bottle:

'Come now, Johnny, don't be a fool – it's rum, I tell yer, and you Sickies ain't afraid o' rum. Wot! you won't drink 'er 'elth, you mutineering nigger? Then I'll make yer. Feel that – now then, "'Ere's a 'elth unto'w her Majesty."'

Beneath the buoyant humour of 'At the Great Durbar', and of "London" as well, there is a remarkably accurate portrait of the Indian peasant and his agrarian problems. We learn something about his fatal attachment to the land, the complicated ownership laws, the power of the money-lender, and the caprices of nature on which ultimately the harvest depends. But never for a moment do we feel that the author is instructing us at the cost of the story itself. Not a sentence, not a word, seems out of place.

Though Steel admits that she prefers the Muslims to the Hindus (as indeed did most Anglo-Indians), she never reveals her personal preferences in her stories. Her even-handedness is most evident in 'The Gift of Battle', where two hereditary enemies, a Hindu and a Muslim, are appointed to the Bench as honorary magistrates. Despite their hatred for one another, they find themselves on the same side while dispensing justice. And they go down together when in their zeal for absolute justice they overreach themselves. The story refutes the cliché *divide et impera* as applied to British rule in India; moreover, it is an admission that Hindus and Muslims can work together for the betterment of both people. But to draw a moral is to deprive the story of its subtlety, and its many nuances.

The stories of Alice Perrin in this volume do not by themselves illustrate her versatility and should therefore be read in conjunction with four of her other stories included in my previous two Raj anthologies: 'The Rise of Ram Din', 'The Centipede', 'Justice' and 'The White Tiger'. In the first two, Perrin offers brilliant satiric portraits of the English and the Indians. Without revealing any of her own biases, she brings the two races into contact and allows them to settle their differences. In the latter two, she reveals the Indian fondness for duplicity and intrigue. In the story 'Justice', no justice is done, for the English judge cannot comprehend how any man 'black or white' could murder his own mother to be avenged on his neighbour. In 'The White Tiger', a villager, Kowta, steals the mangled body of his half-brother, Mar Singh, to use it as a bait to kill the famed tiger and claim the reward. Her Indian characters live up to the description found in a phrase of Kipling's: 'half devil and half child'.

Kipling's influence on Perrin is particularly strong. The title of her very first collection of short stories, *East of Suez* (1901), is taken from Kipling's famous lines:

> Ship me somewheres east of Suez, where the best is like the worst,
> Where there aren't no Ten Commandments an' a man can raise a thirst.

Like Kipling's, many of her stories are set in remote places and, like Kipling, she is interested in the occult and the supernatural. Of her four stories included in this collection, the supernatural in one form or another is present in three. It is strongest in 'Caulfield's Crime', where an Englishman is haunted by a jackal that has earlier fed on the corpse of a *fakir* whom he (the Englishman) had wantonly killed. But Perrin is rarely interested in the supernatural for its own sake. 'Caulfield's Crime' focuses on what happens to an Englishman when he loses his moorings, and the way India often brutalizes its rulers. The theme of brutalization is also central to Bithia Mary Croker's 'Jack Straw's Castle', but it finds its most extensive treatment in the portrayal of the timber merchant Ellis in Orwell's *Burmese Days* (1934). However, with Orwell there was a straightforward solution to the problem – get out of India and let the Indians manage their own affairs. With this solution, Perrin could never have agreed. She was a true daughter of the Raj, but it is a measure of her integrity as an artist that she never sought answers to the questions she posed in her writings.

Much of Perrin's fiction is marked by violence, sudden deaths and disasters. This comes as no surprise in a land where death from smallpox, cholera, plague, rabies and snake-bites was not uncommon, and where malaria alone is estimated to have accounted for a million fatalities a year. In 'Ann White' we learn something of the horrors of the Indian Mutiny and the ever-present British fear of another massacre. In 'The Fakirs' Island' we are given a frightening picture of the Hindu Khoom Festival (as vividly recapitulated as the festival of the Great Eclipse in Steel's 'The Squaring of the Gods'), and the dreadful curse a *fakir* puts upon the young Englishwoman. But there is one story of quite a different kind – 'Mary Jones'. Its theme is exile. Mary Jones's unintelligible mutterings in Hindustani, her deathbed song and dance, made grotesque by her cracked nasal voice and withered body, speak of the exile's unrest better than any intelligible utterance might.

Christine Weston, the only surviving woman writer of the Raj, does not share the imperial zeal of the other women writers. She has a deep affection for India, which she describes as a 'beautiful, brown, kindly land'. Her novel, *Indigo* (1943), praised by E. M. Forster and often compared to Forster's own *A Passage to India* (1924), provides a compassionate awareness of the social, political, racial and religious issues that dominate the sub-continent. Her delightful short stories, many of which were first published in *The New Yorker* and later put together in a volume entitled *There and Then* (1947), are created from episodes taken mainly from her childhood. They are narrated from the viewpoint of a young girl in the company of her brother, and her brother and parents often appear as principal characters.

The stories are built on small happenings, but when seen through the eyes of children they grow large and haunting. In the child's perception of the world there is wonder, candour, astonishment – all of which Weston conveys admirably. But what gives the stories their unique flavour is the interplay between the children's intuitive wisdom on the one hand and their limited perception on the other. In 'The Mangoes Are Gone', the children rightly surmise that Mahala, the keeper of the mango grove, has fled from shame because the mangoes were stolen. But the possibility that the household servants might have connived in the theft does not occur to them. The story thus works on two different planes: that of the children and that of the adult reader.

The best of Weston's stories carry a meaning far beyond the obvious. 'The Mud Horse', for instance, which deals with the make-believe world of children, contrasts the self-assurance and confidence of Kulloo, the six-year-old Indian boy, with the arrogance and hysteria of the slightly older white boy. But for the perceptive reader it accomplishes something far more significant than this simple contrast: it reveals in miniature an ugly picture of the British incivility towards Indians; it exposes the infection that has poisoned relationships between the two races for generations and now forebodes the end of the Raj. Kulloo and the white boy of today's 'The Mud Horse' may well grow up to be the susceptible Vasi and the bullying white lawyer of tomorrow's 'A Game of Halma' – another of Weston's disturbing stories.

Among the other stories in this volume is Maud Diver's 'Sunia: A Himalayan Idyll'. It deals with the vexed question of intermarriage (and concubinage) between the two races and shows the strong influence of Kipling's 'Lispeth' and 'Without Benefit of Clergy'. There was a time when it was not uncommon for Englishmen to marry Indian girls or enter into liaisons with them. But with the arrival of Englishwomen in large numbers by the early years of the nineteenth century, intermarriage came to be looked upon with extreme disfavour. The reasons given were many – political, social and cultural. The cultural differences were often emphasized and the Indian girl was shown as an emotional creature whose secretive love and single-minded devotion a Westerner could not fathom. In Diver's story, Sunia gives her life to save that of the Englishman Brodie, and Brodie, even while lamenting her death, cannot help realizing 'that he had narrowly escaped committing an act of sentimental folly, which would probably have ruined his career'. Even in an 'idyll' the Anglo-Indian writer found miscegenation difficult to accept.

Ethel Winifred Savi, in 'The Interloper', gives us a

glimpse into the minds of the Indian servants – a class that has figured more frequently in Anglo-Indian fiction than any other. Herself devotedly served by native servants for twelve years in the wilds of Bihar, Savi portrays a faithful Muslim bearer who risks his life to save that of his newly arrived mistress. But what engages the reader is the hope and consolation he proffers to the other household servants who have so far had an easy time with their bachelor master and now dread being put to work by the new arrival:

'Like as not, this woman he is bringing from across the Black Water will have no tolerance for this land of ours. Many have I seen come and go . . . and it's generally fear that turns their livers to water, for such have no stomach for difficulties. She will hear this and that. She will tremble when a thunderstorm breaks overhead with deafening crashes. The sight of a snake will paralyse initiative. Insects will be as pins in her flesh. She will be afraid to eat or drink lest she be seized with the Bad Sickness, and naught will content her but to sojourn in the mountains the moment the weather gets hot and the sun blisters the skin. Then, when it is established beyond doubt that a child is on the way, of a truth, she will turn and flee. Our Sahib will escort her to the docks and breathe a sigh of satisfaction when the vessel departs, realizing that freedom and contentment are only for the unwed, and that cursed is the man who yields his neck to the yoke of marriage when he is of the race that has ceased to uphold the supremacy of the male.'

For all its humour and unconscious cynicism, the above passage reveals the physical hardships of the memsahib in India. As for the memsahib's emotional hardships, few speak better than Sara Jeannette Duncan in 'The Pool in the Desert'. It is the story of one woman's courageous bid to recapture her youth and her sense of joy in the midst of the arid Frontier and among people who have become 'sepulchres of themselves'. Judy Harbottle accepts a young subaltern, Somers Chichele, 'as the contemporary of her soul if not of her body'. She neither wins nor loses, but in her dignified struggle one sees the emotional trauma that Anglo-Indian women experienced. The story is a strong rebuttal of the commonly held notion that many Anglo-Indian women deserted their husbands during the scorching summer months to make merry with young army officers in the Indian hills. Duncan, in quiet tone and with ironic understatement, gives the woman's point of view – a point of view mainly absent in fiction by men writers of the Raj.

University of Regina
Regina, Canada, 1990

FLORA ANNIE STEEL
The Doll-Maker

'Christmas Eve!' echoed Mrs Langford. 'Yes! I suppose it is; but I had forgotten – there isn't much to remind one of it in India – is there?'

As she paused half-way up the verandah steps she glanced back at the creeper-hung porch where the high dogcart, in which she had come home from the club, waited for its owner to return to the box-seat. He seemed in no hurry to do so, and his glance followed hers as he stood on the step below her. He was a tall man, so his face was on a level with hers, and the two showed young, handsome – hers a trifle pale, his a trifle red.

There was a stretch of garden visible beyond the creepers. It was not flowerful, since Christmas, even in India, comes when the tide of sap, the flow of life, is at its lowest; yet, in the growing dusk, the great scarlet hands of the poinsettias could be seen thrusting themselves out wickedly from the leafy shadows as if to clutch the faint white stars of the oleanders blossoming above them; and there was a bunch of Maréchal Niel roses in the silver belt of the woman's white tennis dress, which told of sweeter, more homelike blossom.

'And it is just as well,' she continued, with a bitter little laugh, 'that there isn't, for it's a deadly, dreary time – '

'All times are dreary,' assented the tall man in a low voice, rapidly, passionately, 'when there is no one who cares – '

'There is my husband,' she interrupted, this time with a nervous laugh. The answer fitted doubly, for she turned to a figure which at that moment came out of the soft rose-tinted light of the room within, and said in a faintly fretful tone, 'You don't mean to say, George, surely, that you've been working till now?'

'Working!' echoed George Langford absently. 'Yes! why not? Ah! is that you, Campbell? Brought the missus home, like a good chap. Sorry I couldn't come, my dear; but there was a beastly report overdue, so now I must just get out for a bit before dinner. By the way, Laura, you'd better send off your home letter without mine. I really haven't had time to write to the boys this mail.'

He was busy now, in the same absent, preoccupied, yet energetic way, in seeing to the bicycle, which a red-coated servant held for him; but he looked up quickly at his wife's reply – '

'I haven't written either.'

'Haven't you? That's a pity,' he began, then paused, with a vaguely unquiet look at her and her tall companion, which merged, however, into a good-natured smile. 'Well, they won't know it was Christmas mail anyhow. 'Pon my soul, I'd forgotten it myself, Campbell, or I'd have made a point . . . But there's the devil of a crush of work just now, though I shall clear some of the arrears off tomorrow. That's about the only good of a holiday to me!' He was off as he spoke – a shadow gliding into the shadows, where the red hands of the poinsettias and the white stars of the oleanders showed fainter as the dusk deepened.

But he left a pair of covetous, entreating hands and a white face behind him in the verandah, between the rosy light of comfort from within and the grey gloom of the world without.

'It cannot go on – this sort of thing – for ever,' said the man, still in that low, passionate voice. 'It will kill – '

'Kill him? Do you think so?' she interrupted, still with

that little half-nervous, half-bitter laugh. 'I don't; he's awfully strong and awfully clever, you know.'

The owner of the dogcart turned to it impatiently.

'You will come tomorrow at eleven, anyhow,' he said, bringing the patience back to his voice with an effort, for it seemed to him – as it so often seems to a man – that the woman did not know what she would be at. 'It will be a jolly drive; and, as they are sending out a mess tent, we need not come back till late. Your husband said he was to be busy all day.'

He waited, reins in hand, for an answer. It came after a pause; came decidedly.

'Yes; at eleven, please. It will be better anyhow than stopping here. There isn't even tennis on Christmas Day, you know; and the house is – is so deadly quiet.' She turned to it slowly as she spoke, passed into the rose light, and stood listening to the sound of the dogcart wheels growing fainter and fainter. When it had gone an intense stillness seemed to settle over the wide, empty house – that stillness and emptiness which must perforce settle round many an Englishwoman in India; the stillness and emptiness of a house where children have been, and are not.

It made her shiver slightly as she stood alone, thinking of the dogcart wheels.

Yet just at the back of the screen of poinsettias and oleanders which hid the servants' quarters from the creeper-hung porch there were children and to spare. Dozens of them, all ages, all sizes, belonging to the posse of followers which hangs to the skirts of bureaucracy in India.

Here, as the lights of the dogcart flashed by, they lit up for an instant a quaint little group gathered round a rushlight set on the ground. It consisted of a very old man, almost naked, with a grey frost of beard on his withered cheeks, and of a semicircle of wide-eyed, solemn-faced, brown babies – toddlers of two and three, with a sprinkling of demure little maidens of four and five.

The centre of the group lay beside the rushlight. It was a rudimentary attempt at a rag doll; so rudimentary indeed that as the passing flash of the lamps disclosed its proportions, or rather the lack of them, a titter rose from the darkness behind, where some older folk were lounging.

The old doll-maker, who was attempting to thread a big packing-needle by the faint flicker, turned towards the sound in mild reproof: 'Lo! brothers and sisters,' he said, 'have patience awhile. Even the Creator takes time to make His puppets, and this of mine will be as dolls are always when it is done. And a doll is a doll ever, nothing more, nothing less.'

'Yet thou art sadly behind the world in them,' put in a pale young man, with a pen-box under his arm, who had paused on his way to the cook-room, whither he was going to write up the daily account for the butler; since a man must live even if he has a University degree, and, if Government service be not forthcoming, must earn a penny or two as best he can. 'That sort of image did for the dark ages of ignorance, but now the mind must have more reality; glass eyes and such-like. The world changes.'

The old man's face took an almost cunning expression by reason of its self-complacent wisdom. 'But not the puppets which play in it, my son. The Final One makes *them* in the same mould ever; as I do my dolls, as my fathers made theirs. Aye! and thine too, *baboo-jee*! As for eyes, they come with the sight that sees them, since all things are illusion. For the rest' – here he shot a glance of fiery disdain at the titterers – 'I make not dolls for these scoffers, but for their betters. This is for the little masters on their Big Day. Tomorrow I will present it to the sahib and the mem, since the little sahibs themselves are away over the Black Water.

For old Premoo knows what is due. This dust-like one, lame of a leg and blind of an eye, has not always been a garden coolie – a mere picker of weeds, a gatherer of dried leaves, saved from starvation by such trivial tasks. In his youth Premoo hath carried young masters in his bosom, and guarded them night and day after the manner of bearers. And hath found amusement for them also; even to the making of dolls as this one. Aye! it is true,' he went on, led to garrulous indignation by renewed sounds of mirth from behind; 'dolls which gave them delight, for they were not as some folk, black of face, but *sahib-logue* who, by God's grace, grew to be *ginerâls* and *jedges*, and commissioners, and – and even *Lât-sahibs*.'

The old voice, though it rose in pitch with each rise in rank, was not strong enough to overbear the titter, and the doll-maker paused in startled doubt to look at his own creation.

'I can see naught amiss,' he muttered to himself; 'it is as I used to make them, for sure.' His anxious critical eye lingered almost wistfully over the bald head, the pincushion body, the sausage limbs of his creature, yet found no flaw in it; since fingers and toes were a mere detail, and as for hair, a tuft of wool would settle that point. What more could folk want, sensible folk, who knew that a doll must be always a doll – nothing more, nothing less?

Suddenly a thought came to make him put doubt to the test, and he turned to the nearest of the solemn-faced, wide-eyed semicircle of babies.

'Thou canst dandle it whilst I thread the needle, Gungi,' he said pompously, 'but have a care not to injure the child, and let not the others touch it.'

The solemnity left one chubby brown face, and one pair of chubby brown hands closed in glad possession round the despised rag doll. Old Premoo heaved a sigh of relief.

The Doll-Maker

'Said I not so, brothers and sisters?' he cried exultingly. 'My hand has not lost its art with the years. A doll is a doll ever to a child, as a child is a child ever to the man and the woman. As for glass eyes, they are illusion – they perish!'

'Nevertheless, thou wilt put clothes to it, for sure, brother,' remonstrated the fat butler, who had joined the group, 'ere giving it to the Presences. 'Tis like a skinned fowl now, and bare decent.'

Premoo shook his head mournfully. 'Lo! *khânjee*, my rags, as thou seest, scarce run to a big enough body and legs! And the *Huzoor*'s tailor would give no scraps to Premoo the garden coolie; though in the old days, when the little masters lay in these arms, and there was favour to be carried by the dressing of dolls, such as he were ready to make them, male and female, kings and queens, fairies and heroes, memsahibs and *Lât-sahibs* after their kind. But it matters not in the end, *khânjee*, it matters not! The doll is a doll ever to a child, as a child is a child ever to the man and the woman, though they know not whether it will wear a crown or a shroud.'

So as Christmas Eve passed into Christmas night, Premoo stitched away contentedly as he sat under the stars. There was no Christmas message in them for the old man. The master's Big Day meant nothing to him save an occasion for the giving of gifts, notably rag dolls! There was no vision for him in the velvet darkness of the spangled sky of angels proclaiming the glad tidings of birth; and yet in a way his old heart, wise with the dim wisdom which long life brings, held the answer to the great Problem, as in vague self-consolation for the titterings he murmured to himself now and again: 'It is so always; naught matters but the children, and the children's children.'

And when his task was over, he laid the result for safety on the basket of withered leaves which he had swept up from the path that evening, and wrapping himself in his thin cotton shawl, lay down to sleep in the shelter of the poinsettia and oleander hedge.

So the Christmas sun peering through the morning mists shone upon a quaint crèche indeed – on the veriest simulacrum of a child lying on a heap of faded red hand-like leaves and white starlike blossoms. Perhaps it smiled at the sight. Humanity did, anyhow, as it passed and repassed from the servants' quarters to its work in the house. For in truth old Premoo's creation looked even more comical in the daylight than it had by the faint flicker of the lamp. There was something about it productive of sheer mirth, yet of mirth that was tender. Even the fat butler, on his way to set breakfast, stopped to giggle foolishly in its face.

'God knows what it is like,' he said finally. 'I deemed it was a skinned fowl last night, but 'tis not that. It might be anything.'

'Aye!' assented the bearer, who had come out, duster in hand. 'That is just where it comes. A body cannot say what it might or might not be. Bala Krishna himself, for aught I know.' Whereupon he *salaamed*; and others passing followed suit, in jest at first, afterwards with a suspicion of gravity in their mirth, since, when all was said and done, who knew what anything was really in this illusory world?

So the rag doll held its levée that Christmas morning, and when the time came for its presentation to the *Huzoors* there were curious eyes watching the old man as he sat with his offering on the lowest step of the silent, empty house, waiting for the master and mistress to come out into the verandah. Premoo had covered the doll's bed of withered flowers with some fresh ones, so it lay in pomp in its basket, amid royal scarlet and white and gold; nevertheless he waited till the very last, until the smallest platter of sugar and oranges and almonds had been ranged at the master's feet, ere he crept up the steps, *salaaming* humbly, yet with a vague confidence on his old face.

'It is for the child-people,' he said, in his cracked old voice. 'This dust-like one has nothing else, but a doll is always a doll to them, as a child is a child to the man and the woman.'

Then for an instant the rag doll lay, as it were, in state, surrounded by offerings. But not for long. Someone laughed, then another, till even old Premoo joined doubtfully in the general mirth.

'The devil is in it,' chuckled the fat butler apologetically; 'but the twelve *Imâms* themselves would not keep grave over it during the requiem!'

'By jove, Laura,' cried George Langford, 'we must really send that home to the kids. It's too absurd!'

'Yes,' she assented, a trifle absently, 'we must indeed.' She stooped to take the quaint travesty from its basket, and as she did so one of the red hands of the poinsettias clung to its sausage legs. She brushed the flower aside with a smile which broadened to a laugh; for in truth the thing was more ludicrously comical than ever seen thus, held in mid-air. George Langford found it so, anyhow, and exploded into a fresh guffaw.

She flushed suddenly, and gathered the unshapen thing in her arms as if to hide it from his laughter.

'Don't, George,' she said, 'it – it seems unkind. Thank you, Premoo, very much. We will certainly send it home to the little masters; and they, I am sure – ' Here her eyes fell upon the doll again, and mirth got the better of her gravity once more.

Half an hour afterwards, however, as she stood alone in the drawing-room, ready dressed for her drive, the gravity had returned as she looked down on the quaint monstrosity spread out on the table, where on the evening before the rose-shaded lamp had been. It was ridiculous, certainly, but beneath that there was something else. What was it? What had the old man said: 'A doll is always a doll' . . . He had said that and something more: 'As the child is always a child to the man and the woman.' It ought to be – but was it? Was not that tie forgotten, lost sight of in others . . . sometimes?

Half-mechanically she took the rag doll, and sitting down on a rocking-chair laid the caricature on her lap among the dainty frills and laces of her pretty gown. And this was Christmas Day – the children's day – she thought vaguely, dreamily, as she rocked herself backwards and forwards slowly. But the house was empty save for this – this idea, like nothing really in heaven or earth; yet for all that giving the Christmas message, the message of peace and goodwill which the birth of a child into the world should give to the man and the woman:

'Unto us a child is born.'

She smiled faintly – the thing on her lap seemed so far from such a memory – and then, with that sudden half-remorseful pity, she once more gathered the rag doll closer in her arms, as if to shield it from her own laughter.

And as she sat so, her face soft and kind, her husband, coming into the room behind her, paused at what he saw. And something that was not laughter surged up in him; for he understood in a flash, understood once and for all, how empty his house had been to her, how empty her arms, how empty her life.

He crossed to her quickly, but she was on her feet almost defiantly at the first sight of him. 'Ridiculous monster!' she exclaimed, gaily tossing the doll back on the table. 'But it has an uncanny look about it which fascinates one. Gracious! Where are my gloves? I must have left them in my room, and I promised to be ready at eleven!'

When she had gone to look for them, George Langford took up the rag doll in his turn – took it up gingerly, as men take their babies – and stared at it almost fiercely. And he stood there, stern, square, silent, staring at it until his wife came back. Then he walked up to her deliberately and laid his hands on hers.

'I'm going to pack this thing up at once, my dear,' he said, 'and take it over this morning to little Mrs Greville. She starts this afternoon, you know, to catch the Messageries steamer. She'll take it home for us; and so the boys could have it by the Christmas mail, which I forgot.'

The words were commonplace, but there was a world of meaning in the tone.

'I – I thought you were busy,' she said indistinctly, after a pause in which the one thing in the world seemed to her that tightening hold upon her hand. 'If you are – I – I could go . . .'

There was another pause – a longer one.

'I thought you were going out,' he said at last, and his voice, though distinct, was not quite steady; 'but if you aren't, we might go together. My work can easily stand over, and – and Campbell can drive you out some other day when I can't.'

She gave an odd little sound between a laugh and a sob.

'That would be best, perhaps,' she said. 'I'd like the boys to have this' – she laid her other hand tenderly on the rag doll – 'by the Christmas mail I had forgotten.'

Old Premoo was sweeping up the withered leaves and flowers from the poinsettia and oleander hedge, when first one and then another high dogcart drove past him. And when the second one had disappeared, he turned to the general audience on the other side of the hedge, and said with great pride and pomp –

'Look you! The scoffers mocked at my doll, but the

Huzoors understand. The sahib himself has taken it to send to the little sahibs, and the mem packed it up herself and went with him, instead of going in the Captain-sahib's dogcart. That is because a doll is always a doll; as for glass eyes and such like, they perish.'

And with that he crushed a handful of withered red poinsettias into the rubbish basket triumphantly.

FLORA ANNIE STEEL
At the Great Durbar

He sat, cuddled up in a cream-coloured cotton blanket, edged with crimson, shoo-ing away the brown rats from the curved cobs of Indian corn. The soft mists of a northern November hung over the landscape in varying density: heavy over the dank sugarcane patch by the well, lighter on the green fodder crop, dewy among the moisture-loving leaves of the sprouting vetches, and here, in the field of ripening maize, scarcely visible between the sparse stems. He was an old man with a thin white beard tucked away behind his ears, and a kindly look on his high-featured face. Every now and then he took up a little clod of earth from the dry, crumbling ridge of soil which divided the field he was watching from the surrounding ones, and threw it carefully among the maize, saying in a gentle, grumbling voice, '*Ari*, brothers! Does no shame come to you?'

It had no perceptible effect on the rats, who, owing to the extreme sparsity of the crop, could be seen every here and there deliberately climbing up a swaying stem to seat themselves on a cob and begin breakfast systematically. In the calm, windless silence you could almost hear the rustle and rasp of their sharp white teeth. But Nânuk Singh – as might have been predicted from his seventy and odd years of life in the fields – was somewhat hard of hearing, somewhat near of vision also. For when so many years have been spent watching the present furrow cling to the curves of the past one, in sure and certain hope of similar furrows in the future, or in listening to the endless lamentations of a water-wheel ceasing not by day or night to proclaim an eternity of toil and harvest, both eyes and ears are apt to grow dull towards new sights and sounds. Nânuk's had, at any rate, even though the old familiar ones no longer occupied them, fate having decreed that in his old age the peasant farmer should have neither furrows nor water-wheel of his own. How this had come about needs a whole statute-book of Western laws to understand. Nânuk himself never attempted the task. To him it was, briefly, the will of God. His district officer, however, when the case fell under his notice by reason of the transfer of the land, thought differently; and having a few minutes' leisure from office drudgery to spare for really important work, made yet one more representation regarding the scandalous rates of interest, the cruelty of time-foreclosures, and the general injustice of applying the maxim '*caveat emptor*' to transactions in which one party is practically a child and the other a Jew. A futile representation, of course, since the Government, so experts affirm, is not strong enough to attack the Frankenstein monster of Law which it has created.

In a measure, nevertheless, old Nânuk was right in attributing his ruin to fate, since it had followed naturally from the death of his three sons: one, the eldest, dying of malarial fever in the prime of life, leaving, alas! a young family of girls; another, the youngest, swept off by cholera just as his hand began to close firmly round his dead brother's plough-handle; the third, when on the eve of getting his discharge from a frontier regiment in order to take his brothers' places by his father's side, being struck down ingloriously in one of the petty border raids of which our Punjab peasant soldiers have always to bear the brunt.

And this loss of able hands led inevitably to the loss of ill-kept oxen; while from the lack of well cattle came that gradual shrinkage of the irrigated area where some crop is certain – rain or no rain – which means a less gradual sinking further and further into debt, until, as had been the case with Nânuk, the owner loses all right in the land save the doubtful one of toil. Even this had passed from the old man's slackening hold after his wife died, and the daughters-in-law, with starvation staring them in the face, had drifted away back to their own homes, leaving him to live as best he could on the acre or so of unirrigated land lent to him out of sheer charity. For public opinion still has some power over the usurer in a village of strong men, and all his fellows respected old Nânuk, who stood six feet two, barefoot, and had tales to tell of the gentle art of singlestick as applied to the equitable settling of accounts in the old days, before Western laws had taken the job out of the creditor's hands.

Strangely enough, however, Nânuk, as he sat coping inadequately with the brown rats, felt less resentment against the usurer who had robbed him, or the law which permitted the robbery, than he did against the weather. The former had made no pretence of favouring him; the latter, year after year, had tempted his farmer's soul to lavish sowings by copious rain at seedtime, and thereinafter withheld the moisture necessary for a bare return of measure for measure. Briefly, he had gambled in grain, and he had lost. Lost hopelessly in this last harvest of maize, since, when the sound cobs should be separated from those which the wanton teeth had spoilt, they would not yield the amount of Government revenue which the old man had to pay; certainly would not do so if the cobs became scarcer day by day and the rats more throng. In fact, the necessity for action ere matters grew worse appeared to strike Nânuk, making him, after a time, draw out a small sickle and begin to harvest the remaining stalks one by one.

'*Bullah!* neighbour Nânuk,' cried the new man, who, better equipped for the task with sons and cattle, was driving the wheel and curving the furrows for the usurer, 'I would, for thy sake, the task was harder. And as if the crop were not poor enough, the dissolute rats must needs play the wanton with the half of it. But, 'tis the same all over the land, and between them and the revenue we poor folk of the plough will have no share.'

Nânuk stood looking meditatively at a very fine cob out of which a pair of sharp white teeth were taking a last nibble, while a pair of wicked black eyes watched him fearlessly.

'They are God's creatures also, and have a right to live on the soil as we others,' he said slowly.

'Then they should pay the revenue,' grumbled Dittu. 'Why should *you*, who have no crop whereon to pay? O infamous one!' he added sharply to one of the oxen he was driving to their work, 'sleepest thou? and the well silent! Dost want to bring me to Nânuk's plight?'

So, with a prod of the goad, he passed on, leaving old Nânuk still looking at the brown rat on the corn-cob. Why, indeed, should he have to pay for God's other creatures? In the old days justice would have been meted out to such as he. The crop would have been divided into heaps, so many for the owner of the soil, so many for the tiller, so many for the State. Then, if *Purmêshwar* sent rats instead of rain, the heaps were smaller. That was all. And if the equity of this had been patent to those older rulers, who had scarcely given a thought in other ways to the good of their subjects, why should it not be patent to those new ones who – God keep them! – gave justice without respect of persons, so far as in them lay? There must be a mistake somewhere; the facts could not have been properly placed before the *Lât-sahib* – that vice-regent of God upon earth. This conviction came home slowly to the old man as he finished his harvesting; slowly but surely, so that when he had spread the cobs out to dry on his cotton blanket he walked over to the well, and, between the whiffs of the general pipe, hinted that he thought of laying the matter before the authorities. 'I will take the produce of my field,' he said, 'in my hand – it will not be more than five *seers* when the good is sifted from the bad – and I will say to the *Lât-sahib*, "This is because *Purmêshwar* sent rats instead of rain. Take your share, and ask no more."'

Dittu, the new man, laughed scornfully. 'Better take a rat also, since all parties to the case must be present by the law.'

He intended it as a joke, but Nânuk took it quite seriously. 'That is true,' he assented; 'I will take a rat also; then there can be no mistake.'

That evening, when he sat with his cronies on the mud dais beneath the peepul tree, where he was welcome to a pull out of anybody's pipe, he spoke again of his intention. The younger folk laughed, but the seniors thought that it could at least do no harm. Nânuk's case was a hard one; it was quite clear he could not pay the revenue, and it was better to go to the fountainhead in such matters, since underlings could do nothing but take fees. So, while the stars came out in the evening sky, they sat and told tales of Nausherwân, and many another worthy whose memory lingers in native minds by reason of perfectly irrational acts of despotic clemency, such as even Socialists do not dream of nowadays. The corn-cobs then being harvested, dried, and shelled, he set to work with the utmost solemnity on rat-traps; but here at once he realized his mistake. By harvesting his own crop he had driven the little raiders farther afield; and though he could easily have caught one in his neighbour's patch, a desire to deal perfectly fairly with those who, in his experience, dealt perfectly fairly with facts, made him stipulate for a rat out of his own.

This necessitated the baiting of his property with some of the corn in order to attract the wanton creatures again; and even then, though he sat for hours holding the cord by which an earthen dish was to be made to fall upon the unsuspecting intruder, he was unsuccessful.

'Trra! not catch rats!' cried a most venerable old pantaloon to whom he applied for advice, remembering him in his boyhood as one almost god-like in his supreme knowledge of such things. 'Wait awhile; 'tis a trick – a mere trick – but when you once know it you cannot forget it.' All that day the old men sat together in the sunshine, profoundly busy, and towards evening they went forth together to the field, chattering and laughing like a couple of schoolboys. It was long after dusk ere they returned, full of mutual recrimination. The one had coughed too much, the other had wheezed perpetually; there was no catching of rats possible under such circumstances. Then the old pantaloon went a-hunting by himself, full of confidence, only to return dejected; then Nânuk, full of determination, sat up all one moonlight night in the field where – now that he had no crop to benefit by it – the night-dew gathered heavily on every leaf and blade – on Nânuk, too, as he sat crouched up in his cotton blanket, thinking of what he should say to the *Lât-sahib* when the rat was caught, which it was not. Finally, with angry misgivings as to the capabilities of the present generation of boys, the old pantaloon suggested the offering of one whole anna for the first rat captured in Nânuk's maize-field. Before the day was over a score or two of the village lads, long-limbed, bright-eyed, were vociferously maintaining the prior claims of as many brown rats, safely confined in little earthen pipkins with a rag tied round the top. They stood in a row, like an offering of sweets to some deity, round Nânuk's bed, for – as was not to be wondered at after his night-watch – he was down with an attack of the chills. That was nothing new. He had had them every autumn since he was born; but he was not accustomed to be surrounded on such occasions by brown rats appealing to him for justice. It ended in his giving, with feverish hands, one anna to each of the boys, and reserving his selection until he was in a more judicial frame of mind. Still, it would not do to starve God's creatures, so every morning while the fever lingered – for it had got a grip on him somehow – he went round the pipkins and fed the rats with some of the maize. And every morning, rather to his relief, there were fewer of them to feed, since they nibbled their way out once they discovered that the top of their prison was but cloth. So as he lay, sometimes hot, sometimes cold, the idea came to him, foolishly enough, that this was a process of divine selection, and that if he only waited the day when but one rat should remain, his mission would bear the seal of success. An idea like this only needs presentation to a mind, or lack of mind, like old Nânuk's. So what with the harvesting and the rat-catching, and the fever and the omen-awaiting, it was close on the new year when, with a brown rat, now quite tame, tied up in a pipkin, some five *seers* of good grain tied up in the corner of his cotton blanket, and Heaven knows what a curious conglomeration of thought bound up in his still feverish brain, the old man set out from his village to find the *Lât-sahib*. Such things are still done in India, such figures are still to be seen, making some civilized people stand out of the road bare-headed, as they do to a man on his way to the grave – a man who has lived his life, whose day is past.

Owing also to the fever and the paying for rats, etc., old Nânuk's pockets were ill-provided for the journey, but that mattered little in a country where a pilgrimage on foot is in itself presumptive evidence of saintship. Besides, the brown rat – to which Nânuk had attached a string lest one of the parties to the suit might escape him on the road – was a perpetual joy to the village children, who scarcely knew if it were greater fun to peep at it in its pipkin, or see it peeping out of the old man's cotton blanket, when in the evenings it nibbled away at its share of Nânuk's dinner. They used to ask endless questions as to why he carried it about, and what he was going to do with it, until, half in jest, half in earnest, he told them he was the *mudâ-ee* (plaintiff) and the rat the *mudee-âla* (defendant) in a case they were going to lay before the *Lât-sahib*; an explanation perfectly intelligible to even the babes and sucklings, who in a Punjabi village nowadays lisp in numbers of petitions and pleaders.

So the *mudâ-ee* and *mudee-âla* tramped along together amicably, sometimes by curving wheel-tracks among the furrows – ancient rights-of-way over the wide fields, as transient yet immutable as the furrows themselves; and there, with the farmer's eye-heritage of generations, he noted each change of tint in the growing wheat, from the faintest yellowing to the solid dark green with its promise of a full ear to come. Sometimes by broad lanes, telling yet once more the strange old Indian tale of transience and permanence, of death and renewed birth, in the deep grass-set ruts through which the traffic of centuries had passed rarely, yet inevitably. And here with the same knowledgeable eye he would mark the homing herds of village cattle, and infer from their condition what the unseen harvest had been which gave them their fodder. Finally, out upon the hard, white highroad, so different from the others in its self-sufficient straightness, its squared heaps of nodular limestone ready for repairs, its elaborate arrangements for growing trees where they never grew before, and where even Western orders will not make them grow. And here

At the Great Durbar

Nânuk's eyes still found something familiar in the great wains creaking along in files to add their quota of corn sacks to the mountain of wheat cumbering the railway platforms all along the line. Yet even this was in its essence new, provoking the wonder in his slow brain how it could be that the increased demand for wheat and its enhanced price should have gone hand-in-hand with the financial ruin of the grower.

To say sooth, however, such problems as these flitted but vaguely through the old man's thought, and even his own spoliation was half forgotten in the one great object of that long journey which, despite his cheerful patience, had sapped his strength sadly. To find the *Lât-sahib*, to make his *salaam*, and bid the *mudee-âla-jee* do so likewise, to lay the produce of the field at the Sahib's feet, and say that *Purmêshwar* had sent rats instead of rain – that in itself was sufficient for the old man as he trudged along doggedly, his eyes becoming more and more dazed by unfamiliar sights, as he neared the big city.

'*Bullah!*' said the woman of whom he begged a night's lodging. 'If we were to house and feed the wanderers on this road, we should have to starve ourselves. And thou art a Sikh. Go to thine own people. 'Tis each for each in this world.' That was a new world to Nânuk.

'Doth thy rat do tricks?' asked the children critically. 'What, none? Trra! we can see rats of that mettle any day in the drains, and there was a man here yesterday whose rat cooked bread and drew water. Ay! and his goat played the drum. That was a show worth seeing.'

So Nânuk trudged on.

'See the *Lât-sahib*,' sneered the yellow-legged police constable when, after much wandering through bewildering crowds, the old Sikh found himself at a meeting of roads, each one of which was barred by a baton. 'Which *Lât-sahib* – the big one or the little?'

'The big one,' replied Nânuk stoutly. There was no good in underlings; *that* he knew.

Police Constable number Seventy-five called over to his crony, number Ninety-six, on the next road.

'Ho, brother! Here is another *durbari*. Canst let him in on thy beat? I have no room on mine.' And then they both laughed, whereat old Nânuk, taking courage, moved on a step, only to be caught and dragged back, hustled, and abused. What! was the Great Durbar for the like of him – the Great Durbar on which lakhs and crores had been spent – the Great Durbar all India had been thinking of for months? *Wâh!* Whence had he come if he had not heard of the Great Durbar, and what had he thought was the meaning of the Venetian masts and triumphal arches, the flags and the watered roads? Did he think such things were always? If it came to such ignorance as that, mayhap he would not know what *this* was coming along the road.

It was a disciplined tramp of feet, an even glitter of bayonets, a straight line of brown faces, a swing and a sweep, as a company of the Guides came past in their khaki and crimson uniform. Old Nânuk looked at it wistfully.

'Nay, brother,' he said, 'I know that. 'Twas my son's regiment, God rest him!'

'Thou shouldst sit down, old man,' said a bystander kindly. 'Of a truth thou canst go no farther till the show is over. Hark! there are the guns again. 'Twill be Bairânpore likely, since Hurriâna has gone past. *Wâh!* it is a show – a rare show!'

So down the watered road, planted out in miserable attempts at decoration with barbers' poles unworthy of a slum in the East End, came a bevy of Australian horses, wedged at a trot between huge kettledrums, which were

At the Great Durbar

being whacked barbarically by men who rose in their stirrups with the conscientious precision of a newly imported competition-*wallah*. Then more Australian horses again in an *orfévré* barouche lined with silver, where, despite the glow of colour, the blinding flash of diamonds in an Indian sun, despite even the dull wheat-green glitter of the huge emerald tiara about the turban, the eye forgot these things to fix itself upon the face which owned them all; a face haggard, sodden, superlatively handsome even in its soddenness; indifferent, but with an odd consciousness of the English boy who – dressed as for a flower show – sat silently beside his charge. Behind them with a clatter and flutter of pennons came a great trail of wild horsemen, showing, as they swept past, dark, lowering faces among the sharp spearpoints.

And the guns beat on their appointed tale, till, with the last, a certain satisfaction came to that sodden face, since there were none short in the salute – *as yet*. The measure of his misdoings was not full *as yet*.*

The crowd ebbed and flowed irregularly to border the straight white roads, where at intervals the great tributary chiefs went backwards and forwards to pay their State visits, but Nânuk and his rat – the plaintiff and the defendant – waited persistently for their turn to pass on. It was long in coming; for even when the last flash and dash of barbaric splendour had disappeared, the roar of cannon began louder, nearer, regular to a second in its even beat.

'That is the *Lât* salute,' said one man to another in the crowd. 'Let us wait and see the *Lât*, brother, ere we go.'

Nânuk overheard the words, and looked along the road anxiously, then stood feeling more puzzled than ever; for

---

* A reduction in the number of guns is the first punishment for bad administration.

there was nothing to see here but a plain closed carriage with a thin red and gold trail of the bodyguard behind it and before. The sun was near to its setting, and sent a red, angry flare upon a bank of clouds which had risen in the east, and the dust of many feet swept past in whirls before a rising wind.

'It will rain ere nightfall,' declared the crowd contentedly, as it melted away citywards. 'And the crops will be good, praise to God.'

Once more Nânuk overheard, and this time a glad recognition seemed to rouse him from a dream. Yes! the crops would be good. Down by the well, on the land he and his had ploughed for so many years, the wheat would be green – green as those emeralds above that sodden face.

'The *Lât* has gone out,' joked Constable Seventy-five as he went off duty; 'but there are plenty of other things worth seeing to such an ignoramus as thou.'

True; only by this time Nânuk was almost past seeing aught save that all things were unfamiliar in those miles and miles of regiments and rajahs, electric lights and newly macadamized roads, tents and make-believe gardens, all pivoted, as it were, round the Royal Standard of England, which was planted out in the centre of the Viceroy's camp. As he wandered aimlessly about the vast canvas city, hustled here, sent back there, the galloping orderlies, the shuffling elephants, the carriages full of English ladies, the subalterns cracking their tandem whips, and the native outriders had but one word for him.

'*Hut! Hut!*' ('Stand back! – stand back!')

A heavy drop of rain came as a welcome excuse to his dogged perseverance for sheltering awhile under a thorn bush. He was more tired than hungry, though he had not tasted food that day; and it needed a sharp nip from the defendant's teeth, as it sought for something eatable in the

At the Great Durbar

folds of his blanket, to remind him that others of God's creatures had a better appetite than he. But what was he to give? There was the five *seers* of grain still, of course; but who was to apportion the shares? Who was to say, 'This much for the plaintiff, this much for the defendant, this much for the State'? The familiar idea seemed to give him support in the bewildering inrush of new impressions, and he held to it as a drowning man in a waste of unknown waters clutches at a straw.

Nevertheless, the parties to the suit must not be allowed to starve meanwhile, and if they took equal shares surely that would be just.

The rain now fell in torrents, and the bush scarcely gave him any shelter as, with a faint smile, he sat watching the brown rat at work upon the corn, and counting the number of grains the wanton teeth appropriated as their portion. For so much, and no more, would be his also. It was not a sumptuous repast, but uncooked maize requires mastication, and that took up time. So that it was dark ere he stood up, soaked through to the skin, and looked perplexedly at the long lines of twinkling lights which had sprung up around him. And hark! what was that? It was the dinner bugle at a mess close by, followed, as by an echo, by another and another and another – quite a chorus of cheerful invitations to dinner. But Nânuk knew nothing of such feasts as were spread there in the wilderness. He had lived all his life on wheat and lentils, though, being a Sikh, he would eat wild boar or deer if it could be got, or take a tot of country spirits on occasion to make life seem less dreary. He stood listening, shivering a little with the cold, and then went on his way, since the *Lât-sahib* must be found, the case decided, before this numbing forgetfulness crept over everything.

Sometimes he inquired of those he met. More often he

did not, but wandered on aimlessly through the maze of light, driven and hustled as he had been by day. And as he wandered the bands of the various camps were playing, say, the march in *Tannhäuser*, or 'Linger longer, Loo'. But sooner or later they all paused to break suddenly into a stave or two of another tune, as the colonel gave 'The Queen' to his officers.

Of all this, again, Nânuk knew nothing. Even at the best of times, he had been ignorant as a babe unborn of anything beyond his fields, and now he remembered nothing save that he and the brown rat were suitors in a case against *Purmêshwar* and the State.

So the night passed. It was well on into the chilliest time before the dawn, when the slumber which comes to all the world for that last dead hour of darkness having rid him of all barriers, he found himself beneath what had been the goal of his hopes ever since he had first seen its strange white rays piercing the night – the great ball of electric light which crowned the flagstaff whereon the Standard of England hung dank and heavy; for the wind had dropped, the rain had ceased, and a thick white mist clung close even to the round bole of the mast, which was set in the centre of a stand of chrysanthemums. The colours of the blossoms were faintly visible in the downward gleam of the light spreading in a small circle through the mist.

So far good. This was the '*Standard of Sovereignty*', no doubt – the '*Lamp of Safety*' – the guide by day and night to faithful subjects seeking justice before the king. This Nânuk understood; this he had heard of in those tales of Nausherwân and his like, told beneath the village peepul tree.

Here, then, he would stay – he and the defendant – till the dawn brought a hearing. He sat down, his back to the flowers, his head buried in his knees. And as he sat, immovable, the mist gathered upon him as it had gathered in the field. But he was not thinking now what he should say to the *Lât-sahib*. He was past that.

He did not hear the jingle and clash of arms which, after a time, came through the fog, or the voice which said cheerfully –

"'Appy Noo Year to you, mate!'

'Same to you, Tommy, and many of 'em; but it's rather you nor I, for it's chillin' to the vitals.'

They were changing guards on this New Year's morning, and Private Smith, as he took his first turn under the long strip of canvas stretched as a sun-shelter between the two sentry-boxes, acknowledged the truth of his comrade's remark by beating his arms upon his breast like any cabman. Yet he was hot enough in his head, for he had been singing 'Auld Lang Syne' and drinking rum for the greater part of the night, and, though sufficiently sober to pass muster on New Year's Eve, was drunk enough to be intensely patriotic. So, as he walked up and down, there was a little lilt in his step which attempted to keep time to the stave of 'God Save our Gracious Queen' which he was whistling horribly out of tune. On the morrow – or, rather, today, since the dawn was at hand – there was to be the biggest review in which he had ever taken part: six-and-twenty thousand troops marching up to the Royal Standard and saluting! They had been practising it for weeks, and the thrill of it, the pride and power of it, had somehow got into Private Smith's head – with the rum. It made him take a turn beyond that strip of canvas, round the flagstaff he was supposed to guard.

"'Alt! 'oo goes there?"

The challenge rang loudly, rousing Nânuk from a dream which was scarcely less unreal than the past twelve hours of waking had been to his ignorance. He stumbled up stiffly – a head taller than the sentry – and essayed a *salaam*.

"Ullo! What the devil are you doin' here? *Hut*, you! Goramighty! wot's that?"

It was the defendant, which Nânuk had brought out to *salaam* also, and which, alarmed at the sudden introduction, began darting about wildly at the end of its string. Private Smith fell back a step, and then pulled himself together with a violent effort, uncertain if the rat were real; but the cold night air was against him.

'Wash'er-mean? – Wash'er doin'-'ere? – Wash'er-got?' he asked conglomerately; and Nânuk, understanding nothing, went down on his knees the better to untie the knot in the corner of his blanket. '*Poggle*,' commented Private Smith, recovering himself as he looked down at the heap of maize, the defendant, and the old man talking about *Purmêshwar*. Then, being in a benevolent mood, he wagged his head sympathetically. 'Pore old Johnny! wot's 'e want, with 'is rat and 'is popcorn? Fine lookin' old chap, though – but we licked them Sickies, and, by gum! we'll lick 'em again, if need be!'

The thought made him begin to whistle once more as he bent unsteadily to look at something which glittered faintly as the old man laid it on the top of the pile of corn.

It was his son's only medal.

'Hillo!' said Private Smith, bringing himself up with a lurch, 'so that is it, eh, mate? Gor-save-a-Queen! Now wot's up, sonny? 'Orse Guards been a-doing wot they didn't ought to 'ave done? Well, that ain't no noos, is it, comrade? But we'll drink the old Lady's 'elth all the same. Lordy! if you've bin doin' extra dooty on the rag all night you won't mind a lick o' the lap – eh? Lor' bless you! – I don' want it. I've 'ad as mush as me and Lee-Metford can carry 'ome without takin' a day-tour by orderly room – Woy! you won't, won't yer? Come now, Johnny, don't be a fool – it's rum, I tell yer, and you Sickies ain't afraid o' rum. Wot! you won't drink 'er 'elth, you mutineering nigger? Then I'll make yer. Feel that – now then, "'Ere's a 'elth unto'w her Majesty."'

Perhaps it was the unmistakable prick of a bayonet in his stomach, perhaps it was the equally unmistakable smell of the liquor arousing a craving for comfort in the old man, but he suddenly seized the flask which Private Smith had dragged from his pocket, and, throwing his head back, poured the contents down his throat, the action – due to his desire not to touch the bottle with his lips – giving him an almost ludicrous air of eagerness.

Private Smith burst into a roar of laughter.

'Gor-save-the-Queen!' And as he spoke the first gun of the hundred and one which are fired at daybreak on the anniversary of her Most Gracious Majesty's assumption of the title *Kaiser-i-Hind* boomed out sullenly through the fog.

But Nânuk did not hear it. He had stumbled to his feet and fallen sideways to the ground.

'I gather, then,' remarked the surgeon-captain precisely, 'that before gun-fire this morning you found the old man in a state of collapse below the flagstaff – is this so?'

Private Smith, sober to smartness and smart to stiffness, saluted; but there was an odd trepidation on his face. 'Yes, sir – I done my best for 'im, sir. I put 'im in the box, sir, and give 'im my greatcoat, and I rub 'is 'ands and feet, sir. I done my level best for 'im, not being able, you see, sir, to go off guard. I couldn't do no more.'

'You did very well, my man; but if you had happened to have some stimulant – any alcohol, for instance.'

Private Smith's very smartness seemed to leave him in a sudden slackness of relief. 'Which it were a tot of rum, sir, as I 'appened to 'ave in my greatcoat pocket. It done 'im no 'arm, sir, did it?'

The surgeon-captain smiled furtively. 'It saved his life, probably; but you might have mentioned it before. How much did he take?'

'About 'arf a pint, sir – more nor less.' Private Smith spoke under his breath with an attempt at regret; then he became loquacious. 'Beggin' your pardon, sir, but I was a bit on myself, and 'e just poured it down like as it was milk, an' then 'e tumbled over and I thought 'e was dead, and it sobered me like. So I done my level best for 'im all through.'

Perhaps he had; for old Nânuk Singh found a comfortable spot in which to spend his remaining days when the regimental doolie carried him that New Year's morning from the flagstaff to the hospital. He lay ill of rheumatic fever for weeks, and when he recovered it was to find himself and his rat quite an institution among the gaunt, listless convalescents waiting for strength in their long dressing-gowns. The story of how the old Sikh had drunk the Queen's health had assumed gigantic proportions under Private Smith's care, and something in the humour and the pathos of it tickled the fancy of his hearers, who, when the unfailing phrase, 'An' so I done my level best for him, I did,' came to close the recital, would turn to the old man and say –

'Pore old Johnny – an' Gord knows what 'e wanted with 'is rat and 'is popcorn!'

That was true, since Nânuk Singh did not remember even the name of his own village; and, though he still talked about the plaintiff and the defendant, *Purmêshwar* and the State, he was apparently content to await his chance of a hearing at another and greater durbar.

FLORA ANNIE STEEL
The Gift of Battle

'Then you recommend them both,' said the mild little Commissioner, doubtfully; he was a vacillating man, by nature lawful prey to his superiors.

Tim O'Brien, CIE – the uncoveted distinction had been, to his great disgust, bestowed on him after a recent famine, in which his sheer vitality had saved half a province, removed his long Burmah cheroot from his lips and smiled brilliantly. He was a thin brown man with a whimsical face.

'And what would I be doing with wan of them on the Bench and the other in the dock? For it would be that way ere a week was past. It is very kind of the LG to suggest putting either Sirdar Bikrama Singh or Khân Buktiyar Khân on the Honorary Magistracy, but he doesn't grasp that they are hereditary enemies and have been the same for eight hundred years. Ever since the Pathans temporarily conquered the Rajputs, in the year av' grace 1256! So you couldn't in conscience expect wan of them not to commit a crime if the other was to be preferred before him. Ye see, he'd just have to kill someone. But, if ye appoint them both, the dacencies of Court procedure and the hair-splittin' formalities of the local Bar will conduce to dignity – to say nothing of their own sense of justice, which, I'll go bail, is stronger than it is in most people ye could appoint. Equity's apt to go by the board if ye've too much legal knowledge; and they have none of that last. But I'll give them a good Clerk of the Court and guarantee they come to no harm. Yes, sir, I recommend them both – to sit *in banco*.'

When Tim O'Brien spoke, as he did in the last sentence,

curtly and without a trace of his usual rollicking Irish accent, his superior officers invariably fell in with his views; it saved trouble.

So, in due course, what answers to a JP's commission at home (with no small extra powers thrown in) was sent to Sirdar Bikrama Singh, Rajput, at his castle of Nagadrug (the Snake's Hole), and also to Khân Buktiyar Khân at his fortress of Shakingarh (the Falcon's Nest).

Both buildings had been for some centuries in a hopeless state of dilapidation, as, from a worldly point of view, were their owners' fortunes. But, just as the crumbling walls still commanded the wide arid valley which lay between the rocky steeps of the sandhills on which they stood, so the position of the two most ancient families of Hindus and Muhammadans in the district still commanded the respect of the whole sub-division. Of course, they were antagonistic. Had they not been so always? But, in truth, the old story of how they came to be so was such a very old story that none knew the rights of it: not even the two high-nosed, high-couraged old men, who, having in due time succeeded to the headship of their respective families, had done as their fathers had done; that is to say, glared at each other over their barren fields, formulated every possible complaint they could against their neighbour, and denied any good quality to him, his house, his wife, his oxen, or his ass.

Yet the two had one thing in common. They were both soldiers by race. Their sons were even now with the colours of Empire, and in their own youth both had served John Company, and afterwards the Queen. This bond, however, was not one of union, but rather of discord. For the one had belonged to the crack Hindu and the other to the crack Muhammadan corps of the Indian army, and their respective sons naturally followed in their fathers' footsteps.

Indeed, on occasions the pair of dear old pantaloons would appear in the uniforms of a past day, hopelessly out of date as regards buttons and tailoring, but still worn with the distinctive cock of the turban and swagger of high boots that had belonged of old days and still belonged to the 'rigimint'.

Bikrama Singh was seated on the flat roof which had sheltered him and his for centuries when he received the little slip of silk paper, so beautifully engrossed, which appointed him to the Honorary Magistracy. It was a barren honour, since he was not one of those – and there are many – who make a stipend out of an unpaid post; but his thin old fingers trembled a little and his eye lost the faintly blue film which age draws between the Real and the Unreal. Whether his mind reverted at once to his hereditary enemy – who was not mentioned in the paper – is doubtful, but he felt it to be an honour in these miserable days, when a money-lender had more chance of being elected to a district council than a gentleman of parts to be chosen by the *Sirkar*. It was a thousand times better than being 'puffed by rabble votes to wisdom's chair'.

'It is well,' he said simply, but with a superior air, to his womenfolk – the wife and daughters and grand-daughters and daughters-in-law and their kind who filled up the wide old house. 'I shall do my duty and punish the evil doer; notably those who do evil to my people and my land, since true justice begins at home.' And he curled his thin grey moustache to meet his short grey whiskers and looked fierce as an old tiger.

Over in Shakingarh also the commission met with approval. 'It is well!' said Buktiyar Khân, as he sat amongst his crowding womenfolk with a poultice of leaves on his short beard to dye it purple. 'I shall do my duty and punish the evil doer; notably him who has done evil to my people and my land, since that is the beginning of justice.' And his hawk's eye travelled almost unconsciously from his flat roof to that other one far over the valley.

Yet, when they met, a few days afterwards, duly attired in their uniforms on the threshold of Brine sahib's verandah, whither they had repaired full of courteous acknowledgements to one whom they recognized as being at the bottom of the appointment, a faint frown came to their old faces. But Brine sahib broke it to them gently, with the graceful tact which gained him so much confidence. Government, recognizing their many and great excellencies, had found it impossible to do otherwise than elevate them both to the Bench, where they would doubtless remain, as they were now, the best representatives of Hindu and Muhammadan feeling in the district. And then Tim O'Brien made a few remarks about the King-Emperor and devoted service which sent both old hands out in swift stiff salute.

Doubtless it was a shock to find themselves equally honoured; but regarding the '*in banco*', they both admitted instantly to themselves that it was better to sit next a hereditary enemy than a stinking scrivener or a mean money-lender. So Bikrama Singh twirled his grey moustache and said, 'It is well,' and Buktiyar Khân twirled his purple one and said the same thing.

Thereinafter they began work. The women of both houses made the first court day a regular festival, and sent the two old men from home dressed and scented and decorated as if for a bridal. The purple of Buktiyar's beard was positively regal, while the points of Bikrama's thin trembling fingers were rosy as the dawn.

They were fearsomely stately with each other, of course, but that only added to the dignity of the Bench. An excellent Clerk of the Court had been provided for them,

The Gift of Battle

and their first cases had been carefully chosen by Tim O'Brien for their simplicity.

Thus there had seemed no possibility of friction; yet the two new judges returned to their womenkind vaguely dissatisfied, dimly uneasy.

'The Muhammadan is no fool,' remarked Bikrama Singh thoughtfully, 'he saw as quickly as I did that truth lay with the defendant, lies with the plaintiff.'

'By God's truth,' admitted Buktiyar Khân grudgingly, 'the Hindu is not such a blockhead as I deemed him. He saw as quickly as I did that lies were with the plaintiff, truth with the defendant.'

It was almost intolerable; but it was true. The hereditary enemies had agreed about something on God's earth. And as time went on this unanimity of opinion became the most salient feature of the newly constituted court. They agreed about everything. Of different race, different religion, something deeper in them than these surface variations coincided. Their innate sense of justice, fostered by the fact that they had both been brought up in the India of the past, that they represented its laws, its morals, its maxims, made their judgements identical.

'We waste time, *babu-jee*,' broke in old Bikrama Singh on the lengthy peroration of a newly passed pleader, eager to air his eloquence. 'Words are idle when facts stare you in the face. "Who knows is silent, he who talks knows not", as the proverb hath it. That is enough. We are satisfied.'

'*Wâh Wâh*,' assented Buktiyar Khân at once, acquiescent and regretful. 'Truly, pleader-*jee*! thou hast said that before. Why say it again? If sugar kills, why try poison? We are satisfied, so that is enough.'

It was more than enough for the local Bar. They went in a body to Tim O'Brien and complained that they were not treated as lawyers should be treated.

As usual, Brine sahib met them with sympathy; but it was the sympathy of inaction.

'I sincerely regret, gentlemen,' he said softly, 'that sufficient time is not allowed you to get all the words you have at command off your stomachs – I beg pardon, your minds. But, ye see, the judgements of the Bench are unfortunately quite sound; they'd be watertight against the full forensic flood of the whole High Court Bar. So I don't see what the divvle is to be done – do you?'

They did not. In sober truth the sense of equity in the hereditary enemies was too strong for the lawyers. The old men were honestly fulfilled with the desire of punishing the evil doer and praising those who did well. Such flimsy overlays as race and tribe and caste and family and creed did not touch their agreement on all things necessary to salvation.

The fact was rather a pain and grief to them. It did not make them treat each other with less stately dignity or cause them to be one whit more friendly out of court.

Sirdar Bikrama Singh went home to his womenfolk and railed as ever against his neighbour, and Khân Buktiyar Khân, as he rolled his little opium pill betwixt finger and thumb, would do the same thing. But in their heart of hearts they knew that, since a judge must always be 'an ignorant man between two wise ones' (the plaintiff and defendant), it must be some common ground in themselves which made their views coincide.

Meanwhile the fame of the collective wisdom grew amongst the litigants, and indignation at its brevity increased amongst the lawyers. Tim O'Brien, however, when the timid little Commissioner showed him a numerously signed petition from the local Bar protesting against the 'strictly non-regulation curtailment of eloquence', only smiled suavely. 'They get at the rights of a case by congenital intuition, sir. The High Court have upheld their judgements in the few appeals the pleaders have cared to make; so I don't see what the div – I mean, sir, I don't see what is to be done – do you?'

Once again there was no answer, and Tim O'Brien, as he dashed off here and there to institute inquiries in obedience to the cipher telegrams which came pouring in from Calcutta by day and by night, felt comfort in knowing that one sub-division of his district at any rate was being well-administered.

For they were troublous days for officers in charge. Someone somewhere had been unwise enough to take the thumb-marks of a peripatetic preacher who was suspected of being an anarchist. He was proved to be an apostle of unrest; he was also unfortunately a man not only of thumb-mark, but of mark. A professor, briefly, in some far-away college. So the official who had ordered the indignity in the interests of public order was degraded; and thereinafter, naturally, began a campaign of would-be terrorism amongst the schoolboys and students of the province which shattered the nerves of government.

'By the Lord who made me,' ejaculated Tim O'Brien angrily, as he flung aside the last urgent *communiqué* from headquarters, 'one would think from that bosh, we were in danger of losing India tomorrow. Can't they see it's only schoolboy rot, sheer daredevil schoolboy mischief, like throwing caps under a motor-car and heads you win, tails I lose, you're over last. I'll tell you what it is, Smith,' – here he addressed his assistant, a pale-faced boy not yet recovered from the strain of examinations – 'if I was worth my salt and had the courage of my opinions I'd have up those boys' masters and give 'em each thirty with the cane for not keeping their pupils in order. That 'ud stop it. Instead of that, I have to arrest a poor child of thirteen who threw a badly made bomb, as harmless – it turned out – as a squib. However! my pension stares me in the face. There isn't even a House of Lords left to which I could appeal. So here goes for the innocent victim av' education! Inspector! arrange the arrest, please!'

Naturally, of course, as Tim O'Brien had known, every other schoolboy in the district marched about singing patriotic songs and doing wanton mischief to their hearts' content; thus there was quite a crop of minor arrests.

In fact, when the Bench of Hereditary Enemies held its next sitting it was confronted with a lengthy police case against a gang of boys whose ages varied from ten to thirteen.

Bikrama Singh listened gravely to the details and twirled his grey moustache. Buktiyar Khân also listened gravely and stroked his purple beard. They listened very patiently, yet a vague impatience came to their old faces. Then they looked in each other's eyes, and at last the wisdom of their hearts found speech.

'Where is the teacher of these children? Bring him hither that he may show cause for himself.'

To be brief. That night the head-master of the sub-divisional school could neither sit down nor stand up comfortably. But the streets were quiet; the boys peacefully in their beds.

'Glory be to them,' cried Tim O'Brien exultantly, when the news was brought to him. 'They've more spunk than I have – so now to get them out of the scrape.'

He did his best, and that was a good deal, but the law and lies were against him. The schoolmaster happened to be somebody's nephew by marriage, and though there was ample evidence to prove that he had misused his position as a Government servant, the utmost favour Tim O'Brien could screw out of the Powers was permission for the offenders to retire instead of being dismissed from the Honorary Magistracy.

He broke this to the old men with his usual tact, applauding them between the lines for their courage. To his surprise and relief they accepted the position calmly. The better the subordinate, they said, the less likely he was to be always in agreement with others. During their three years' work, which, in truth, had been laborious, not one of their decisions had been upset on appeal. How many judges could say the same! And as for head-master-*jee* – ? Would Brine sahib, if he could, remove those thirty stripes from the miscreant's back. 'Ye have me there, *sahiban*,' Tim O'Brien replied, with conviction, 'I would not; an' that's God's truth.'

So the old men sent in their resignations; not altogether regretfully. For one thing, the unanimity of their opinions had been disturbing; the old antagonism seemed more natural. And there the matter should have ended. Unfortunately for all, it did not. Tim O'Brien was asked one day, as District Officer, to sign a warrant for the arrest of Sirdar Bikrama Singh and Khân Buktiyar Khân on a charge of assault and battery against the head-master-*jee*, who turned out to be related to half the local Bar.

There is no reason to go into the legal points of the incident, or to tell of the vain efforts of Tim O'Brien to save the whilom Bench from this last affront. An epidemic of cases against magistrates had set in, and late one evening the District Officer started to ride over and break the news of the coming arrest to the Hereditary Enemies.

Nagadrug stood on the nearest scarp of sand, so he went there first. He found the old Sirdar, looking rather frail, engaged as usual in glaring out over the arid fields to Shakingarh.

But this time all Tim O'Brien's tact did not avail for

calm. Incredulous anger, half-dazed indignation, took its place. It could not be true. What! was he, Rajput of Rajput, to be dragged to court at the bidding of a miserable hound whom he had whipped, and rightly whipped? Had not Brine sahib himself applauded the act? Had they not done right? – the plural pronoun came out naturally. Was not a false guru God's basest creature? Did not the law say so: 'He who teaches false teaching, who kills his own soul and another, let him die.' Why had they not given the vile reptile a hundred stripes and so got rid of him altogether.

And now were they to have a degree (decree) against them? Shivjee! It should never be, never! never! They would not have it! The old tongue found no difficulty in thus claiming companionship in revolt, the old heart knew it was certain of sympathy in the ancient enmity.

Utterly sickened at a tragedy he could not prevent, the District Officer went, tactfully as ever, to Shakingarh; only to meet with even deeper indignation. Innocent though he knew himself to be, the Englishman positively writhed under the contemptuous unsparing scorn of the old Pathan. What! was the *Sirkar* not strong enough to protect itself? Then let it pack up its bundle and get out of Hindustan. Let it leave India and its problems to *his* people – those northern folk who had harried Bengal in the past, who, God willing, would harry it again. Had Brine sahib not heard the saying: 'He who uses his public office to betray the State commits a crime against himself, his country, and his God.' And had not the base hound betrayed the State? A thousand times, yes! It was a pity they had not flogged him to death.

The moon rose over the low sandhills before the District Officer, bruised and broken by the verdict of past India on the present, rode back to the sessions bungalow, where he meant to pass the night. For with the dawn he would go up with the police officer and so soften the arrest of the Hereditary Enemies so far as it could be softened.

They would be let out on bail, of course, and, at the worst, a fine more or less heavy would see them through. It was not so bad – not so very bad.

The District Officer tried to comfort himself with such reflections; in his heart he knew they were futile; that nothing would soften the degradation to those two old warriors.

Nothing! unless it was the calm moonlight that lay over the arid valley and turned the round old fortresses to dim mysterious palaces of light.

Perhaps the peace of it sank into the wearied hot old eyes that looked out from the ancestral roofs with a new feeling of comradeship, each for each, dulling the hereditary hatred, yet bringing with it old memories, old tales of past enmity.

'Bring me my uniform, women!' said Bikrama Singh suddenly. Half a dozen weeping daughters and daughters-in-law and an old wife too blind to see did as they were bid, and in a short time the old man stood arrayed as for a bridal, his sword buckled tight to his bowed back. 'And the shield, women – the shield of my fathers that hangs in the entry. I shall need it, too!'

Over in Shakingarh, Buktiyar Khân, impelled likewise by those memories of the past, that hatred of the present, had donned his uniform likewise; and so the moonlight shone on cold steel and damascened gold as, silently obeying some inward community of thought, the two old men started silently alone, leaving all behind them, to seek for Peace in their own way.

Steadily over the arid fields, nearer and nearer to each other. The fields had been cut and carried; the harvest was over; it was nigh time to plough again for a fresh crop –

Of what?

'The Peace of the Unknown be upon you, O mine enemy,' said Bikrama Singh, when at long last they stood face to face in the open.

'And the Peace of the Most Mighty be on you, my foe,' answered Buktiyar Khân.

So for a moment there was silence. Then the Rajput spoke, his old voice full of fire, full of vibration.

'In the old days to which we belong, O Muhammadan! did brave men wait for Fate?'

'They did not wait, O Hindu,' came the answer. 'When brave men found sickness or dishonour before them: when there was no longer hope of victory: when that which lay ahead was hateful, and they left sons to carry on the race, did not the ancestors of my race claim of their enemies the glorious gift of battle?'

'They did so claim it, O Bikrama Singh! Dost claim it now?'

The reply, quick, vibrant, rang through the moonlight; a veritable challenge.

'Yea, Pathan – robber! thief! I claim it now! *Jug-dân*, *Jug-dân* – the Gift of Battle to the Death.'

'Take it, pig of an idolater! *Jug-dân*, *Jug-dân* – the Gift of Battle!'

The still, hot air became full of faint chinkings, as buckles were settled straight, scabbards thrown aside. Then there was an instant's silence as the two old warriors faced each other.

'Art ready . . . friend?' The question came softly.

'Yea! I am ready . . . friend!' The reply was almost a caress.

So, with a quick clash of sword on sword, youth and health and strength came back to the Hereditary Enemies.

* * *

The Gift of Battle

It matters little if the combat ended in quarter of an hour, half an hour, or an hour; whether Bikrama Singh or Buktiyar Khân got in the first blow. The moon shone peacefully on the Gift of Battle. She still hung a white shield on the grey skies of dawn when Tim O'Brien and the police officer, coming to do their disagreeable duty, found the two old men lying stone dead within sword's thrust of each other on the stubble.

'They are really an incomprehensible lot,' said the police officer, almost mournfully; 'why the deuce should the two poor old buffers come out and kill each other, as presumably they have – '

Tim O'Brien smiled a grim smile. 'You haven't heard, I suppose – why should ye – of what they call the Gift of Battle? Well! I have. It's an ould Rajput custom by which a man who feared he'd die in his bed or be put to it any way by any other stupid inept limitations, could claim a decent death from his nearest foe.'

'Well! they've done it. That's all, and small blame to them.'

'By God who made me, it's a protest with a vengeance. But the worst of it is, the Government won't see it and I can't explain it. Cipher telegrams won't run to it. So . . . peace be with you, friends!'

FLORA ANNIE STEEL
The Shâhbâsh Wallah

'*Shâhbâsh, bhaiyan, shâhbâsh!*'

The words, signifying 'Bravo, boys, bravo!' came in a despondent drawl from the coolie leaning against the ladder – one of those crazy bamboo ladders with its rungs tied on with grass twine at varying slants and distances, whereon the Indian house-decorator loves to spend long days in company with a pot of colour-wash and a grass brush made from the leavings of the twine.

There were two such ladders in the bare, oblong, lofty room, set round with open doors and windows, and on each was balanced a man, a pot, and a brush – all doing nothing. So was the coolie below.

He was a small, slight man, with a dejected expression. Stark naked, save for two yards or so of coarse muslin wisped about his short hair and a similar length knotted about his middle. What colour either had been originally could not be guessed, since both were completely covered with splashes of colour-wash – blue, green, yellow, and pink. So was his thin body, which, as he stood immovable at the bottom of the ladder, looked as if it was carved out of some rare scagliola.

For they were doing up the hospital in Fort Lawrence, and Surgeon-Captain Terence O'Brien, of the 10th Sikh Pioneers – then engaged in making military roads over the Beloochistan frontier – had an eye for colour. Not so, however, Surgeon-Major Pringle, who that very morning had marched in with the detachment of young English recruits which had been sent to take possession of the newly enlarged fort. It was a queer mud building, looking as if it were a part of the mud promontory which blocked a sharp turn in the sun-dried, heat-baked mud valley, through which the dry bed of a watercourse twisted like the dry skin of a snake. Everything dry, everything mud, baked to hardness by the fierce sun. It was an ugly country in one way, picturesque in another, with its yawning fissures cracking the mud hills into miniature peaks and passes, its almost leafless flowering shrubs, aromatic, honeyful, and its clouds of painted butterflies. A country in which colour was lost in sheer excess of sunshine.

That, however, was not the reason why Surgeon-Captain O'Brien had painted his wards to match Joseph's coat. As he explained to Surgeon-Major Pringle, who, as senior officer, took over charge, it was wiser, in his opinion – especially with youngsters about – to call wards by the colour of their walls rather than by the diseases to be treated in them; since if a patient 'wance found out what was really wrong with his insoide, he was sure to get it insthanter.'

The Surgeon-Major, fresh from England and professional precisions – fresh also to India and its appeals to the imagination – had felt it impossible to combat such statements seriously. Besides, there was no use in doing so. The walls were past remedy for that year, and even the *post-mortem* house – that last refuge of all diseases – was being washed bright pink; a colour which, according to Terence O'Brien, was 'a nice, cheerful tint, that could not give anyone, not even a corpse, the blues'.

In the course of which piece of work the small man at the foot of the ladder was becoming more and more like a statue in *rosso antico*, as he repeated: '*Shâhbâsh, bhaiyan, shâhbâsh!*' at regular intervals.

His voice had no resonance, and not an atom of enthusiasm about it; but, like a breeze among rain-soaked trees, it always provoked a pitter-patter of falling drops – a patter of pink splashes like huge tears – upon the concrete floor and the scagliola figure. For the words set the brushes above moving slowly for a while; then the spasm of energy passed, all was still again, until a fresh 'Bravo, boys, bravo!' was followed by a fresh shower of pink tears.

'Lazy brutes!' came a boy's voice from the group of young recruits who were enjoying a well-earned rest after having marched in fifteen miles, carrying their kits as if they had been born with them, and settling down into quarters as if they were veterans. For they were smart boys, belonging to a smart regiment, whose recruiting ground lay far from slums and scums; one whose officers were smart also, and kept up the tone of their men by teaching them a superior tolerance for the rest of the world. 'Jest look at that feller – like an alley taw. He ain't done a blessed 'and's turn since I began to watch 'im.' They were seated on some shady mud steps right over against the hospital compound, and the *post-mortem* house being separate from the wards, and having all its many windows and doors set wide, the inside of it was as plainly visible as the out.

'Rum lot,' assented another voice with the same ring of wholesome self-complacency in it. 'I arst one of the Sickies, as seems a decent chap for a nigger and knows a little decent lingo, wot the spotted pig was at with his everlastin' *shabbashes*, an' 'e says it's to put courage to the Johnnies up top. Not that I don't say I shouldn't cotton myself much to them ladders, that's more like caterpillars than a decent pair o' 'ouse-steps. A poor lot – that's wot they are, as doesn't know the differ in holt between a nail and a bit o' twine.'

'Well, mates,' said a third voice, 'all I can say is that if they ain't got no more courage than *shâhbâsh* can put to

The Shâhbâsh Wallah

them, it's no wonder we licks the blooming lot of them – as we does constant.'

There was a faint laugh first, and then the group sucked at their pipes decisively as they watched the doings in the *post-mortem*. Though they would have scouted the suggestion, the *shâhbâsh wallah* had justified his calling; for patriotism brings courage with it.

He did not trouble his head about justification, however. Someone, in his experience, always did the shouting, and it suited him better than more active occupation, for he was lame; stiff, too, in his back. Surgeon-Major Pringle, coming in later to find the *post-mortem* very much as it had been hours before, looked at him distastefully, and began a remark about what two English workmen could have done, which Surgeon-Captain Terence O'Brien interrupted with his charming smile: 'Sure, sir, the sun rises a considerable trifle airlier East than West, an' that's enough energy for wan hemisphere. Besides, ye can't get on in India without a *shâhbâsh wallah*. Or elsewhere, for that matter. Ye always require "the something not ourselves which makes for righteousness" – '

'Makes for fiddlesticks!' muttered the senior under his breath, adding aloud: 'Who the dickens is the *shâhbâsh wallah* when he is at home, and what's his work?' He asked the question almost reluctantly, for his junior's extremely varied information had, since the morning, imparted a vague uncertainty to a round world which had hitherto, in Dr Pringle's estimation of it, been absolutely sure – cocksure!

'What is he? Oh! he's a variety of names. He's objective reality, moral sanction, antecedent experience, unconditioned good. Ye can take yer choice of the lot, sir; and if ye can't win the thrick with metaphysics – I can't, and that's the thruth – play thrumps. Sentiment! – sympathy! Ye can't go wrong there. Ye can't leave them out of life's equation, East or West. Just some one – a fool, maybe – to say ye're a fine fellow, an' no misthake, at the very moment whin ye know ye're not. Biogenesis, sir, is the Law of Life. As Schopenhauer says, the secret that two is wan, is the – '

His senior gave an exasperated sigh, and preferred changing the subject. So at the appointed time, no sooner, no later, the last patter of pink tears fell from the brushes upon the floor of the *post-mortem* and upon the still figure, which might have been a corpse save for its drowsy applause – 'Bravo, boys, bravo!' Then the caterpillar ladders, with the decorators and the pots of colour-wash and the brushes still attached to them, crawled away, and the *shâhbâsh wallah* followed in their wake, his skin bearing mute evidence to the amount of work he had provoked.

His turban and waistcloth testified to it for days – in lessening variety of tint as the layers of pink, green, blue, and yellow splashes wore off – for at least a fortnight, during which time Surgeon-Major Pringle, busy in making all things conform to his ideal, constantly came across the *shâhbâsh wallah* bestowing praise where, in the doctor's opinion, none was deserved. What right, for instance, had the water-carriers filling their pots, the sweepers removing the refuse, to senseless commendation for the performance of their daily round, their common task?

Especially when it was so ill performed; even in the matter of *punkah*-pulling, a subject on which the native might be credited with some knowledge. Surgeon-Major Pringle seethed with repressed resentment for days over the intermittent pulse of the office *punkah*, and finally, in a white heat of discomfort and indignation, burst out into the verandah, harangued the coolie at length, and in the fullness of Western energy went so far as to show him how to keep up a regular, even swing. His masterly grasp of a till then untouched occupation not only satisfied himself but also the *shâhbâsh wallah*, who, as usual, was lounging about in the verandah doing nothing. So, of course, his *'Shâhbâsh, jee, shâhbâsh,'* preceded Surgeon-Major Pringle's hasty return to the office and prepared Terence O'Brien for the dictum that the offender must be sent about his business; for *if* he was a camp-follower he *must* have some business, some regular work.

'Worrk, is it?' echoed Terence with his charming smile of pure sympathy. 'Be jabers! yes. Worrk – plenty, but not regular, as a rule. The man's a torch-bearer. If it happens to be a dark night, and annybody wants a *dhooli*, he carries the torch for it.'

Dr Pringle's resentful surprise made him stutter: 'Do you mean to say that – that – that – that – the public money – the ratepayers' money – is wasted in entertaining a whole man for so trivial a task?'

'Trivial, is it? When he's a pillar of fire by night an' a cloud of witnesses by day? And then he isn't a whole man, sir, at all at all. Wan of his legs is shorter than the other. I had to break it twice, sir, to get it as straight as it is. Thin, I've grave doubts about his spinal column; and as I trepanned him myself, I know his head isn't sound. It was two ton of earth fell on him, sir, last rains, when he was givin' a drink to wan of the Sikhs that got hurt blasting. It's nasty, shifty stuff, sir, is the mud in these low hills – nasty silted alluvial stuff, with a bias in it. So, poor divvle! seeing he wasn't fit for much but the hospital, I put him to the staff of it. And he kapes things going. Indeed, I wouldn't take it upon myself to say that he doesn't do the native patients as much good as half the drugs I exhibit to the unfortunate craythurs, since for sheer mystherious dispensations of Providence commend me to the British pharmacopoeia.'

Once again Surgeon-Major Pringle felt that professional

dignity could best be served by silent contempt, and orders that the offender was, at least, not to loaf about the verandahs.

But the fates were against the fiat. In the moonless half of May, driest of all months, a Hindu returning from Hurdwar fell sick, and half-an-hour after the report, Surgeon-Captain Terence O'Brien, going out of the ward with his senior, paused in his cheerful whistling of 'Belave me, if all those endearing young charms', to say under his breath, 'Cholera, mild type.' Now cholera, no matter of what type, has an ugly face when seen for the first time, especially when the face which looks into it, wondering if it means life or death, has youth in its eyes. So in the dark nights the *dhooli* came into requisition, and with it the torch-bearer, until the green and the blue and yellow wards overflowed into the verandahs, and even the pink *post-mortem* claimed its final share of boys. Not a large one, however, since, as Terence O'Brien said, 'It was wan of those epidemics when ye couldn't rightly say a man had cholera till he died of it.'

It was bad enough, however, to make the Surgeon-Major, who had never seen one before, set to work when it passed, suddenly as it had come, to cipher out averages, and tabulate treatments, with a view to what is called future guidance. And so, as he confided to his assistant with great complacency, it became clear as daylight that the largest percentage of recoveries, their rapidity, and as a natural corollary the incidence of mildness in the attack itself, seemed in connection with the position of the cots. Those close to the doors, or actually on the verandahs, were the most-fortunate, and so he was inclined to believe in the value of currents of fresh air.

'Fresh air, is it?' echoed Terence, with an encouraging smile. 'Maybe; maybe not. God knows, it may be anything in the wide wurrld, since there's but wan thing you can bet your bottom dollar on in cholera, sir, and that is that ye can't tell anything about it for certain, and that your experience of wan epidemic won't be that of the next.'

'Neither does your experience, Mr O'Brien,' retorted his senior sarcastically, 'militate against mine being more fortunate. I mean to leave no stone unturned to arrive at reliable data on points which appear to me to have been over-looked. For instance, I shall begin by asking those cases of recovery if they remember anything which seemed at the time to bring them relief, to stimulate in them that vitality which it is so essential to preserve.'

In pursuance of which plan he went out then and there to the verandah, where a dozen or more lank boys were lounging about listlessly, just beginning to feel that life might soon mean more than a grey duffle dressing-gown and a long chair.

'No, sir,' said the first firmly. 'I disremember anythin' that done me good. I jest lay with a sickenin' pain in my inside, an' a don't-care-if-I-do feelin' outside.' He paused, and another boy took up the tale sympathetically.

'So it was. A reg'lar, don't care except w'en that little 'eathen – 'im that's always saying *shâhbâsh*, sir, come along; an' that seem to me most times. 'E made me feel a blamed sight – beggin' pardon, sir – worse. For I kep' thinkin' of where I see 'im first, like a alley taw in the dead 'ouse; and the dead 'ouse isn't a cheerful sorter think w'en you ain't sure but wot you're going there. It made me – ' he paused in his turn.

'Made you what?' asked Terence O'Brien, who had followed to listen.

'Give me the 'orrors, sir, till I'd 'ave swopped all I knew to kick 'im quiet; but not bein' able, I jest lay and kep' it for 'im against I could, till it seemed like as I must; an' so I will.'

'In cases of extreme nervous depression, sir,' began the junior mischievously, 'a counter irritant – '

'Pshaw!' interrupted Dr Pringle angrily, and walked back with great dignity to the office.

But the conversation thus started lingered among the grey dressing-gowns, the result of comparing notes being a general verdict that 'Alley Taw' deserved that kicking. He did not actually get it, however; the boys were too big, and he too small for that. But he sank into still greater disrepute, becoming, in truth, that most unenviable of all things not made nor created, but begotten of idle wit – a garrison butt. Not that he seemed to care much. He grew more furtive in his lounging, but nothing seemed to disturb the divine calm of his commendation for the world which he had created for himself with his 'Bravo, boys, bravo!' Behold, all things in it were very good! That, at least, was Terence O'Brien's fanciful way of looking at the position. As he went about his work whistling 'Belave me, if all those endearing young charms' – a tune which, he said, cheered the boys – he would often pause to smile at the *shâhbâsh wallah*. After a time, however, the smile would change to a quick narrowing of the eyes, as if something in the bearing of the man was puzzling. Finally, one day, coming upon the man sidling along a bit of brick wall, which had been built to strengthen a crack in the mud one overhanging the dry watercourse, he pulled up, asked a few rapid questions, and then lifted the man's eyelids and peered into the soft brown eyes, as if he wanted to see through them to a crack he knew of in the back of the man's skull.

'And you are sure you see as well as ever?' he asked again.

'Quite as well, *Huzoor*,' came the answer, with a faint

tremor in it. 'I can see to carry the torch on the darkest of nights if it is wanted, *Huzoor*!'

'Hm!' said Dr O'Brien doubtfully, promising himself to test the truth of this statement. But the fates again decreed otherwise. The next day's mail brought orders for him to go and act elsewhere for a senior on two months' leave.

Dr Pringle was not sorry. How could you collaborate properly with a man who calmly admitted that at a pinch he had used a bullet-mould to extract a tooth?

The monsoon had long since broken in the plains ere the young doctor returned; but in the arid tract in which Fort Lawrence lay rain came seldom at any time. And that was a year of abnormal drought. The fissures in the mud seemed to widen with the heat, and the fringe of green oleanders which followed every turn of the dry watercourse, mutely witnessing to unseen moisture below, wilted and drooped. In the new-built fort itself a crack or two showed in the level platform jutting out across the low valley on which the building stood, and in more than one place portions of the low mud-cliffs crumbled and broke away. The whole earth, indeed, seemed agape with thirst.

But water in plenty came at last. On the very day, in fact, when Terence O'Brien returned to the fort, which he reached on foot, having had to leave his *dhooli* behind, owing to a small slip on the road; nevertheless, as he crossed over from the mess to his quarters close to the hospital that evening, he told himself that he had the devil's own luck to be there at all. For the rain was then hitting the hard ground with a distinct thud, and spurting up from it in spray, showing white against the black murk of the night. And the rush of the stream filling up the dry bed of the watercourse, and playing marbles with the boulders, was like a lion's roar.

It did not keep him awake, however, for he was dead

tired. So he slept the sleep of the just. For how long he did not know. It was darker than ever when he woke suddenly – why he knew not, and with the same blind instinct was out into the open, quick as he could grope his way.

Not an instant too soon, either. A deafening crash told him that, though he could not see his own hand. The rain had ceased, but the rush of the river dulled hearing to all lesser sounds. As he stood dazed, he staggered, slipped, almost fell. Was that an earthquake, or was the solid ground parting somewhere close at hand? And if his house was down, how about the hospital and the sick folk?

He turned at the thought and ran till, in the dark and the silence of that overwhelming roar, he came full tilt upon someone else running in the dark also. It was the Surgeon-Major.

'The hospital's down. Have you a light – anything – a match?' panted Dr Pringle. 'We must have a light to see –'

'Oh, *masâl*! Oh, *masâl-jee*!' (Oh, the torch! Oh, the torch-bearer!) shouted Terence at the top of his voice as he ran on till stopped by something blocking the way. Ruins! And that was the sound of voices.

'What's up?' he cried.

'Don' know, sir,' came from unseen hearers. 'Part o' the 'orspital's down, but we can't see. It's a slide o' some sort, for there's a crack right across nigh under our feet. If we could get a light!'

'Oh, *masâl*! Oh, *masâl-jee*!' The doctor's voice rang out again towards the camp-followers' lines, but the roar was deafening. And in the night, when all men are asleep, the news of disaster travels slowly. Yet without a light it was impossible even to realize what had happened, still less to help the sick who might lie crushed.

'Oh, *masâl*! Oh, *masâl-jee*! – thank God! there's a light at last.'

There was, in the far distance across the quadrangle. But it was not a torch; it was only an officer in a gorgeous sleeping-suit running with a bedroom candle. Still it was a light!

'Come on, man!' shouted Terence O'Brien, as it slackened speed, paused, stopped dead. His was the only voice that seemed to carry through the roar.

But the gay sleeping-suit stood still, waving its candle.

'It's the crack, sir,' called someone in Terence O'Brien's ear. 'It goes right across, I expect – we'd best find out first.'

It did. A yawning fissure, twenty feet wide, had cut the hospital compound in two, and isolated one angle of the fort – that nearest the river – from the rest. Twenty feet wide, at least, judged by the glimmer of light! And how deep? Had the river cut it? Was it only a matter of time when the mud island on which they stood should be swept away? And what were the means of escape? There was more light now; more bedroom candles and sleeping-suits; a lamp or two, and others behind, as the boys – last to wake – came running, to pause like the first-comers, at the unpassable gulf; for the more it could be seen, the more difficult seemed the task of crossing it at once. By-and-by, perhaps, with ladders and ropes it would be possible – but now? Terence O'Brien, feeling the 'now' imperative, skirted the crumbling edge almost too near for safety in his eagerness to find some foothold for a daring man; but there was none. True, the brick wall, built to strengthen the cracked mud one, still bridged the extreme end of the fissure, looking as if the mud had deliberately shrunk from its intrusion. It hung there half seen, on God knows what slender foundation – perhaps on none. But it could give no help. To trust it would be madness; a touch might send it down into the river below. No! Since none could cross the gap there must be more light on the farther side; torches, a bonfire, anything to pierce the dark and let men see how to help themselves and other men!

'Oh, *masâl*! Oh, *masâl-jee-ân*!' The cry went out with all the force of his lungs. Surely the camp-followers must be awake by now.

One was, at any rate; for, surrounded by a halo from the faggot of blazing pitch-pine it carried, a figure showed upon the path worn, close to the mud walls of the native quarters, by the foot-tracks of those whose duty took them to the hospital. It was the *shâhbâsh wallah*, coming slowly, almost indifferently, in answer to the call; coming as if to his ordinary duty towards the growing fringe of ineffectual candles and eager men bordering the impossible. That was better! Given half-a-dozen more such haloes – and there were plenty if they would only come – and eager men on the other side would see how to help themselves and their comrades!

But no other halo appeared behind the one which followed the foot-track of others so closely; and so once again the call was given –

'Oh, *masâl*! Oh, *masâl-jee-ân*! Oh, *masâl*! Oh, *masâl-jee*!'

'*Hâzr, Huzoor!*' (Present, sir).

The nearness of the voice made Terence O'Brien look up, for it was the first voice he had heard clearly from the other side against that roar of the river. But as he looked another voice beside him said hurriedly –

'My God! he's coming across!'

He was. Surrounded by the halo of his own light, and keeping religiously to the beaten path, the *shâhbâsh wallah*, leaving the mud wall of the quarters, had struck the outer brick one as it stood, supported for a few yards by a spit of earth upon which the foot-track showed as the light passed.

A spit narrowing to nothing – no! not to nothing, but to a mere ledge of earth and mortar clinging like a swallow's nest to the brick – wider here, narrower there, yet still able to give faint foothold upon the traces of those feet which had passed and repassed so often to their trivial round, their common task. Foothold! Ay! But what of the brain guiding the feet? What of the courage guiding the brain?

And even then, what of the foundation?

A sort of murmur rose above the roar. 'He can't do it – impossible – tell him. Call to him, O'Brien. Tell him not to try.'

The doctor stood for one second watching the figure centring its circle of light against the background of wall; then, even though there was no need for it, his voice fell to a whisper. 'Hush!' he said. 'Don't hustle him. By the Lord who made me, he doesn't know; he's feeling his way every inch by the wall! He's blind, and by God! if anybody can do it, he will.'

He did. Step by step, slowly, confidently, in the footsteps of others.

And the great cry of 'Bravo, brother, bravo!' which went up from both sides of the gap as he and his torch stepped on to firm ground, brought him as much surprise as a voice from heaven might have done.

'Pressure on the brain!' said Surgeon-Captain Terence O'Brien, about three weeks after this, when he and Dr Pringle had had a consultation over the *shâhbâsh wallah*. He was not only blind now, but there was a drag in the good leg as he limped about, over which both doctors shook their heads. 'And there's nothing to be done that I can see. The bhoys will miss him!'

That was true. Alley Taw had come into favour since the night when, as Terence phrased it, 'he had done a brave deed without doing it,' and by failing to see the evil, had enabled other men to do good. For the torch had not disclosed irretrievable disaster, and by timely rescue not a life had been lost.

Surgeon-Major Pringle frowned. He was beginning to understand his India a little, but the idea of the *shâhbâsh wallah* being a useful member of society was still as a red rag to a bull. And so, out of sheer contrariety, he began to talk doctor's talk as to the possibility of this or that.

'It's life or death, annyhow,' said the junior, shaking his head, 'but I don't see it. I wouldn't thry it myself – not now at any rate.'

Perhaps not then. But after a month or two more he said, 'It's your suggestion; I don't belave it can be done; but you may as well thry.'

For the *shâhbâsh wallah*, half paralysed, had even given up his cry. So, part of the hospital being still under repair, they took him to the pink *post-mortem* house and set all the doors and windows wide for more light. He was quite unconscious by that time, so Terence O'Brien only had the chloroform handy, and kept his finger on the pulse. Half-a-dozen or more of the boys were on the mud steps over against the hospital compound waiting to hear the *shâhbâsh wallah's* fate. But you might have heard a pin drop in the *post-mortem*, save for the occasional quick request for this or that as the Surgeon-Major, with the Surgeon-Captain's eyes watching him, set his whole soul and heart and brain on doing something that had never been done before.

So the minutes passed. Was it to be failure or success? The Surgeon-Major's fingers were deft – none defter.

The minutes passed to hours. That which had to be done had to be done with one touch light as a feather, steady as a rock, perfect in its performance, or not at all.

And still the minutes passed. Terence O'Brien's face was

losing some of its eagerness in sympathy, Dr Pringle's gaining it in anxiety; for clear, insistent, not-to-be-silenced doubt was making itself heard. Only the *shâhbâsh wallah* cared not at all as he lay like a corpse.

It had come to the last chance. The last; and Dr Pringle, with a pulse of wild resentment at his own weakness, realized that his nerve was going, his hand shaking. Still, it had to be done. The splinter of bone raised – the whole process he had thought out as the last chance gone through. He steadied himself and began. Failure or success? Failure – failure – failure! The word beat in on his heart and brain, bringing unsteadiness to both.

'Dresser, the chloroform,' said Terence O'Brien sharply; for there was a quiver in the man's eyelids.

But ere the deadening drug did its work, the *shâhbâsh wallah*'s brain, set free to work along familiar lines by the raising of that splintered bone, had sent its old message to his lips –

'*Shâhbâsh, bhaiyan, shâhbâsh!*'

In telling the story Dr Pringle says no more; generally because he cannot.

But after a time, if you are a brother craftsman, he will give you all details of the biggest and most successful operation he ever did.

And though he is slow to allow the corollary, he never denies that the *shâhbâsh wallah*'s verdict put courage into him.

FLORA ANNIE STEEL
Surâbhi
A Famine Tale

She was only a cow, but she was all things, wife and child, earth and heaven, to old Gopâl, the Brahmin who owned her.

And, apart from his estimation, she had value. Connoisseurs in the village, as they looked over the low mud wall which separated the slip of open courtyard, ten feet by six, where there was just room for a crazy four-legged string bed between Surâbhi's manger and the door, would nod and say she must have been a good cow when young; but when that was only God knew!

Whereupon Gopâl would raise his shaven head with its faint frosting of silver hair from Surâbhi's silver flank, as he squatted holding a brass pot in one hand, milking with the other, and smile scornfully.

'Old or young, she is the best milker in the village, and the best-looking one and the best bred,' he would say. 'And wherefore not? Is she not Surâbhi the Great Milk-Mother, whom even the gods worship? Since without her where would the little godlings be?' And then he would pop down the pot and cease milking for a moment, so that both hands might be free for a reverential *salaam* to the old cow who, at the cessation, would turn her mild white face – the real Brahmini zebu face with its wide dewy black nostril, wide dewy black eyes, and long lopping ears – to see what had come to old Gopi; and, as often as not, would give his round frosted black poll a lick round with her black frosted tongue, by way of encouragement to go on, as if he had been a calf!

But the connoisseurs over the wall would snigger, and touch their foreheads, and say that Gopâl Das was getting quite childish and mixed up things. Though, no doubt, the great Surâbhi must have been just such another cow, since the old man said right. There was not her like in the village. No! not even now that Govinda had brought home the brown cow with five teats, which had taken the prize at the *Huzoor*'s big show. It was younger, of course, but Surâbhi would outlast the old man, and what more could *he* want? Then who, before these latter days, had ever heard tell of a brown cow? And as for the five teats, they might portend more milk, but were they lawful?

So, long-limbed, whole-hearted, dull-headed, the villagers went doubtfully about their business scarcely less confused than old Gopi between facts and fancies, realities and unrealities; tied and bound, as their like are in hamlet and village, by the allegories of a faith whose inner teaching has been forgotten.

But old Gopâl stayed with Surâbhi. His life was bounded by her. How he lived was one of the many mysteries of Indian village life. He did nothing but look after his cow, but he must have inherited some fractional share of the village land from his fathers, or been entitled, by reason of his race, to some ancestral dues, for twice a year at harvest time he would come back to the courtyard, like a squirrel to its nest, with so many handfuls of this grain and so many handfuls of that, so many bundles of wheat straw, millet stalks, or pea stems. And on these, and the milk she gave, he and Surâbhi lived contentedly. He was very old; if he had had wife and children in the past he had quite forgotten them. Yet it was typical of village life that no one forgot old Gopi or his rights. Whatever was due to him from well or unwatered land, even if it were only so many leaves of tobacco or chilli pods, came to the courtyard as regularly as the sunshine.

And, regularly as the sunshine, too, the old man, after he had milked Surâbhi in the early dawn, would go with his solitary blanket and a little spud and spend the whole day till sunset in gathering succulent weeds for the great Milk-Mother's supper. It was his religion. And under the broad blue sky, edging a plantigrade path over the parched plain, leaving, like a locust, not a green leaf behind him, old Gopi's mind would be full of confused piety and mystical meanings.

This was the highest service of man, this was Faith and Hope and Charity all combined; since everyone knew that Surâbhi was the World-Mother, and without her –

Here the old Brahmin's memory of words would fail him, and he would fall back on deeds, by digging at the biggest weed within reach.

From year's end to year's end he seldom fingered a coin, and if he did, it was Surâbhi who brought it to him. Her last calf had long since become an ox, and drifted away from the village to fill a gap in the great company of the ploughers and martyrs who give the coffer of the Empire all its gold and die in thousands – long before famine touches humanity – without a penny piece from that coffer being spent to save them from starvation. Yet she still, after the fashion of her race, gave milk and to spare. The latter went, as a rule, to folk poorer still than the old Brahmin, especially to children; but when he sold it, part of the money was always spent on a new charm for Surâbhi's neck. And it might be noted that whenever, by looking over the low mud walls which separated the village courtyards one from the other, he found that Govinda's brown cow had a fresh bell or disposition of cowries round her neck, there was always enough milk over and above Gopi's wants next day to procure a similar adornment for the white one with its heavy dewlap.

The rivalry grew, by degrees, into a definite challenge between their owners, so that when, after a time, Govinda's beast fell off in her milk, Gopi's delight was palpable, and he scouted all reasonable explanations of the fact.

The cow, he said, was underbred. You could see by her hoofs that she had been accustomed to wander about and pick up her own living like low-caste folk; while Surâbhi bore token of her lifelong seclusion in every polished ring of her long-pointed black toes.

But before the question at issue could be decided, that came about which dried up every cow in the village, and made even old Gopi's brass pot cease to brim.

There was no rain. Even in December and January, though the skies were dappled as the partridge's breast, the clouds carried their moisture elsewhere. Where, did not affect the villagers. It was not here, and that was all they knew. The autumn crop, which means fodder, had been a scant one, the cattle were thrown entirely on the still scantier growth of grass in the waste land; and when that failed, custom did not fail. The herds were driven forth from the thorn enclosures every morning to the wilderness and taken back from it at eve, just as if that wilderness were still a grazing-ground. What else could be done, seeing that when cattle starve it is not a famine? *That* is a time when help is given by the new master. God knows why, since the old masters never gave any.

Such time of help must come, of course, ere long, if the clouds remained dry; but meanwhile the flocks and herds went out to graze on mud, and if some failed to return in the evening, what else was to be expected?

So the long dry days dragged on. That spring-harvest old

Gopâl's share of garnered grain was scarcely worth the bringing home. The squirrel's hoard in the little courtyard was scanty indeed, and very soon he had to stint his own share, and rise an hour earlier to go weed-grubbing, and return an hour later, so that Surâbhi should not low her discontent at short commons. For that would be shame unutterable, even though the brown cow had long since been driven from high-class seclusion to fend for herself with the common herd from dawn till eve.

Thus old Gopâl's lank anatomy was appreciably more lank, more skeleton-like, when one day the headman of the village, as he smoked his pipe in front of the house of faith where strangers were lodged, announced that the famine had really come at last. Over in Chotia Aluwala there were piles of baskets and spades. Some *Huzoors* were there in white tents, so doubtless ere long, God knows why, they would begin digging earth from one place and putting it in another, so that a distribution of grain could be made in the evening.

That was the headman's idea of relief-works, and his hearers had no other.

Now Chotia Aluwala was ten miles at least from Surâbhi's stall, but of late Gopi had scarce found a weed within twice that distance.

So the very next day, when, backed by a pile of forlorn-looking earth on one side and a not much smaller pile of baskets with which the earth had, during the day's toil, been conveyed to its present resting-place, one hungry face after another came up in file to the distribution of food, old Gopi's frosted head was among the number. But he was bitterly disappointed at his dole of cooked dough-cake. He had expected grain. Though more than enough for his old appetite, what would Surâbhi, with her seven stomachs, say to such concentrated food?

Surâbhi

After his long trudge home he passed a miserable night seeking, by every means in his power, to supply the bulk necessary for the satisfying of those clamorous stomachs. He even chopped up the grass twine of his string bed and tempted the old cow to chew it by soaking the fibre in some of her own milk.

Thus, once more, he came off second best, for the milk should have been his share. So he could scarcely manage to stagger along with his basket next day. Not that this mattered, for already the Englishmen who, in their khaki clothes and huge pith helmets, were supervising the work, were saying tentatively, with a glance at the totterers, that it might have been better to start relief a little sooner. And down in one hollow Gopi saw a woman being carried away, while the babe which had been at her breast yelled feebly in an orderly's arms.

The sight did not affect Gopi in the least. He had thought out a plan which filled his confused old soul with a heavenly joy. So when his two dough-cakes were given him that evening he hurried off with them to the contractor in the background, through whom the *Huzoors* had arranged for this supply, and exchanged them – at a loss, inevitably – for the coarse husks, the bran, the sweepings, the absolute waste which could not be used even in famine bread.

The arrangement suited both parties, the contractor and old Gopi, who day after day trudged home, hungry, with a bulky bundle of fodder for Surâbhi. It was a fair exchange all round, even with the old cow, who turned the fodder into milk. Not much, it is true, since the bundle was not overlarge, but enough to keep Gopi's soul and body together.

And the soul grew if the body wasted. How could it be otherwise, when one was permitted to be the babe and suckling, as it were, of the Great Milk-Mother? The Great

World-Mother, whose sacred work it was to nourish all things, even the little godlings?

The old Brahmin's eyes grew softer, more trustful, more like the eyes of a child, as the days went by; and as he milked her, Surâbhi's black frothed tongue often licked more than his shaven poll, as if she were concerned at the bones which showed through the skin of her calf.

Gopâl himself, however, took this licking as a mark of Divine favour; and, as for the thinness, were not all the babes and sucklings growing thin?

That was true. The Englishman in head charge of the Chotia Aluwala relief-work canal had that thinness on his conscience. But what could man do in a wilderness, without mothers, without milk?

He had it on his heart too, because he was a father; and because, despite a mother and milk, doctors and skilled care, it was not two months since he had seen his first-born waste away mysteriously to death, as children will waste.

So his mind was full of it, when, for the sake of seeing a lonely wife and mother, he rode forty miles after nightfall to the little bungalow so empty of a child's voice.

'I've got quite a nursery of 'em now,' he said grimly, 'but they beat me. I can't get the men in charge to mix that tin-milk stuff right, you know, and the little beggars won't look at a teaspoon.'

Perhaps it was his ride that had tired him. Anyhow, he crossed his hands on the table, and laid his head on them wearily.

He roused, however, at her touch on his shoulder.

'Let me come,' she said; 'I've – I've nothing to do here.'

He looked at her for a moment, then turned his eyes away. 'Will you?' he said in an odd voice; 'that – that will be awfully jolly.'

So in a day or two, armed with the dead baby's bottles,

feeding-cups, God knows what, and such mother's lore as the dead child had taught her, she was at work in a white tent set in the shade of the only tree at Chotia Aluwala.

'I must have more milk,' she said decidedly, and there was a new light in her eyes, a new tone in her voice, when they brought her yet another whimpering brown baby. 'That is the end of it; by hook or by crook I *must* have more milk. There *must* be some, somewhere. Send out and see!'

So, because when a woman is standing between death and children, her orders are the orders of 'She-who-must-be-obeyed', they sent. And, of course, one of the first discoveries made by the Indian underling to whom the inquiry was entrusted, was Surâbhi. In other words, that an old Brahmin, in receipt actually of relief, was the possessor of a remarkably fine cow, if not in full milk, yet capable of supporting an infant or two. It needs the vicious flair of an underpaid orderly to find such chances for tyranny and extortion at the first throw off. But this one was found, and when Gopi returned that evening to the little courtyard, an official with a brass pot was waiting for milk. It would be paid for, of course, by and by. Gopi could keep an account, and the *Sirkar* no doubt would pay, provided the *proper official* certified it by a counter-sign.

The old man was too confused, too tired to be ready with protest at a moment's notice. So that night he went supperless to bed. But in the white tent over at Chotia Aluwala, an Englishwoman's pale face had quite a colour in it.

'Fancy!' she said, 'two whole quarts of the most beautiful, rich milk! I would reward that man if I were you, dear. I am to have the same every day. It – it means two lives at least!'

Possibly, for a baby takes less to keep it alive than an old man.

Small tragedies of this sort are common enough in India, but it is difficult to give all their fineness of detail to English eyes.

Old Gopâl was at once cunning as a fox, guileless as a child; and through both the guile and the innocence ran that bewildered belief in Surâbhi as something beyond ordinary cows. He tried to escape the *impasse* by not milking her dry, so as to leave some for himself; but though Surâbhi resented any other hand finishing the task, it was impossible for an experienced onlooker to be deceived. The result of that, therefore, was abuse and blows. Then he tried keeping back one dough-cake from his daily dole for himself, and only exchanging the other for fodder. That reduced the milk in reality, but it also reduced Surâbhi to lowing; and his sense of sin, in consequence, became so acute that he was forced into going back to the old plan. But these tactics had, by this time, roused the petty official's ire. The memsahiba had spoken sharply to him because the milk had fallen off in quantity and quality; for he had not scrupled, despite old Gopi's tears and distracted prayers, to take away the Milk-Mother's character by filling up the measure with water.

And so he lost patience. Thus one day he avenged himself and attained his object by first reporting that Gopi, Brahmin, was wrongfully and fraudulently obtaining relief, seeing that he was, amongst other things, possessor of a remarkably fine cow, whose milk he was selling to the *Huzoors*, and then seizing Surâbhi, on the ground that Gopi, having no means of supporting her, was not fit to take care of so valuable an animal!

These two blows, followed by the sight of Surâbhi being walked off on her dainty toes into the rough, outside world, quite upset the frail balance of the old man's mind.

Surâbhi

He crouched shivering all night in the empty stall, feeling himself accursed. He was not worthy. Surâbhi had gone.

How long he remained there speechless, famine-stricken, yet not hungry, he did not know. It was early afternoon when the white garment and brass badge of authority showed again at the door in the low wall, and a voice said sullenly –

'Thou must come. Thy cursed cow is a devil for kicking, and the mem is a fiend for temper. My badge is gone if thou come not. My pony will carry two.'

The sun was showing red behind the great piles of earth which in that wide level plain rose like a range of hills, when the oddly assorted pair rode into the shade of the Chotia Aluwala tree. There was no need to announce the arrivals. Surâbhi declared who one was, almost ere he stumbled to the ground, stiff, dazed, bewildered. All the more bewildered for that vision of something undreamt of, unseen hitherto in Gopâl Das' ignorant village life – a woman fair as milk herself, smiling at him gladly, calling with quaint, strange accent: 'Quick – quick! we wait, we are hungry – are we not, babies?'

There were dark toddlers round the white dress, a dark head on the white bosom, and old Gopi muttered something about the Milk-Mother, the World-Mother, as, with a brass vessel someone thrust into his hand, he squatted down beside Surâbhi.

He scarcely needed to milk her; perhaps that was as well, for he was very tired. But the pot brimmed, and another had to be called for, while Surâbhi's black frosted tongue licked the black frosted head between her '*moos*' of satisfaction.

And beyond, in the shadiest part of the shade, there was more satisfaction and to spare.

After a while old Gopi crept stiffly to watch it, squatting

in the dust with dry, bright, wistful eyes fixed on the bottles, the babies; above all on the milk-white face full of smiles.

Until suddenly he gave a little cry.

'Me too, Mother of mercy! Great Milk-Mother of the world, me too!' he said, like any child, and so fell forward insensible with outstretched, petitioning hands.

But that was the end of his troubles.

When he came to himself, the Great Milk-Mother was feeding him with a teaspoon. Nor when he recovered his strength would she let him out of the nursery, for by that time the whole story had been told, with the curious calm acquiescence of villagers in such pitiful tales of mistake and wrong. Everyone had known the truth, of course, but what then? The *Huzoors* wanted the milk for the babies, and Gopi was old –

'He is only a baby himself,' interrupted a woman's voice indignantly when this explanation was being given; 'why, this morning I made him as happy as a king by letting him suck one of the bottles! He said that there was nothing left now to be desired, nothing wanting, except – '

'Except what?' asked the man's voice.

'That he could see no little godlings like – like me.'

Then there was silence.

FLORA ANNIE STEEL
'London'

The rains had fallen late, bringing unusual greenness to the stretches of waste land, and unusual promise of harvest to the bare, brown fields where man and beast were hard at work, day and night, ploughing, harrowing, sowing, watering. Waiting – that integral part of Indian husbandry – had yet to come, but the memory, almost the dread of it, lurked ever in the slow brains of the labourers. In mine also, alien and uninterested though it was; for surely no one who has seen a Jât cultivator, tall, meagre, soft-eyed, wandering amongst his green wheat, waiting for Râm to send rain, can ever forget the incarnate tragedy of the sight.

The sun was setting cloudless in a sea of light, that still flooded the scene with the brightness of noon, though the shadows lengthened in swift strides. I was sitting on a wide flight of steps leading down into a small tank closed in on all sides by masonry. Viewed thus, with the mass of brickwork surrounding it, this square of placid water reflecting back the lemon-coloured sky, the fringe of dull *farâsh* trees, and the gilded spires of the temple rising above them, showed like a small Dutch picture set in a heavy, deep-recessed frame. On the opposite side a woman in a saffron veil was filling her brass pot, and on the trumpery stucco arcades of the temple-plinth were painted blue elephants, gingerbread tigers and spidery monkeys. Round and round the central spire the iridescent breasts of the whirling pigeons glinted in the level rays.

It was peaceful, colourful, almost in its way beautiful, especially after a long day's work in the office tent which rose a few hundred yards away. Suddenly the clear-cut silence of the scene was marred by a deprecatory voice behind me.

'The Presence will not think it so fine as '*Ide Park*, doubtless?'

'So fine as what?' I echoed carelessly, being accustomed to the thousand and one interruptions of a district officer's life.

'So fine as your '*Ide Par-k* in the town of London.'

'Hyde Park! – why! what the deuce do you know of Hyde Park?'

Intense surprise had replaced my indifference, for there was nothing to account for the strangeness of his words either in the face or figure of the man who stood behind me leaning on a long staff over which his hands were crossed. It was just such a face and figure as I saw every day. A typical Jât – in other words, a farmer by race and heritage – tall, high-shouldered, lank, with a bushy-shaped turban adding to his height, and straight folds of heavy unbleached cotton cloth suggesting the lean, bony frame beneath. A face well cut, but not refined, marked, but not strong, in which the most noticeable features were the large dreamy eyes like those of Botticelli's *Moses* in the Sistine Chapel.

Immovable from the knee downwards he squatted, as the Americans say, 'in his tracks', keeping his submissive face towards mine like a dog awaiting his master's pleasure.

'By the mercy of the Presence I have seen 'Ide Park. Yes, I have been there – in the city of London – where the sahibs and the memsahibs sit and walk.'

A vision of the figure before me planted out amongst flower-decked mashers and powdery belles aroused such a sense of incongruity in my mind that I could only echo feebly –

'So you have been to London!'

'Yes!' he replied cheerfully, 'I've been to London to see the great Queen.'

For the life of me I could not help reverting to the sequence of childish days: *'Pussy cat, pussy cat, what saw you there?'* and his reply fitted in so neatly that my query lost its lightness and became serious.

'I saw the *Sikattar* (secretary) who sits in her chair.'

I laughed then; I could not help it, for I felt convinced that no other words could have expressed the whole incident more truthfully.

'I went to London, O Protector of the Poor!' continued the stranger softly, 'because I wanted to get back the land. The Presence knows we Jâts cannot live without our land.'

Involuntarily his eyes turned to a neighbouring field, where a couple of plough bullocks were slowly scoring the levels into feeble furrows, whilst the ploughman – just such a man as the one before me – held his hookah in one hand, his goad in the other.

'So you did not get the land after all? How was that?' God knows I was not always so ready of access to the native (as the departmental pastorals put it), but then one does not meet a Jât who has been to Hyde Park every day.

'Perhaps if it had not been a *Sikattar*,' replied the low soft voice – 'perhaps if it had been the great Queen herself – ' Here the plough bullocks he was watching turned too sharply, and his hand closed mechanically on the stick he held between his knees, as if he were responsible for the mistake. 'If the Presence has not heard it all before, I will tell it why Dewa Râm the Jât went to London.'

I give the story in his own words, for mine might fail to transmit the perfection of his patience.

'The land was my father's, and my father's father's from Mahratta times. In those days no one could sell the land or prevent the sons from following the father's plough. To begin with, no one wanted to sell good land, and then they could not if they would. That was before the great *Sirkâr* – life and prosperity be with it always – came to lift the hearts of the poor and set their heads high. There was much land, and on some of it in olden days a mortgage had been put. The Presence will know the kind of mortgage, where for a hundred rupees or so of loan another man is allowed to till the soil worth thousands. Only if it is wanted back, then the owner returns the hundred rupees. That is all. It is done when a family is small and has too much land to till properly. So the village accountant's people held the land because they were relations by marriage. It was in my father's time that the great *Sirkâr* came, and we began paying the dues to it instead of to the Maharajah. Then, when my father fell into evil ways because of drugs, my mother took her sons – we were twins, Sewa Râm and I – if the Presence pleases, back to her people far away beyond Amritsar. For she was of a high, proud family, and when the hemp gets into a man's head he does unclean things. So my father was alone, and the accountant made him do as he liked, bribing him with drugs. That was how it happened, as the Presence will doubtless perceive. So when my father neglected his own land, the accountant's people cultivated it for him and gave him what was due. My mother heard of this, but she said nothing, because we were but little lads, and the land could not run away – it was better that it should be tilled than left to rack and ruin. At last my father died, but they sent no word to Amritsar, because the great *Sirkâr* was coming to count the village, and make a map of it with all the holdings of the proper shape, and all the fields coloured green. If the Protector of the Poor will forgive his dust-like slave, he will remember that fields are not green always, and so likewise the holdings are not always right, no matter how carefully they are put on the map. There was the old mortgage, a man who lied tilling the soil, and no one to come to the *Sirkâr* and say, "Here is the hundred rupees, give us back the land and write it in our names," because, as I have said, Sewa Râm and I were away beyond Amritsar, and our mother thought the land could not run away. It was no wonder the *Sirkâr* was deceived, no wonder at all, but when we came to claim the land even our names were not on the list. They had written the wrong thing because the mortgage had been foreclosed, and there were no heirs. After this one judge – may he become the *Lât-sahib* – said he would put it right, but the accountant was rich and made it into an appeal. The Presence knows what an appeal is, doubtless, and how, when a little thing like this – just a mistake in a map – gets up amongst the pleaders and the *Sikattars*, it is sometimes too small for them to see. It would have been different if the *Sirkâr* had seen two big noisy boys when it counted the village. Then Sewa Râm was set free from the prison of life, and I was alone; for the Presence knows a Jât cannot marry without land, or have sons when there is no plough to keep the furrow of existence straight. So I sold my mother's jewels and went to show the great Queen herself that my father really had a son. Thus I came to 'Ide Park in London city, and saw the *Sikattar*.'

'Then you did not succeed?'

'The Presence knows that the *vizier* is not as the *badshah*. He was very kind, sending me back by ship P and O. And writing! God knows how many letters he wrote, and he bade me wait. That is two years gone, so I am waiting still.'

'Have you a case in my Court?'

He shook his head with a certain pride. 'Oh no! it is in the big Court, or with the Financial, or a *Sikattar* just now; but it will come to the Presence sooner or later. That is why I journey with the Protector of the Poor. When that day comes the Presence will remember how Dewa Râm the Jât went to 'Ide Park.'

As I strolled back to the tent he followed at a discreet distance. Afterwards, as I sat smoking outside, I saw him wandering in the fields listlessly, his tall figure standing out against the sky as he paused to look at the sprouting wheat. When I questioned my underlings as to his story, they smiled obsequiously, as the native will smile before the master's face. The case, it appeared, had grown to be quite a standing joke in the office, nor was this the first cold weather that Dewa Râm had haunted the camp of the Deputy Commissioner and waited for news of his land. They hemmed and hawed, however, over the rights and wrongs of his claim, until I asked them point blank what their own impressions were; then habit gave way to truth, and they frankly declared their belief in some miscarriage of justice. A man, they said, would not go all the way to London for nothing. As I inclined to the same view, I took the trouble to try working the oracle by the back stairs – a method no less successful in India than elsewhere. Replies, more or less hopeful as to some ultimate settlement of the question, came from various friends in high places. Some of these I communicated, in a guarded way, to 'London', who as the sowing time passed fell a victim to fever and deferred hope. It was impossible for mortal man to see those dreamy eyes of his watching the crops of other men without feeling an insane desire to bring the promised land within his reach. He was very grateful. So condescending a Presence, he said, had never before dwelt in the tents of the great *Sirkâr*; and often on Sunday afternoons, when the camp was at rest, he would steal ostentatiously to a spot about thirty yards from where I was sitting, and if opportunity offered, enter into conversation – generally beginning by some apologetic allusion to 'Ide Park, but ending with a vast amount of information. He was a perfect mine of folk-lore, and many a half-hour did he beguile by old-world stories and traditions. One, in particular, I will retail in his own words, because it seems to me to give insight into the nature of the man and of his race.

I had been having my Sunday cup of afternoon tea in the shade of a huge banyan tree, and was idly amusing myself by throwing crumbs to a bright-eyed, bushy-tailed palm squirrel that had crept down the trunk not two yards from me. Attracted, partly by hunger, but more by the sheer light-hearted cussedness which makes the Indian squirrel so charming a companion, the little creature came nearer and nearer, its tail in an aggressive pluff, its large eyes scanning my face knowingly. A pause, a dart, and it was chirruping on the branch above my head with the crumb in its deft fingers.

'The Presence is a friend of Râm's,' said 'London' deferentially; 'that is why the heart of the Presence is so soft.'

'And why do you say I am a friend of Râm's?' I asked.

'Because the Presence is a friend to Râm's friend. Has the *Huzoor* never heard how the squirrel people come to have four black marks on their golden backs? Then I will tell. It was in the old days when Râm's parents fastened the silken bracelet on his wrist, and sent him out to find Seeta his wife. The Presence will have heard of that, and how each year our womenfolk tie the *râm rukkhi* to our wrists for luck. Well, when Râm, the King of all men, came to Sanderip, he found the great Monkey had carried off Seeta the Queen of women. Then, being in distress, he bid all the birds and beasts and fishes come to help him for great Râm was the Lord of the whole earth. Now the first to answer his call was the squirrel. In those days it was all golden, like corn in the sunlight, and light-hearted beyond all mortal things, as it is now. It leapt on to Râm's sword and cried, "Master! I am ready." But the great god's eyes grew soft as he saw the little thing's slender beauty, and perceived that it had the bravest heart of all his creatures. So he laid his hand on it in blessing, saying softly –

'"Nay! tender little warrior! thou art too pretty for strife and death. Live on, brave and careless for ever, so that weary men may see the beauty of the life great Râm has given."

'But, lo! when he raised his hand the squirrel's shining coat bore the shadow of Râm's tired fingers, for even golden life is dimmed by the touch of care.'

This and many another tale he told to me, while the green pigeons bustled about in the branches, and the squirrels lay yawning amongst the mango flowers. For the winter had flown, the camping season was at an end, and still 'London' was waiting. He never complained; only when rain fell, or when there was a heavy dew, or a good winnowing wind, – anything, in short, calculated to gladden the heart of a farmer, – he used to talk of 'Ide Park, and bewail the fact that *Sikattar* sahibs had penetrated even there. The hot weather passed, as usual, in a stagnation of mind and body more or less modified by individual energy, and during it 'London' paid me but occasional visits, and was fairly cheerful. No sooner, however, did the stir of coming cultivation begin again in the high, unirrigated soils, than he followed suit with a growing restlessness. And still no answer came. Just then a small piece of Government land, – that is to say, land in which no cultivator had a vested interest, – fell vacant in a village not far from 'London's' ancestral home, and I bethought me of putting him in as tenant if I could. But it is no easy task to find soil to cultivate in India, since farms are not 'to be let' as they are in England, and the State, though in reality owner, has no power to turn out one man or his heirs in favour of another, or in any way to manipulate the holdings of hereditary cultivators. Why, knowing this, it could have delegated the power to the money-lender, in giving the right of alienation by sale or mortgage to the cultivator, is one of those abstruse mysteries over the elucidation of which volumes have been and are still to be written. A mystery, moreover, which is responsible for half the growing poverty of those whose patient labour is the bulwark of the State.

The particular village in which I hoped to find a more or less temporary outlet for poor 'London's' hereditary instinct – which made the sight of a plough have much the same effect on him as a clutch of eggs has on a broody hen – had earned an unenviable notoriety from the number of mutineers it produced in the '57. Nearly one-half of the land had come under direct Government control by confiscation, and as the country settled down, had been leased at fixed rentals, to the loyal families, or in many cases to the heirs of the dead offenders.

One of these, the son of a notorious mutineer, had just died childless, and it was into his place that I determined, if possible, to put 'London'. The case 'Dewa Râm *versus* the Empress and others' had come back to me for the third time, with a request for further inquiry and evidence. There was none to give, for in a country where birth and marriage certificates are unknown quantities, and registers of all kinds are inaccurate legal proof of a case like 'London's' is almost impossible. As he himself invariably said, it was no wonder the *Sirkâr* had been deceived by the foreclosed mortgage, and the lying man who tilled the soil, joined to the newly invented theory that the peasant proprietor had a right to alienate the ancestral property of his descendants. So, with the prospect of another cold weather camp before me, I felt an almost morbid desire to get rid of

'London', and those patient eyes that seemed to me as if they were ever on the look-out for the promised land.

I was told afterwards by my superiors, in set terms, that my behaviour was illegal and indiscreet, and that I should have gone round the mutinous crew one by one, giving them the option of leasing the land, before offering it to anyone else, above all, before putting in a man whose claim to other ground was 'in course of settlement'. I believe my superiors to have been quite right theoretically, and I know that, practically, my philanthropic experiment proved a disastrous failure. Not a week after 'London', glowing with gratitude, set out for the village in which his new holding was situated, he was brought back to the hospital on a stretcher with a broken arm and several clouts on the head. Indeed, I have always felt it to be the crowning mercy of my career, that no one was actually killed in the free fight which ensued on my protégé's arrival in the mutineers' village; for he had some friends, stalwart as himself, and the Jâts, once aroused from their usual calm placidity, fight like devils with their long quarterstaves. On this occasion they gave the truculent crew as good as they got, until overpowered by numbers. When the incident occurred I was in a very out-of-the-way part of the district, and I well remember having to send a special messenger thirty miles with an urgent telegram in order to allay still more urgent inquiries as to the 'serious agrarian riot in B – '.

When I returned to headquarters I found 'London' convalescent and distinctly cheerful. He was sitting on the hospital steps whittling a new staff, and expressed his determination of going back to the village as soon as possible with a larger supply of friends. I felt constrained, however, to deny him his revenge. To begin with, my official reputation could not have stood another agrarian riot; in addition, the mutineering village had appealed against my action *en masse*, so the matter had passed beyond my control. 'London' was sorrowful, but sympathetic, seeming to enjoy the idea that I too might become a prey to *Sikattars* ere long. He took great pride in his broken arm and new stick, and more than once suggested that if the great Queen only knew how he had clouted the heads of the misbegotten, unfaithful devils, she might believe that his father had indeed left a son.

After this I made several attempts to bring a plough-handle within 'London's' reach, but my philanthropy was guarded, and my efforts uniformly unsuccessful. Once, a small atom of land on which I had my eye was taken up by a newly-made Municipal Committee as a public institute. It was Jubilee year, and various things of the kind were being started. When I saw this particular one last, a stuffed crocodile, two spinning wheels, some tussar silk cocoons, and a specimen card of aniline dyes, occupied what they were pleased to call the Industrial Department. In the reading room opposite an interesting collection of seditious journalism lay on the table, and a chromo of the *Kaiser-i-Hind* hung over the fireplace.

Then once again, when I thought I had found a resting-place for those dreamy eyes, the Military Department stepped between hope and fruition with a stout *Subadar-major* who had done the State good service. Finally, sick leave – the end of so many kindly plans and hopes for those who, living amongst the peasantry, learn to admire them as they deserve to be admired – came to put an end to all my plans for 'London'.

He bore the tidings with gentle regret. The Presence, he said, had not been well for some time; It would be the better of seeing 'Ide Park again, and perhaps as It was to be away so long – a whole year he was told – there would be a chance of seeing not only the *Sikattar*, but the great Queen herself.

'And if,' he continued, standing up and leaning on his staff as I had first seen him, whilst his eyes followed the ploughing for yet another harvest, – 'and if the Presence is so fortunate, perhaps It might find time to remember that Dewa Râm the Jât is waiting for his land.'

The reason for my writing this absolutely true experience is one of those distressing inconsistencies which are part and parcel of poor humanity. One might have thought the facts sufficient to excuse a resort to pen, ink and paper on the part of one really interested in that peasant life of which the rulers and governors know so little. But it needed an unreality, a mere feverish fancy, to supply the motive power.

I was in Hyde Park yesterday at the close of a bright afternoon. No need to describe what I saw. To those who live in London the scene is as familiar as their own faces, while those who do not, have at their disposal a thousand descriptions far better than any I could give. An unusually thick sprinkling of clerical attire among the crowd testified to the attraction of missionary meetings when combined with London at its best. Indeed, as I had come down Piccadilly the vast number of sandwich men advertising lectures, meetings, and addresses on every conceivable subject, struck me as favourable evidence of the growing intelligence and sympathy of the many for things beyond the daily round of English life.

I sat down, and being a comparative stranger, amused myself, as many have done before me, in listening to the scraps of conversation which fell from the lips of the passers-by – the flotsam-jetsam left by the stream of humanity; and as usual my initial curiosity and interest died down before the growing perception of some strange likeness underlying all the atoms of thought and speech.

Slowly, uncertainly, as the confused tints of a child's magic lantern focus into some horrid monster, or as the ebbing tide discloses the drowned face of a victim, the half-heard assertions, denials, protestations of the pleasure-seeking crowd, gave up their individual form and colour, and were lost in the one unchangeable, indestructible characteristic of humanity – its selfishness. On every face an interest, a smile, a frown, a thought; below these, the one source of all. Inevitable, no doubt, but depressing in the masks are men and women claiming to be the cream of culture and civilization. I wondered if, when the best was said and done, the art of widening our vitality by our sympathies had made much progress.

A stir in the crowd, a murmur, a look of expectation, roused me from idle moralizings. A couple of outriders in red came down the drive, and people paused to look.

'By Jove! it's the Queen herself,' said someone hurriedly, as a brougham drove past giving a glimpse from behind closed windows of grey hair and a widow's cap. The murmur swelled to a roar, almost a cheer. Every hat was off, and some country cousins stood up in their chairs in order to see better.

Now, what followed will, I know, be set down to the attack of Indian fever which some ten minutes afterwards sent me home to shiver in bed. Nevertheless, I am prepared to swear that there, amongst the flower-decked mashers and the powdery belles, I saw the tall, gaunt form of 'London' leaning on his quarterstaff. The gentle, deprecatory smile I had so often seen when he spoke of 'Ide Park was on his face, as if he knew the incongruity of his own appearance in such a scene. His eyes were not on the modest carriage in which the *Kaiser-i-Hind* was being partially displayed to her faithful subjects. They were fixed on me! On me, the tape-tied, sealing-waxed representative of a paternal despotism in India. The myriad tongues resumed their civilized shibboleths, but above them came a well-known cadence, 'And if the Presence is so fortunate, perhaps it might find time to remember that Dewa Râm the Jât is waiting for his land.'

As I said before, I went home to bed. What else could I do? Perhaps if other people could have seen what I saw, Dewa Râm and his kind would not be so often in difficulties about their land.

FLORA ANNIE STEEL
The Squaring of the Gods

It was the night before the great Eclipse. A vast, vague expectancy brooded over the length and breadth of India. Of prophesying there had been no lack, for signs and wonders had been as blackberries in September.

So, far and near, east, west, south, and north, the people of Hindustan – many-hued, many-raced, many-faithed – were watching for they knew not what, watching with grave, silent, yet curious composure.

But there was no outward sign of this inward expectation on either side. The millions of dark faces behind which it lay were as inscrutable as the telegraph wires through which the mere fraction of white faces responsible for the safety of those millions of dark ones were flashing silent messages of warning and preparation.

And here, in the Sacred City, beside the Sacred River, in which multitudes of those millions hoped to bathe on the morrow during the fateful moments of the sun's eclipse, the dim curves of the world had never been outlined against a calmer, more restful sky – a sky almost black in its intensity of shadow. Yet the night was clear, full of starlight that could be seen, which showed the bend of the broad river, angled on one side by the straight lines of its curved sequence of bathing-steps that swept away to the horizon on either side.

The steps themselves, shadowy, vague, were spangled as with stars by the little trembling lamps of the myriads on myriads of pilgrims already gathered on them waiting for the dawn. The reflection of these lamps lay in the water beside the reflection of the stars, making it hard to tell where heaven ended, where earth begun.

Behind this long length of bathing-steps – irregular in height, in slope, in everything save an inevitable crowning by the tall temple spires – lay Benares. Benares, the only city in the world – since the reputation of Rome lives by works as well as faith – whose every stone tells of that search after righteousness which lies so close to the heart of humanity. Benares, with its sunless alleys, full of the perfume of dead flowers and spent incense – alleys which thread their way past shrine after shrine, holy place after holy place; mere niches in a worn stone, perhaps, or less even than that; only the bare imprint of a bloody hand on the tall, blank walls of the crowded tenement houses which seem to narrow God's sky as they rise up toward it. Benares, where the alien master steps into the gutter to let a swinging corpse pass on its way to the Sacred River, but where the priest behind it – his dark forehead barred with white, or smeared with a bold patch of ochre – steps into the opposite gutter, and clings to the shrine-set wall like a limpet, lest he be defiled by a touch, a shadow. Benares, which is, briefly, the strangest, saddest city on God's earth.

It lay this night, far as the eye could reach along the outward curve of the Ganges, dreamful exceedingly, dimly paler than the sky. But on the other side of the river, where the land bulged into the stream, lay a scene as dreamful; yet dreamful in a different way; for here, almost from the water's edge, the young green wheat stretched away into that level plain of India, the most densely populated agricultural country in the world, where myriads and myriads of men live content as the cattle with which they till the soil.

So a whole world lies between these two banks of the Ganges; between the men of whom pilgrims are made, and the pilgrims made of those men. And spanning them, joining them, aggressively, unsympathetically, is the railway bridge built by the alien 'Bridge-builders'.

Seen in the starlight, with its lattice of dark girders showing against the sky, its white piers blocking the waterslide at intervals, this bridge looked quaintly like a fell and monstrous hairy caterpillar out for a night-walking, one of those caterpillars with turreted excrescences at its former and its latter end. The hinder one here was clearly outlined against a distant block of greater darkness. This was a dense grove of mango trees; and through its far-off shadow shone twinkling coloured lights, while from it came fitfully, at the wind's caprice, a faint sound of drumming, a twangling of *sitaras*; for, in the shelter of the grove, some of the white faces who were responsible for the dark ones were in camp – in a pleasure-camp full of guests come to see the show, and whither the telegrams of warning flashed and whence the answers flashed back, even while the *nautch*, bidden to amuse those guests, went on and on in twanglings, drummings, screechings, posturings.

Such details, however, were hidden even from the nearest point of the angled curve of bathing-steps which swept right away to the starlit horizon on the opposite side of the river. The only movement visible thence by the waiting crowd, as it looked across the river, was a curious dazzling flicker, as if the bridge were shivering, which was caused by the continuous stream on its outer footway of arriving pilgrims, showing now against the dark girders, now against the paler sky.

'*Mai* Gunga hath her hands full!' murmured one of the group squatting immovable on these nearest steps; 'they come, and come.'

A face or two, patient, dark, turned to the bridge, and another voice came, calm, passive.

'Ay! 'tis easier for folk to find salvation with "rails" and bridges than, as of old, with blistered feet and boats.' A dark hand nearest the water's lip, as it lapped a lazy, silvery whisper on the worn stone steps, slid into the sacred flood with a sort of tentative caress.

'Yet they said *She* would revenge Herself for the rending of Her bosom, for the burden of bricks laid on Her; but She hath not. She gives and takes as ever.'

The long, dark fingers gathered some of the fallen petals which the river was returning to those who had cast their flower-offering on its surface, and the dark eyes watched a white-swathed corpse that was drifting down stream, a faint streak in the slumbering shadow.

'True!' came another passive voice; 'but the time is not past. There is tomorrow yet.'

The absolutely unrepresentable *chuck*! made by the tongue against the roof of the mouth, which is the most emphatic denial of India, echoed suddenly, aggressively, into the peaceful air.

It came from the blackness of a low masonry abutment which, traversing the last three steps, projected a few feet into the river, like a pier. A yard maybe above the water, some three long, and perhaps a couple broad, there was just room on its outer end for a small square temple with a rude spiked spire – the plainest of temples, guiltless of ornament, looking out over the Ganges blankly. For its only aperture, a low arched doorway, faced the steps and showed now as a blot of utter darkness.

'Not She, brethren!' said a cracked voice following on the denial. 'She or Her like will never harm the *Huzoors*! They have paid their toll, see you, they have squared the gods.'

A dozen or more faces turned to the voice, the figures

The Squaring of the Gods

belonging to them remaining immovable, as if carved in stone.

'Dost think so really, *Baba-jee?*' came a question. 'I have heard that tale before – and that 'tis done in the "Magic-houses".'*

The emphatic denial rose again. 'Not so! These eyes saw it done – here in this very place, forty years ago! here, at *Mai* Kâli's shrine!'

In the pause that followed, a pair of claw-like hands could be seen above the bar of shadow, wavering *salaams* to the little temple, in the perfunctory manner of priesthood all over the world.

''Tis old Bishen, the flower-seller,' said a yawning voice. 'He was here in the Time of Trouble [the Mutiny], and he tells tales of it – when he remembers!'

'Then let him tell,' yawned another, 'since the night is long and the dawn lingers. How was't done, *Baba-jee?*'

There was a pause.

'Many ways, doubtless. Here and there different ways. But here, one way. Forty years ago, brothers! Yea, forty years ago, these eyes saw the squaring of the gods. In this wise . . .'

There was another dreamful pause, and then, from the shadow, came the old thin voice once more.

'Yonder, where the bridge stands now, was Broon-sahib's house – '

'Broon-sahib?' echoed a curious listener. 'Dost mean Broon-sahib who built the bridge?'

'Who built the bridge?' hesitated the tale-teller. 'God knows! More like his son; for the years pass – they pass, *Mai* Gunga! and I grow old. Grant me this last cleansing, Mother! Wash me from sin ere I go hence . . .'

---

* The natives call Freemasonry Lodges by this name.

'Lo! thou hast made him forget the rest,' reproved another listener, 'as if there were not Broon-sahibs ever! Even now, here in Benares! Yes! *Baba-jee*, of a certainty, Broon-sahib's house stood here, where the bridge stands now.'

The old memory, started afresh, went on.

'It was a boy, the child. A toddler, but with the temper of tigers. Lo! it would scream and yell in the *ayah*'s arms, and beat her face to be let crawl down the steps to pull the spent bosses of the marigolds out of the water and fling them back like balls. A mite of a boy; white as jasmine in the face, yellow as the marigolds themselves in hair. The mem, its mother, had the like face and hair. I used to see her in the verandah over the river, and driving above the steps. There were many sahibs came and went to the house, after their fashion, and she smiled and spoke to them all. There was one of them – so young, he might have been a son almost – who came often; and she smiled on him, too, as he played, like a boy, with the child. He was one of the sahibs who have eyes; so, after a time, he would nod to me and say "*Râm! Râm!*" with a laugh as he passed above me, sitting here in the shadow, selling my garlands.

'So, one day, as he came by, there was the baby screaming in its *ayah*'s arms to be let crawl to the water, and she was denying it by the mem's orders. What the young sahib said at first I know not; but after a bit he came running down the steps, the child in his arms, calling back to the woman, in her tongue, "Trouble not, *ayah*! I'll square it, never fear!"

'And there he was beside me, the two white faces, the yellow heads – for he was but a boy himself, slim, white, yellow-haired – close together, brother-like, buying a garland of the biggest marigolds I had. So down at the water's edge, he teaching the child how to throw them in like a thrower.

'"No underhand work, brotherling," he said in our tongue, for the baby, after the fashion of the *baba-logue*, knew none other. "So! straight from the shoulder. Bravo! Thou wilt play crickets, by-and-by, like a man."

'After that first time, he would often come down from the house with the child, and I had to keep the biggest marigolds for the game, since, see you, they held the bits of brick better with which he weighted them.

'Thus it went on till one day all the sahibs and mems were at the house yonder, for God knows what amusement! and in the cool they strolled down here – the mems dressed so gay, the sahibs all black and smoking – to see how well the toddler, who could scarce speak, had learnt to throw. At least, so it seemed, for they watched and laughed; but after a time they took to throwing the flowers themselves, laughing more and jesting, until not a marigold was left. Then they began on Shivjee's *dhatura* blossoms, filling their white horns with pebbles, and hurling them far, far into the stream.

'So, when paying time came, the young sahib – he had the child by the hand – flung rupees into my empty basket, and said, "Lo! Bishen" – for he was one of those who remember names – "those who seek to curry favour with the gods will have no chance today. We are beforehand. We have squared them."

'At this the mem, standing close by, frowned and spoke some reproof; maybe because she was of those who drive to church often. But the boy only laughed, and, catching the child up, cried "Lo! brotherling, then are we sinners indeed; since we do it so often, you and I!"

'And with that he raced up the steps with the child calling "*Râm, Râm!*" and "*Jai Kâli Ma!*" like any worshipper; so that the mem and the others strolling after could not but laugh. And some echoed the cry as they went up the steps.'

The old voice paused in its even sing-song; and when it began again, there was a new note in it which seemed to bring a sense of hurry and stress even to that uttermost peace.

'But they came down again. How long after matters not. I see them so in my old eyes. Going up, laughing in the sunset, then returning. It was starlight when they came down, the mems and the sahib and the *baba-logue*. Starlight as it was now, brethren, but not still, like this. There were cries, and flames yonder, and folk running.

'The boats lay here below the temple. And one – a Muhammadan – came with them, promising safety. So they began to get into the boats, and one moved off, the crowd looking on. Then suddenly, God knows why! it ceased looking on, and began to kill. They were half in, half out of the boat; the *sahib-logue* and some cried to stop, some to go on. But the mems made no noise; only you could see their faces white out of the shadows.

'And his, the young sahib's, was whiter than any, glittering, it seemed, with a white fire. The mem was in the boat, and Broon-sahib on the bottom step, the baby in his arms. But he, the boy, was above him facing the crowd – making time.

'Then, just as the mem stretched her hands for the child, a bullet – they were firing from the top steps – hit Broonsahib, and he fell half in, half out of the water, pushing the boat out in his fall. So it began to slide down stream.

'Some in it would have stopped it, but the mem gave a look at those other mems, those other babies, and laid her hand on one that would have gone back.

'"No!"

The Squaring of the Gods 113

'That was the cry she gave – a great cry; but a greater one rang out through the shadows and the lights, from the boy who had caught up the child as it fell upon the steps.

'I know not what it was, but it was great, and it echoed out as the boat slipped fast to safety. And he held the child to his breast and waved his sword, so that the mem's white face rose from her hands, where she had hidden it, and she looked back. That was the last thing I saw out of the shadows as the boat slipped to safety; but it held me, so that when I looked round, the boy was no longer on the steps.

'He had leaped to the plinth of the temple, and his arms were empty of his burden. Only he, stood in front of the doorway with his glittering white face – his glittering white face, his glittering white sword!

'"Come on, you devils!" he shouted in our tongue. "Come on! *Mai* Kâli shall have blood tonight if she wants it."

'And she had, brothers!

'It ran from the plinth and trickled to the river; for none could touch him from behind, and his sword was in front.

'There was a method in its hackings and hewings. At least so it seemed to me, watching helpless for good or evil, from my place in the shadow. For ever, as its keenest stroke fell, so another body fell blocking the plinth, until he had to stand almost in the arch itself.

'Then a burly Muhammadan trooper challenged him, and I knew not which way the fight was going, till, with a shout that was almost a laugh, the white face and the white sword showed, lunging back at the big body as they broke past. And it fell sidelong, blocking the doorway quite. But none thought of that, of it. None thought of anything save the glittering face and the glittering sword that had burst through the circling crowd, and now, facing it again, was backing up the steps, fighting grimly as it backed.

'Up and up, step by step, and we – even I, brothers, watching helpless – drawn after it perforce to see – to know . . .

'So the steps were left silent in the starlight.

'I did not see the end, brothers. It was beyond my sight. They told me afterwards it was in the bazaar, with half the town to see; but I had crept away, a great shivering on me, for I had remembered the flowers and the young sahib's words about the gods.

'And I remembered the child. What had become of the child?

'Then suddenly I understood. Then I knew what the method of the sword had been – how it had hidden, had lured!

'It was nigh dawn when I remembered; dawn as it is now. Look! The iron of night's scabbard grows into the steel of day's sword upon the water; and hark! that is the cry of the mallards. The world is waking. So it was when I crept down to Kâli's shrine.

'The blood was still dripping into the water, and when I drew the dead mass of flesh from blocking the doorway, the red of it lay in a pool up to Her feet. But the child had crawled on Her knees, brothers, and had cried itself to sleep there.

'Yet when it wakened at my touch it did not cry, for, see you, it knew me; and so, when it saw the milk, set in a bowl before Her as offering, it stretched its hands for it.

'Thus it was made clear. So I gave it *Mai* Kâli's milk, knowing it was true what he had said, "that they had squared the gods".'

The voice paused, and another voice had to ask, 'And then?' before it went on dreamily.

'Yea! it was true indeed, for ere the day ended they were back with guns and soldiers. So, since silence is better than speech when nought is sure, I crept in the night to a Colonel's house and left the child in the garden for them to find.

'Forty years ago, brothers! Forty years is it since the boats slipped down to safety with the *Huzoors*, and now . . .'

There was a sudden stir in the waiting crowd. A boat had slipped up the river shadows from the bridge and was making for the steps.

'That's your station, Brown,' said an English voice; 'the water is a bit deep about the shrine, remember, and the old women are devilish hard to keep back. All right!' it continued, as a man stepped out. 'Go on to the next. We are a bit early on the field; but it is as well to be beforehand, and square things.'

As the boat paddled on, another English voice in the stern said in a low tone, 'Why did you put Brown there? Just where his father was killed, don't you remember?'

'Just why I did! He won't stand any nonsense, and it is a troublesome job. Besides, he wasn't killed, and there's luck in it. That was a queer story. Someone saved him, of course, but why? and how? Now, Smith! there you are. And, as I said to Brown, for Heaven's sake look after the old dodderers, male and female. When they've nothing left to live for . . .'

The rest was lost as the boat went on to a yet farther station.

So, as the sun rose, it rose on that great angled sweep, not of steps, but of humanity; full, pressed down, running over into the spired town behind – on a million and more of dark faces, and a dozen white ones dotted here and there at the most dangerous points.

And Broon-sahib, bearded, a bit burly with his forty and odd years, sat on the plinth, and thought, no doubt, of that past at first, then took out his pipe, and with it some scraps of smoked glass, since the coming eclipse must not be lost, even though one *was* on duty.

The sun climbed up, brilliantly unconscious, or at least regardless, of its coming fate. And after a time boats began to slide up and down, and a big barge came punting up stream sedately. It was full of English women and children; and under its wide awning a table was laid with flowers and sparkling silver against the champagne breakfast which was to follow on a successful performance of duty.

For not even here could there be allowed hint or sign of that expectancy of possible evil. A little girl holding her mother's hand nodded her yellow curls delightedly, as the barge went past, to Dada sitting swinging his legs just where the blood had dripped into the stream forty years ago; but something in the woman's face made a call echo over the water.

'It's all right. Show going A-1!'

As a show there could be no doubt of that. There was a breathlessness in it, a mighty surge of emotion from one end of that bank of humanity to the other, a curious wail in the ceaseless roar of voices, that struck through eyes and ears to the heart.

And now, what was that?

Broad daylight still; not a shadow had shifted, and yet a sense as if a candle had gone out somewhere.

Broon-sahib put his pipe in his pocket, looked through a glass darkly, stood up, raised his helmet, wiped his forehead, and put it on again.

The time had come – there was a nibble of shadow on the ball of light! – the monster had begun his meal!

As he looked round, unarmed, defenceless, on the

hundreds of thousands of dark heads which held this thought, he smiled and nodded with the words.

'Have patience, brethren; there is time!' Doubtless, but not much time to think of other things beyond the mere keeping of that forward crush of bathers, that backward crush of those that had bathed, from inextricable confusion.

So much the better, perhaps. Less time, at any rate, for expectation of the new King who was to fall from the sun and sweep away existing kingdoms. Less time to notice the white horse led out ostentatiously by the Brahmins at the biggest temple, sign that such talk was true, that one aeon had passed away, and another – in which Vishnu should appear in his final incarnation – had begun.

'Have patience! Have patience!'

That was the burden of the cry from the few white faces dotted among the dark ones, and it was caught up and echoed by the connecting links of yellow-legged policemen stationed every ten yards along the lowest step.

'Have patience! Have patience!'

A hard saying indeed.

Broon-sahib slipped down from the plinth and collared an old pantaloon just as he fell, hefted him up like a baby, and set him squatting in safety above. Then an old woman, gasping, gurgling, from the first mouthful of the water into which regardless of depth, she had literally been propelled.

'Have patience, brethren! Have patience!'

A harder saying, now that all things had grown grey; though still – weird, uncanny, beyond belief – not a shadow had shifted.

Hopelessly grey, and hopelessly cold – so cold. So curiously quiet, too; for the great roar of voices seemed to have severed itself from things earthly, and was like a mighty wind from heaven.

'Have patience, brethren! Have patience! There is time!'

A harder saying still, when in the greyness, the coldness, a flock of scared pigeons overhead sent a weird flight of faint grey shadows down that long length of angled curve, packed by expectant humanity.

Was He coming indeed? – that new ruler? Were these the heralds?

There was quite a little row, now, of rescued old dodderers on *Mai* Kâli's plinth, whence the blood had dropped forty years ago.

What was that? Had someone withdrawn a veil? Had someone said, 'Let there be light?'

The greyness, the coldness, lost their character in an instant. There was promise in them now – promise of light to come! The sun was reasserting its sway, and – not half of humanity had bathed!

'Have patience, brethren! Have patience!' shouted Broon-sahib, and there was a certain fierce determination in his tone.

Hardest saying of all, when the precious moments were going – going so fast!

'*Huzoor!*' came a piteous, confused voice behind him from the plinth, 'it is my last chance. I am old – I forget. I have forgotten so much – only this remains. For pity's sake – for the sake of forty years ago – let old Bishen, the flower-seller, find salvation!'

Even in his hurry, in his breathless recognition that here was the crucial instant – that a single mistake might bring disaster – Broon-sahib flung a quick look behind him.

He saw a pathetic old face, humble even in its grief.

'It's all right, *Baba*; there's plenty of time!' he said swiftly. 'Here! look through this bit of glass – you'll see for yourself.'

It only took a moment, those quick words; he was back, ready with hand and voice of command, almost without a

The Squaring of the Gods 119

break; but they did more for peace and order than a regiment of soldiers. For old Bishen, after one look through the smoked glass, rose to his feet and *salaamed* again and again, set, as he was, on high, in sight of all.

'Yea! it is true,' he cried, in his thin old voice. 'There *is* time. Let us wait, brethren; for they know – the gods have told them.'

Half-an-hour afterwards, with its table laid with flowers and silver, the sliding barge held Englishmen as well as Englishwomen; and one of them was drinking deep draughts of iced beer, while a little girl with yellow hair watched him admiringly, and a woman, still rather pale of face, stood looking at him with evident relief.

'I told you it would be all right, my dear,' he said, smiling. 'There never was any rush to speak of but once; and then I gave a bit of smoked glass to an old chap, and he saw through a glass darkly what was up, and told the others. So we squared 'em – gods and Brahmins and all – as I told you we should, in spite of all the talk and the telegrams.'

BITHIA MARY CROKER
Jack Straw's Castle

> 'I have supp'd full with horrors.'
> *Macbeth*

Major Blewe, of the Honourable East India Company's Service, hated all manner of men and loved all blends of whisky; the result of this idiosyncrasy was that, after suffering many things from him for many years, the officers of the South Nellore Regiment revolted *en masse*. Endurance has its limits. If a comrade is a smart soldier and a good fellow, much is overlooked; but Major Blewe was neither, and, after an outrageous scene at an inspection dinner, he received a strong official hint to go.

He left with a substantial pension. He was not 'broke' – and carried away with him the detestation of a large body of men, an unparalleled grievance, and a deathless thirst for strong waters. The Major did not return to his native land, but settled down on a hill station in Madras – whether it was on the Nilgherries, the Pulneys, the Shevaroys, or elsewhere, is immaterial. Suffice to say, that he rented a four-roomed bungalow near a small station. It was cheap, in good repair, out of the way, and solitary – standing on a bare hillside, almost surrounded and concealed by rows of funereal pines, and known by the name of 'Jack Straw's Castle'.

Here Major Blewe took up his abode, and made, as was his custom, life a purgatory to his miserable retainers. He had joined the Service in the days when, among a certain set, cursing and beating one's servants was a fashionable and laudable action, and he prided himself that he was conservative, had never discarded old habits, and that every domestic in his employment had been conscientiously and soundly thrashed. He failed, however, to mention the one grand occasion on which, having dragged an able-bodied chokra into his bathroom – there to belabour him privately and at ease – that too vigorous young man had administered to his employer such a drubbing that he was unable to leave his bed for weeks – and meanwhile the delinquent had decamped with the Major's gold watch, silver spoons, and his pet cane!

This had *not* been a lesson, and was an old story now. Major Blewe was a notoriously bad master; his name was well noted in various bazaars. Why, then, did Hassan, his butler, and Ahmed, his cook (brothers), remain with him year after year? It was true that the wages were considerable, but what wages can repay a man for blows, kicks, curses, and insults? Major Blewe had the gift of tongues, and his invectives were as glib and as coarse as those of any old Tamil grass-cutter. The water-man and *dhoby* had a better time than the indoor domestics, not being so constantly *en evidence*, but no horsekeeper born of woman would remain two days, and the Major kept no pony – fortunately for that quadruped.

He invariably began the day with a hoarse, savage roar, when his early morning peg was first introduced to him. As the hours went by, these roars increased and multiplied – accompanied by kicks and blows. Attendance on him was almost as dangerous as waiting on a wild beast. In fact, he was worse than some, for he threw bottles with a deadly aim – also lamps, and scalding water. Rash, indeed, the bill collector who ventured within his reach. To be brief, Major Blewe was a degraded old savage, and yet some people declared 'that he could be a gentleman when he chose'.

Now and then he appeared in the local reading-room and at church — red-faced, beetle-browed, blustering — but clothed, not to say dressed, and dapper, and in his right mind. But what about those other — alas! too frequent — occasions when he was to be met, singing and staggering along the highroad, with the top button of his coat fastened in the lowest button-hole of the said garment, and a guilty black bottle protruding from his pocket?

He had no occupation; he made no attempt at gardening, beyond cultivating some red chilis; and his reading was confined to the local paper, which often accumulated unopened for weeks. He spent his days in swallowing strong pegs, smoking rank 'Trichys', and harrying his staff by night and day. Foolhardy, indeed, the man who dared to call his soul his own!

The owner of Jack Straw's Castle was a slender, narrow-chested Eurasian, named Ezra Pedro. He collected his rents monthly, and in person. Occasionally he arrived at Major Blewe's at some desperate domestic crisis; and once, when he found his tenant tearing off the butler's turban and coat, he ventured to expostulate, and privately asked the Major 'if he was not afraid of appearing before the cantonment magistrate — not afraid of law proceedings?'

'Law action? I'd like to see them try to bully old Joe Blewe! I am in my own house, where I do as I please! My house is my castle — Joe Blewe's Castle!'

'If I were you, my honoured sir, I would send away your cook and butler, and the water-man. I have heard things' — lowering his voice — 'in the bazaar — hints, whispers — '

'That they rob me? Of course they do!'

'If I may humbly venture to suggest, I would counsel more gentle and polite treatment, honourable sir; and I implore you to get rid of your present servants at once. You may be sorry if you keep them — and — so may I. I do not wish to lose an excellent tenant, now you have been here thirteen years.'

'Who the devil said I was going to leave?' bawled the Major. 'Wait till I give you notice! Keep your opinions to yourself, you snivelling, meddling, pudding-faced black brute! Here! get out of the place at once, or I'll help you!'

And poor, timid, well-meaning Mr Ezra Pedro was fain to retire with undignified celerity.

After a short time, there were whispers and vague rumours that Major Blewe – Blue Devil, as he was called – had been worse than usual with respect to violence, language, and liquor. He had broken the water-man's head, kicked the cook's wife's mother, and drowned the butler's beloved and only dog. Of late he had not been encountered slanting about the highways, and his absence was a relief; nor had he appeared in church or reading-room. The individual most interested in his welfare was his landlord, who arrived punctually on the first day of the month, receipt in hand.

He rapped timidly – no answer. Then he hammered boldly. After all, there was a month's rent due, and it was *his* house. Still dead silence. He called to a passing acquaintance, and together they peeped around, listened, whispered, wondered, and finally climbed in through an ill-secured window.

The bungalow proved to be as neat as a new pin, and in apple-pie order (it was let furnished, as are all hill houses). The Major's bedroom was beautifully tidy; long double rows of empty bottles stood as if 'dressed' on parade; his clothes were folded up, his topee and cap hung below his sword-scabbard; his shaving apparatus (razor included) was arranged in tempting order; and a clock was briskly ticking on the chimney-piece. The tiny sitting-room was chiefly filled by a long chair, a teapoy, pipes, and peg tumblers. It was vacant. The little dining-room – ah! here was a promising sign. The cloth was laid in preparation for a meal. There were appointments for two, a cruet-stand and well-filled decanter were set by the Major's seat, and a good-sized covered dish was placed before it. The flies were swarming around this, and some rash impulse of curiosity tempted Pedro to raise the electro-plated lid. He gave a shrill, wild scream as he let it fall with a frightful clang; for, grinning at him, on the dish, was Major Blewe's head!

The landlord and his companion tore out of the bungalow, and, in the language of old story-books, they ran, and they ran, and they ran. They ultimately brought the police, and a vast and excited crowd, to inspect that ghastly dinner-table. The police looked wise – as usual – asked questions, examined the premises, and made copious entries. But from that day to this – a matter of thirty years and more – no trace has ever been found of Major Blewe's servants, or of Major Blewe's body.

Jack Straw's Castle was to let, a bargain, for many seasons; and for many seasons it 'has stood, a roofless ruin'.

SARA JEANNETTE DUNCAN
The Pool in the Desert

I knew Anna Chichele and Judy Harbottle so well, and they figured so vividly at one time against the rather empty landscape of life in a frontier station, that my affection for one of them used to seem little more, or less, than a variant upon my affection for the other. That recollection, however, bears examination badly; Judy was much the better sort, and it is Judy's part in it that draws me into telling the story. Conveying Judy is what I tremble at: her part was simple. Looking back – and not so very far – her part has the relief of high comedy with the proximity of tears; but looking close, I find that it is mostly Judy, and that what she did is entirely second, in my untarnished picture, to what she was. Still I do not think I can dissuade myself from putting it down.

They would, of course, inevitably have found each other sooner or later, Mrs Harbottle and Mrs Chichele, but it was I who actually introduced them; my palmy verandah in Rawul Pindi, where the tea-cups used to assemble, was the scene of it. I presided behind my samovar over the early formalities that were almost at once to drop from their friendship, like the sheath of some bursting flower. I deliberately brought them together, so the birth was not accidental, and my interest in it quite legitimately maternal. We always had tea in the verandah in Rawul Pindi, the drawing-room was painted blue, blue for thirty feet up to the whitewashed cotton ceiling; nothing of any value in the way of a human relation, I am sure, could have originated there. The verandah was spacious and open, their mutual observation had room and freedom; I watched it to and fro. I had not long to wait for my reward; the beautiful candour I expected between them was not ten minutes in coming. For the sake of it I had taken some trouble, but when I perceived it revealing I went and sat down beside Judy's husband, Robert Harbottle, and talked about Pharaoh's split hoof. It was only fair; and when next day I got their impressions of one another, I felt single-minded and deserving.

I knew it would be a satisfactory sort of thing to do, but perhaps it was rather more for Judy's sake than for Anna's that I did it. Mrs Harbottle was only twenty-seven then and Robert a major, but he had brought her to India out of an episode too colour-flushed to tone with English hedges; their marriage had come, in short, of his divorce, and as too natural a consequence. In India it is well known that the eye becomes accustomed to primitive pigments and high lights; the aesthetic consideration, if nothing else, demanded Robert's exchange. He was lucky to get a Piffer [Punjab Frontier Force] regiment, and the Twelfth were lucky to get him; we were all lucky, I thought, to get Judy. It was an opinion, of course, a good deal challenged, even in Rawul Pindi, where it was thought, especially in the beginning, that acquiescence was the most the Harbottles could hope for. That is not enough in India; cordiality is the common right. I could not have Judy preserving her atmosphere at our tea-parties and gymkhanas.

Not that there were two minds among us about 'the case'; it was a preposterous case, sentimentally undignified, from some points of view deplorable. I chose to reserve my point of view, from which I saw it, on Judy's behalf, merely quixotic, preferring on Robert's just to close my eyes. There is no doubt that his first wife was odious to a degree which it is simply pleasanter not to recount, but her malignity must almost have amounted to a sense of humour. Her detestation of her cousin Judy Thynne dated much further back than Robert's attachment. That began in Paris, where Judy, a young widow, was developing a real vein at Julian's. I am entirely convinced that there was nothing, as people say, 'in it', Judy had not a thought at that time that was not based on Chinese white and permeated with good-fellowship; but there was a good deal of it, and no doubt the turgid imagination of the first Mrs Harbottle dealt with it honestly enough. At all events, she saw her opportunity, and the depths of her indifference to Robert bubbled up venomously into the suit.

That it was undefended was the senseless mystery; decency ordained that he and Judy should have made a fight, even in the hope that it would be a losing one. The reason it had to be a losing one – the reason so immensely criticized – was that the petitioning lady obstinately refused to bring her action against any other set of circumstances than those to which, I have no doubt, Judy contributed every indiscretion. It is hard to imagine Robert Harbottle refusing her any sort of justification that the law demands short of beating her, but her malice would accept nothing of which the account did not go for final settlement to Judy Thynne. If her husband wanted his liberty, he should have it, she declared, at that price and no other. Major Harbottle did indeed deeply long for his liberty, and his interesting friend, Mrs Thynne, had, one can only say, the most vivid commiseration for his bondage. Whatever chance they had of winning, to win would be, for the end they had at heart, to lose, so they simply abstained, as it were, from comment upon the detestable procedure which terminated in the rule absolute.

I have often wondered whether the whole business would not have been more defensible if there had been on Judy's part any emotional spring for the leap they made. I offer my conviction that there was none, that she was only extravagantly affected by the ideals of the Quarter – it is a transporting atmosphere – and held a view of comradeship which permitted the reversal of the modern situation filled by a blameless correspondent. Robert, of course, was tremendously in love with her; but my theory is that she married him as the logical outcome of her sacrifice and by no means the smallest part of it.

It was all quite unimaginable, as so many things are, but the upshot of it brought Judy to Rawul Pindi, as I have said, where I for one thought her mistake insignificant compared with her value. It would have been great, her value, anywhere; in the middle of the Punjab it was incalculable. To explain why would be to explain British India, but I hope it will appear; and I am quite willing, remember, to take the responsibility if it does not.

Somers Chichele, Anna's son, it is absurd to think, must have been about fifteen then, reflecting at Winchester with the other 'men' upon the comparative merits of tinned sardines and jam roll, and whether a packet of real Egyptians was not worth the sacrifice of either. His father was colonel of the Twelfth; his mother was still charming. It was the year before Dick Forsyth came down from the neighbourhood of Sheikh-budin with a brevet and a good deal of personal damage. I mention him because he proved Anna's charm in the only conclusive way before the eyes of us all; and the station, I remember, was edified to observe that if Mrs Chichele came out of the matter 'straight' – one relapses so easily into the simple definitions of those parts – which she undoubtedly did, she owed it in no small degree to Judy Harbottle. This one feels to be hardly a legitimate reference, but it is something tangible to lay hold upon in trying to describe the web of volitions which began to weave itself between the two that afternoon on my verandah and which afterwards became so strong a bond. I was delighted with the thing; its simplicity and sincerity stood out among our conventional little compromises at friendship like an ideal. She and Judy had the assurance of one another; they made upon one another the finest and often the most unconscionable demands. One met them walking at odd hours in queer places, of which I imagine they were not much aware. They would turn deliberately off the Maidan and away from the band-stand to be rid of our irrelevant bows; they did their duty by the rest of us, but the most egregious among us, the Deputy-Commissioner for selection, could see that he hardly counted. I thought I understood, but that may have been my fatuity; certainly when their husbands inquired what on earth they had been talking of, it usually transpired that they had found an infinite amount to say about nothing. It was a little worrying to hear Colonel Chichele and Major Harbottle describe their wives as 'pals', but the fact could not be denied, and after all we were in the Punjab. They were pals too, but the terms were different.

People discussed it according to their lights, and girls said in pretty wonderment that Mrs Harbottle and Mrs Chichele were like men, they never kissed each other. I think Judy prescribed these conditions. Anna was far more a person who did as the world told her. But it was a poor negation to describe all that they never did; there was no common little convention of attachment that did not seem to be tacitly omitted between them. I hope one did not too cynically observe that they offered these to their husbands instead; the redeeming observation was their husbands' complete satisfaction. This they maintained to the end. In the natural order of things Robert Harbottle should have paid heavily for interfering as he did in Paris between a woman and what she was entitled to live for. As a matter of fact he never paid anything at all; I doubt whether he ever knew himself a debtor. Judy kept her temperament under like a current and swam with the tides of the surface, taking refreshing dips only now and then which one traced in her eyes and her hair when she and Robert came back from leave. That sort of thing is lost in the sands of India, but it makes an oasis as it travels, and it sometimes seemed to me a curious pity that she and Anna should sit in the shade of it together, while Robert and Peter Chichele, their titular companions, blundered on in the desert. But after all, if you are born blind – and the men were both immensely liked, and the shooting was good.

Ten years later Somers joined. The Twelfth were at Peshawur. Robert Harbottle was Lieutenant-Colonel by that time and had the regiment. Distinction had incrusted, in the Indian way, upon Peter Chichele, its former colonel; he was General Commanding the District and KCB. So we were all still together in Peshawur. It was great luck for the Chicheles, Sir Peter's having the district, though his father's old regiment would have made it pleasant enough for the boy in any case. He came to us, I mean, of course, to two or three of us, with the interest that hangs about a victim of circumstances; we understood that he wasn't a 'born soldier'. Anna had told me on the contrary that he was a sacrifice to family tradition made inevitable by the General's unfortunate investments. Bellona's bridegroom was not a rôle he fancied, though he would make a kind of compromise as best man; he would agree, she said, to be a war correspondent and write picturesque specials for the London halfpenny press. There was the humour of the poor boy's despair in it, but she conveyed it, I remember, in exactly the same tone with which she had said to me years before that he wanted to drive a milk-cart. She carried quite her half of the family tradition, though she could talk of sacrifice and make her eyes wistful, contemplating for Somers the limitations of the drill-book and the camp of exercise, proclaiming and insisting upon what she would have done if she could only have chosen for him. Anna Chichele saw things that way. With more than a passable sense of all that was involved, if she could have made her son an artist in life or a commander-in-chief, if she could have given him the seeing eye or the Order of the Star of India, she would not have hesitated for an instant. Judy, with her single mind, cried out, almost at sight of him, upon them both, I mean both Anna and Sir Peter. Not that the boy carried his condemnation badly, or even obviously; I venture that no one noticed it in the mess; but it was naturally plain to those of us who were under the same. He had put in his two years with a British regiment at Meerut – they nurse subalterns that way for the Indian army – and his eyes no longer played with the tinsel vision of India; they looked instead into the arid stretch beyond. This preoccupation conveyed to the Surgeon-Major's wife the suggestion that Mr Chichele was the victim of a hopeless attachment. Mrs Harbottle made no such mistake; she saw simply, I imagine, the beginnings of her own hunger and thirst in him, looking back as she told us across a decade of dusty sunsets to remember them. The decade was there, close to the memory of all of us; we put, from Judy herself downward, an absurd amount of confidence in it.

She looked so well the night she met him. It was English mail day; she depended a great deal upon her letters, and I suppose somebody had written her a word that brought her that happy, still excitement that is the inner mystery of words. He went straight to her with some speech about his mother having given him leave, and for twenty minutes she patronized him on a sofa as his mother would not have dreamed of doing.

Anna Chichele, from the other side of the room, smiled on the pair.

'I depend on you and Judy to be good to him while we are away,' she said. She and Sir Peter were going on leave at the end of the week to Scotland as usual, for the shooting.

Following her glance I felt incapable of the proportion she assigned me. 'I will see after his socks with pleasure,' I said. 'I think, don't you, we may leave the rest to Judy?'

Her eyes remained upon the boy, and I saw the passion rise in them, at which I turned mine elsewhere. Who can look unperturbed upon such a privacy of nature as that?

'Poor old Judy!' she went on. 'She never would be bothered with him in all his dear hobbledehoy time; she resented his claims, the unreasonable creature, used to limit me to three anecdotes a week; and now she has him on her hands, if you like. See the pretty air of deference in the way he listens to her! He has nice manners, the villain, if he is a Chichele!'

'Oh, you have improved Sir Peter's,' I said kindly.

'I do hope Judy will think him worth while. I can't quite expect that he will be up to her, bless him, she is so much cleverer, isn't she, than any of us? But if she will just be herself with him it will make such a difference.'

The other two crossed the room to us at that, and Judy gaily made Somers over to his mother, trailing off to find Robert in the billiard-room.

'Well, what has Mrs Harbottle been telling you?' Anna asked him.

The young man's eye followed Judy, his hand went musingly to his moustache.

'She was telling me,' he said, 'that people in India were

sepulchres of themselves, but that now and then one came who could roll away another's stone.'

'It sounds promising,' said Lady Chichele to me.

'It sounds cryptic,' I laughed to Somers, but I saw that he had the key.

I cannot say that I attended diligently to Mr Chichele's socks, but the part corresponding was freely assigned me. After his people went I saw him often. He pretended to find qualities in my tea, implied that he found them in my talk. As a matter of fact it was my inquiring attitude that he loved, the knowledge that there was no detail that he could give me about himself, his impressions and experiences, that was unlikely to interest me. I would not for the world imply that he was egotistical or complacent, absolutely the reverse, but he possessed an articulate soul which found its happiness in expression, and I liked to listen. I feel that these are complicated words to explain a very simple relation, and I pause to wonder what is left to me if I wished to describe his commerce with Mrs Harbottle. Luckily there is an alternative; one needn't do it. I wish I had somewhere on paper Judy's own account of it at this period, however. It is a thing she would have enjoyed writing and more enjoyed communicating, at this period.

There was a grave reticence in his talk about her which amused me in the beginning. Mrs Harbottle had been for ten years important enough to us all, but her serious significance, the light and the beauty in her, had plainly been reserved for the discovery of this sensitive and intelligent person not very long from Sandhurst and exactly twenty-six. I was barely allowed a familiar reference, and anything approaching a flippancy was met with penetrating silence. I was almost rebuked for lightly suggesting that she must occasionally find herself bored in Peshawur.

'I think not anywhere,' said Mr Chichele; 'Mrs Harbottle is one of the few people who sound the privilege of living.'

This to me, who had counted Mrs Harbottle's yawns on so many occasions! It became presently necessary to be careful, tactful, in one's implications about Mrs Harbottle, and to recognize a certain distinction in the fact that one was the only person with whom Mr Chichele discussed her at all.

The day came when we talked of Robert; it was bound to come in the progress of any understanding and affectionate colloquy which had his wife for inspiration. I was familiar, of course, with Somers's opinion that the Colonel was an awfully good sort; that had been among the preliminaries and become understood as the base of all references. And I liked Robert Harbottle very well myself. When his adjutant called him a born leader of men, however, I felt compelled to look at the statement consideringly.

'In a tight place,' I said – dear me, what expressions had the freedom of our little frontier drawing-rooms! – 'I would as soon depend on him as on anybody. But as for leadership – '

'He is such a good fellow that nobody here does justice to his soldierly qualities,' said Mr Chichele, 'except Mrs Harbottle.'

'Has she been telling you about them?' I inquired.

'Well,' he hesitated, 'she told me about the Mulla Nulla affair. She is rather proud of that. Any woman would be.'

'Poor dear Judy!' I mused.

Somers said nothing, but looked at me, removing his cigarette, as if my words would be the better of explanation.

'She has taken refuge in them – in Bob Harbottle's soldierly qualities – ever since she married him,' I continued.

'Taken refuge,' he repeated, coldly, but at my uncompromising glance his eyes fell.

'Well?' I said.

'You mean – '

'Oh, I mean what I say,' I laughed. 'Your cigarette has gone out – have another.'

'I think her devotion to him splendid.'

'Quite splendid. Have you seen the things he brought her from the Simla Art Exhibition? He said they were nice bits of colour, and she has hung them in the drawing-room, where she will have to look at them every day. Let us admire her – dear Judy.'

'Oh,' he said, with a fine air of detachment, 'do you think they are so necessary, those agreements?'

'Well,' I replied, 'we see that they are not indispensable. More sugar? I have only given you one lump. And we know, at all events,' I added, unguardedly, 'that she could never have had an illusion about him.'

The young man looked up quickly. 'Is that story true?' he asked.

'There was a story, but most of us have forgotten it. Who told you?'

'The doctor.'

'The Surgeon-Major,' I said, 'has an accurate memory and a sense of proportion. As I suppose you were bound to get it from somebody, I am glad you got it from him.'

I was not prepared to go on, and saw with some relief that Somers was not either. His silence, as he smoked, seemed to me deliberate; and I had oddly enough at this moment for the first time the impression that he was a man and not a boy. Then the Harbottles themselves joined us, very cheery after a gallop from the Wazir-Bagh. We talked of old times, old friendships, good swords that were broken, names that had carried far, and Somers effaced himself in the perfect manner of the British subaltern. It was a long, pleasant gossip, and I thought Judy seemed rather glad to let her husband dictate its level, which, of course, he did. I noticed when the three rode away together that the Colonel was beginning to sit down rather solidly on his big New Zealander; and I watched the dusk come over from the foot-hills for a long time thinking more kindly than I had spoken of Robert Harbottle.

I have often wondered how far happiness is contributed to a temperament like Judy Harbottle's, and how far it creates its own; but I doubt whether, on either count, she found as much in any other winter of her life except perhaps the remote ones by the Seine. Those ardent hours of hers, when everything she said was touched with the flame of her individuality, came oftener; she suddenly cleaned up her palette and began to translate in one study after another the language of the frontier country, that spoke only in stones and in shadows under the stones and in sunlight over them. There is nothing in the Academy of this year, at all events, that I would exchange for the one she gave me. She lived her physical life at a pace which carried us all along with her; she hunted and drove and danced and dined with such sincere intention as convinced us all that in hunting and driving and dancing and dining there were satisfactions that had been somehow overlooked. The Surgeon-Major's wife said it was delightful to meet Mrs Harbottle, she seemed to enjoy everything so thoroughly; the Surgeon-Major looked at her critically and asked her if she was quite sure she hadn't a night temperature. He was a Scotchman. One night Colonel Harbottle, hearing her give away the last extra, charged her with renewing her youth.

'No, Bob,' she said, 'only imitating it.'

Ah, that question of her youth. It was so near her – still, she told me once, she heard the beat of its flying, and the pulse in her veins answered the false signal. That was afterward, when she told the truth. She was not so happy when she indulged herself otherwise. As when she asked one to remember that she was a middle-aged woman, with middle-aged thoughts and satisfactions.

'I am now really happiest,' she declared, 'when the Commissioner takes me in to dinner, when the General Commanding leads me to the dance.'

She did her best to make it an honest conviction. I offered her a recent success not crowned by the Academy, and she put it down on the table. 'By and by,' she said. 'At present I am reading Pascal and Bossuet.' Well, she was reading Pascal and Bossuet. She grieved aloud that most of our activities in India were so indomitably youthful, owing to the accident that most of us were always so young. 'There is no dignified distraction in this country,' she complained, 'for respectable ladies nearing forty.' She seemed to like to make these declarations in the presence of Somers Chichele, who would look at her with a little queer smile – a bad translation, I imagine, of what he felt.

She gave herself so generously to her seniors that somebody said Mrs Harbottle's girdle was hung with brass hats. It seems flippant to add that her complexion was as honest as the day, but the fact is that the year before Judy had felt compelled, like the rest of us, to repair just a little the ravages of the climate. If she had never done it one would not have looked twice at the absurdity when she said of the powder-puff in the dressing-room, 'I have raised that thing to the level of an immorality,' and sailed in to dance with an uncompromising expression and a face uncompromised. I have not spoken of her beauty; for one thing it was not always there, and there were people who would deny it altogether, or whose considered comment was, 'I wouldn't call her plain.' They, of course, were people in whom she declined to be interested, but even for those of us who could evoke some demonstration of her vivid self her face would not always light in correspondence. When it did there was none that I liked better to look at; and I envied Somers Chichele his way to make it the pale, shining thing that would hold him lifted, in return, for hours together, with I know not what mystic power of a moon upon the tide. And he? Oh, he was dark and delicate, by nature simple, sincere, delightfully intelligent. His common title to charm was the rather sweet seriousness that rested on his upper lip, and a certain winning gratification in his attention; but he had a subtler one in his eyes, which must be always seeking and smiling over what they found; those eyes of perpetual inquiry for the exquisite which ask so little help to create it. A personality to button up in a uniform, good heavens!

As I begin to think of them together I remember how the maternal note appeared in her talk about him.

'His youth is pathetic,' she told me, 'but there is nothing that he does not understand.'

'Don't apologize, Judy,' I said. We were so brusque on the frontier. Besides, the matter still suffered a jocular presentment. Mrs Harbottle and Mr Chichele were still 'great friends'; we could still put them next each other at our dinner-parties without the feeling that it would be 'marked'. There was still nothing unusual in the fact that when Mrs Harbottle was there Mr Chichele might be taken for granted. We were so broad-minded also, on the frontier.

It grew more obvious, the maternal note. I began positively to dread it, almost as much, I imagine, as Somers did. She took her privileges all in Anna's name, she exercised her authority quite as Lady Chichele's proxy. She went to the very limit. 'Anna Chichele,' she said actually in his presence, 'is a fortunate woman. She has all kinds of cleverness, and she has her tall son. I have only one little talent, and I have no tall son.' Now it was not in nature that she could have had a son as tall as Somers, nor was that desire in her eyes. All civilization implies a good deal of farce, but this was a poor refuge, a cheap device; I was glad when it fell away from her sincerity, when the day came on which she looked into my fire and said simply, 'An attachment like ours has no terms.'

'I wonder,' I said.

'For what comes and goes,' she went on dreamily, 'how could there be a formula?'

'Look here, Judy,' I said, 'you know me very well. What if the flesh leaps with the spirit?'

She looked at me, very white. 'Oh no,' she said, 'no.'

I waited, but there seemed nothing more that she could say; and in the silence the futile negative seemed to wander round the room repeating itself like an echo, 'Oh no, no.' I poked the fire presently to drown the sound of it. Judy sat still, with her feet crossed and her hands thrust into the pockets of her coat, staring into the coals.

'Can you live independently, satisfied with your interests and occupations?' she demanded at last. 'Yes, I know you can. I can't. I must exist more than half in other people. It is what they think and feel that matters to me, just as much as what I think and feel. The best of life is in that communication.'

'It has always been a passion with you, Judy,' I replied. 'I can imagine how much you must miss – '

'Whom?'

'Anna Chichele,' I said softly.

She got up and walked about the room, fixing here and there an intent regard upon things which she did not see. 'Oh, I do,' she said at one point, with the effect of pulling herself together. She took another turn or two, and then finding herself near the door she went out. I felt as profoundly humiliated for her as if she had staggered.

The next night was one of those that stand out so vividly, for no reason that one can identify, in one's memory. We were dining with the Harbottles, a small party, for a tourist they had with them. Judy and I and Somers and the traveller had drifted out into the verandah, where the scent of Japanese lilies came and went on the spring wind to trouble the souls of any taken unawares. There was a brightness beyond the foot-hills where the moon was coming, and I remember how one tall clump swayed out against it, and seemed in passionate perfume to lay a burden on the breast. Judy moved away from it and sat clasping her knees on the edge of the verandah. Somers, when his eyes were not upon her, looked always at the lily.

Even the spirit of the globe-trotter was stirred, and he said, 'I think you Anglo-Indians live in a kind of little paradise.'

There was an instant's silence, and then Judy turned her face into the lamplight from the drawing-room. 'With everything but the essentials,' she said.

We stayed late; Mr Chichele and ourselves were the last to go. Judy walked with us along the moonlit drive to the gate, which is so unnecessary a luxury in India that the servants always leave it open. She swung the stiff halves together.

'Now,' she said, 'it is shut.'

'And I,' said Somers Chichele, softly and quickly, 'am on the other side.'

Even over that depth she could flash him a smile. 'It is the business of my life,' she gave him in return, 'to keep this gate shut.' I felt as if they had forgotten us. Somers mounted and rode off without a word; we were walking in a different direction. Looking back, I saw Judy leaning immovable on the gate, while Somers turned in his saddle, apparently to repeat the form of lifting his hat. And all about them stretched the stones of Kabul valley, vague and formless in the tide of the moonlight . . .

Next day a note from Mrs Harbottle informed me that she had gone to Bombay for a fortnight. In a postscript she wrote, 'I shall wait for the Chicheles there, and come back with them.' I remember reflecting that if she could not induce herself to take a passage to England in the ship that brought them, it seemed the right thing to do.

She did come back with them. I met the party at the station. I knew Somers would meet them, and it seemed to me, so imminent did disaster loom, that someone else should be there, someone to offer a covering movement or a flank support wherever it might be most needed. And among all our smiling faces disaster did come, or the cold premonition of it. We were all perfect, but Somers's lip trembled. Deprived for a fortnight he was eager for the draft, and he was only twenty-six. His lip trembled, and there, under the flickering station-lamps, suddenly stood that of which there never could be again any denial, for those of us who saw.

Did we make, I wonder, even a pretence of disguising the consternation that sprang up among us, like an armed thing, ready to kill any further suggestion of the truth? I don't know. Anna Chichele's unfinished sentence dropped as if someone had given her a blow upon the mouth. Coolies were piling the luggage into a hired carriage at the edge of the platform. She walked mechanically after them, and would have stepped in with it but for the sight of her own gleaming landau drawn up within a yard or two, and the General waiting. We all got home somehow, taking it with us, and I gave Lady Chichele twenty-four hours to come to me with her face all one question and her heart all one fear. She came in twelve.

'Have you seen it – long?' Prepared as I was her directness was demoralizing.

'It isn't a mortal disease.'

'Oh, for Heaven's sake – '

'Well, not with certainty, for more than a month.'

She made a little spasmodic movement with her hands, then dropped them pitifully. 'Couldn't you do *any*thing?'

I looked at her, and she said at once, 'No, of course you couldn't.'

For a moment or two I took my share of the heavy sense of it, my trivial share, which yet was an experience sufficiently exciting. 'I am afraid it will have to be faced,' I said.

'What will happen?' Anna cried. 'Oh, what will happen?'

'Why not the usual thing?' Lady Chichele looked up quickly as if at a reminder. 'The ambiguous attachment of the country,' I went on, limping but courageous, 'half declared, half admitted, that leads vaguely nowhere, and finally perishes as the man's life enriches itself – the thing we have seen so often.'

'Whatever Judy is capable of it won't be the usual thing. You know that.'

I had to confess in silence that I did.

'It flashed at me – the difference in her – in Bombay.' She pressed her lips together and then went on unsteadily. 'In her eyes, her voice. She was mannered, extravagant, elaborate. With me! All the way up I wondered and worried. But I never thought – ' She stopped; her voice simply shook itself into silence. I called a servant.

'I am going to give you a good stiff peg,' I said. I apologize for the 'peg', but not for the whisky and soda. It is a beverage on the frontier, of which the vulgarity is lost in the value. While it was coming I tried to talk of other things, but she would only nod absently in the pauses.

'Last night we dined with him, it was guest night at the mess, and she was there. I watched her, and she knew it. I don't know whether she tried, but anyway, she failed. The covenant between them was written on her forehead whenever she looked at him, though that was seldom. She dared not look at him. And the little conversation that they had – you would have laughed – it was a comedy of stutters. The facile Mrs Harbottle!'

'You do well to be angry, naturally,' I said; 'but it would be fatal to let yourself go, Anna.'

'Angry? Oh, I am *sick*. The misery of it! The terror of it! If it were anybody but Judy! Can't you imagine the passion of a temperament like that in a woman who has all these years been feeding on herself? I tell you she will take him from my very arms. And he will go – to I dare not imagine what catastrophe! Who can prevent it? Who can prevent it?'

'There is you,' I said.

Lady Chichele laughed hysterically. 'I think you ought to say, "There are you." I – what can I do? Do you realize that it's *Judy*? My friend – my other self? Do you think we can drag all that out of it? Do you think a tie like that can be broken by an accident – by a misfortune? With it all I *adore* Judy Harbottle. I love her, as I have always loved her, and – it's damnable, but I don't know whether, whatever happened, I wouldn't go on loving her.'

'Finish your peg,' I said. She was sobbing.

'Where I blame myself most,' she went on, 'is for not seeing in him all that makes him mature to her – that makes her forget the absurd difference between them, and take him simply and sincerely as I know she does, as the contemporary of her soul if not of her body. I saw none of that. Could I, as his mother? Would he show it to me? I thought him just a charming boy, clever too, of course, with nice instincts and well plucked; we were always proud of that, with his delicate physique. Just a boy! I haven't yet stopped thinking how different he looks without his curls. And I thought she would be just kind and gracious and delightful to him because he was my son.'

'There, of course,' I said, 'is the only chance.'

'Where – what?'

'He is your son.'

'Would you have me appeal to her? Do you know I don't think I could?'

'Dear me, no. Your case must present itself. It must spring upon her and grow before her out of your silence, and if you can manage it, your confidence. There is a great deal, after all, remember, to hold her in that. I can't somehow imagine her failing you. Otherwise –'

Lady Chichele and I exchanged a glance of candid admission.

'Otherwise she would be capable of sacrificing everything – everything. Of gathering her life into an hour. I know. And do you know if the thing were less impossible, less grotesque, I should not be so much afraid? I mean that the *absolute* indefensibility of it might bring her a recklessness and a momentum which might –'

'Send her over the verge,' I said. 'Well, go home and ask her to dinner.'

There was a good deal more to say, of course, than I have thought proper to put down here, but before Anna went I saw that she was keyed up to the heroic part. This was none the less to her credit because it was the only part, the dictation of a sense of expediency that despaired while it dictated. The noble thing was her capacity to take it, and, amid all that warred in her, to carry it out on the brave high lines of her inspiration. It seemed that a literal inspiration, so perfectly calculated that it was hard not to think sometimes, when one saw them together, that Anna had been lulled into a simple resumption of the old relation. Then from the least thing possible – the lift of an eyelid – it flashed upon one that between these two every moment was dramatic, and one took up the word with a curious sense of detachment and futility, but with one's heart beating like a trip-hammer with the mad excitement of it. The acute thing was the splendid sincerity of Judy Harbottle's response. For days she was profoundly on her guard, then suddenly she seemed to become practically, vividly aware of what I must go on calling the great chance, and passionately to fling herself upon it. It was the strangest co-operation without a word or a sign to show it conscious – a playing together for stakes that could not be admitted, a thing to hang upon breathless. It was there between them – the tenable ground of what they were to each other: they occupied it with almost an equal eye upon the tide that threatened, while I from my mainland tower also made an anguished calculation of the chances.

I think, in spite of the menace, they found real beatitudes; so keenly did they set about the business that it brought them moments finer than any they could count in the years that were behind them, the flat and colourless years that were gone. Once or twice the wild idea even visited me that it was, after all, the projection of his mother in Somers that had so seized Judy Harbottle, and that the original was all that was needed to help the happy process of detachment. Somers himself at the time was a good deal away on escort duty: they had a clear field.

I cannot tell exactly when – between Mrs Harbottle and myself – it became a matter for reference more or less overt, I mean her defined problem, the thing that went about between her and the sun. It will be imagined that it did not come up like the weather; indeed, it was hardly ever to be envisaged and never to be held; but it was always there, and out of our joint consciousness it would sometimes leap and pass, without shape or face. It might slip between two sentences, or it might remain, a dogging shadow, for an hour. Or a week would go by while, with a strong hand, she held it out of sight altogether and talked of Anna – always of Anna. Her eyes shone with the things she told me then: she seemed to keep herself under the influence of them as if they had the power of narcotics. At the end of a time like this she turned to me in the door as she was going and stood silent, as if she could neither go nor stay. I had been able to make nothing of her that afternoon: she had seemed preoccupied with the pattern of the carpet which she traced continually with her riding crop, and finally I, too, had relapsed. She sat haggard, with the fight forever in her eyes, and the day seemed to sombre about her in her corner. When she turned in the door, I looked up with sudden prescience of a crisis.

'Don't jump,' she said, 'it was only to tell you that I have persuaded Robert to apply for furlough. Eighteen months. From the first of April. Don't touch me.' I suppose I made a movement towards her. Certainly I wanted to throw my arms about her; with the instinct, I suppose, to steady her in her great resolution.

'At the end of that time, as you know, he will be retired. I had some trouble, he is so keen on the regiment, but I think – I have succeeded. You might mention it to Anna.'

'Haven't you?' sprang past my lips.

'I can't. It would be like taking an oath to tell her, and – I can't take an oath to go. But I mean to.'

'There is nothing to be said,' I brought out, feeling indeed that there was not. 'But I congratulate you, Judy.'

'No, there is nothing to be said. And you congratulate me, no doubt!'

She stood for a moment quivering in the isolation she made for herself; and I felt a primitive angry revolt against the delicate trafficking of souls that could end in such ravage and disaster. The price was too heavy; I would have denuded her, at the moment, of all that had led her into this, and turned her out a clod with fine shoulders like fifty other women in Peshawur. Then, perhaps, because I held myself silent and remote and she had no emotion of fear from me, she did not immediately go.

'It will beat itself away, I suppose, like the rest of the unreasonable pain in the world,' she said at last; and that, of course, brought me to her side. 'Things will go back to their proportions. This,' she touched an open rose, 'will claim its beauty again. And life will become – perhaps – what it was before.' Still I found nothing to say, I could only put my arm in hers and walk with her to the edge of the verandah where the *syce* was holding her horse. She stroked the animal's neck. 'Everything in me answered him,' she informed me, with the grave intelligence of a patient who relates a symptom past. As she took the reins she turned to me again. 'His spirit came to mine like a homing bird,' she said, and in her smile even the pale reflection of happiness was sweet and stirring. It left me hanging in imagination over the source and the stream, a little blessed in the mere understanding.

Too much blessed for confidence, or any safe feeling that the source was bound. Rather I saw it leaping over every obstacle, flashing to its destiny. As I drove to the Club next day I decided that I would not tell Anna Chichele of Colonel Harbottle's projected furlough. If to Judy telling her would be like taking an oath that they would go, to me it would at least be like assuming sponsorship for their intention. That would be heavy indeed. From the first of April – we were then in March. Anna would hear it soon enough from the General, would see it soon enough, almost, in the *Gazette*, when it would have passed into irrecoverable fact. So I went by her with locked lips, kept out of the way of those eyes of the mother that asked and asked, and would have seen clear to any depth, any hiding-place of knowledge like that.

As I pulled up at the Club I saw Colonel Harbottle talking concernedly to the wife of our Second-in-Command, and was reminded that I had not heard for some days how Major Watkins was going on. So I, too, approached Mrs Watkins in her victoria to ask. Robert Harbottle kindly forestalled her reply. 'Hard luck, isn't it? Watkins has been ordered home at once. Just settled into their new house, too – last of the kit came up from Calcutta yesterday, didn't it, Mrs Watkins? But it's sound to go – Peshawur is the worst hole in Asia to shake off dysentery in.'

We agreed upon this and discussed the sale-list of her new furniture that Mrs Watkins would have to send round the station, and considered the chances of a trooper – to the Watkinses with two children and not a penny but his pay it did make it easier not to have to go by a liner – and Colonel Harbottle and I were half-way to the reading-room before the significance of Major Watkin's sick-leave flashed upon me.

'But this,' I cried, 'will make a difference to your plans. You won't – '

'Be able to ask for that furlough Judy wants. Rather not. I'm afraid she's disappointed – she was tremendously set on going – but it doesn't matter tuppence to me.'

I sought out Mrs Harbottle at the end of the room. She looked radiant; she sat on the edge of the table and swung a light-hearted heel. She was talking to people who in themselves were a witness to high spirits, Captain the Hon. Freddy Gisborne, Mrs Flamboys.

At sight of me her face clouded, fell suddenly into the old weary lines. It made me feel somehow a little sick; I went back to my cart and drove home.

For more than a week I did not see her except when I met her riding with Somers Chichele along the peach-bordered road that leads to the Wazir-Bagh. The trees were all in blossom and made a picture that might well catch dreaming hearts into a beatitude that would correspond. The air was full of spring and the scent of violets, those wonderful Peshawur violets that grow in great clumps, tall and double. Gracious clouds came and trailed across the frontier barrier; blue as an idyll it rose about us; the city smiled in her gardens.

She had it all in her face, poor Judy, all the spring softness and more, the morning she came, intensely controlled, to announce her defeat. I was in the drawing-room doing the flowers; I put them down to look at her. The wonderful telegram from Simla arrived — that was the wonderful part — at the same time; I remember how the red, white, and blue turban of the telegraph peon bobbed up behind her shoulder in the verandah. I signed and laid it on the table; I suppose it seemed hardly likely that anything could be important enough to interfere at the moment with my impression of what love, unbound and victorious, could do with a face I thought I knew. Love sat there careless of the issue, full of delight. Love proclaimed that between him and Judith Harbottle it was all over — she had met him, alas, in too narrow a place — and I marvelled at the paradox with which he softened every curve and underlined every vivid note of personality in token that it had just begun. He sat there in great serenity, and though I knew that somewhere behind lurked a vanquished woman,

I saw her through such a radiance that I could not be sure of seeing her at all . . .

She went back to the very first of it; she seemed herself intensely interested in the facts; and there is no use in pretending that, while she talked, the moral consideration was at all present with me either; it wasn't. Her extremity was the thing that absorbed us; she even, in tender thoughtfulness, diagnosed it from its definite beautiful beginning.

'It was there, in my heart, when I woke one morning, exquisite and strange, the assurance of a gift. How had it come there, while I slept? I assure you when I closed my eyes it did not exist for me . . . Yes, of course, I had seen him, but only somewhere at dinner . . . As the day went on it changed – it turned into a clear pool, into a flower. And I – think of my not understanding! I was pleased with it! For a long time, for days, I never dreamed that it could be anything but a little secret joy. Then, suddenly – oh, I had not been perceiving enough! – it was in all my veins, a tide, an efflorescence, a thing of my very life.

'Then – it was a little late – I understood, and since –

'I began by hating it – being furious, furious – and afraid, too. Sometimes it was like a low cloud, hovering and travelling always with me, sometimes like a beast of prey that went a little way off and sat looking at me . . .

'I have – done my best. But there is nothing to do, to kill, to abolish. How can I say, "I will not let you in," when it is already there? How can I assume indifference when this thing is imposed upon every moment of my day? And it has grown so sweet – the longing – that – isn't it strange? – I could more willingly give him up than the desire of him. That seems as impossible to part with as life itself.'

She sat reflective for a moment, and I saw her eyes slowly fill.

'Don't – don't *cry*, Judy,' I faltered, wanting to horribly, myself.

She smiled them dry.

'Not now. But I am giving myself, I suppose, to many tears.'

'God help you,' I said. What else was there to say?

'There is no such person,' she replied, gaily. 'There is only a blessed devil.'

'Then you go all the way – to the logical conclusion?'

She hardly hesitated. 'To the logical conclusion. What poor words!'

'May I ask – when?'

'I should like to tell you that quite definitely, and I think I can. The English mail leaves tonight.'

'And you have arranged to take it?'

'We have arranged nothing. Do you know' – she smiled as if at the fresh colours of an idyll – 'we have not even come to the admission? There has been between us no word, no vision. Ah, we have gone in bonds, and dumb! Hours we have had, exquisite hours of the spirit, but never a moment of the heart, a moment confessed. It was mine to give – that moment, and he has waited – I know – wondering whether perhaps it would ever come. And to-day – we are going for a ride today, and I do not think we shall come back.'

'Oh, Judy,' I cried, catching at her sleeve, 'he is only a boy!'

'There were times when I thought that conclusive. Now the misery of it has gone to sleep; don't waken it. It pleases me to believe that the years are a convention. I never had any dignity, you know, and I seem to have missed the moral deliverance. I only want – oh, you know what I want. Why don't you open your telegram?'

I had been folding and fingering the brown envelope as if it had been a scrap of waste-paper.

'It is probably from Mrs Watkins about the victoria,' I said, feeling its profound irrelevance. 'I wired an offer to her in Bombay. However' – and I read the telegram, the little solving telegram from Army Headquarters. I turned my back on her to read it again, and then I replaced it very carefully and put it in my pocket. It was a moment to take hold of with both hands, crying on all one's gods for steadiness.

'How white you look!' said Mrs Harbottle with concern. 'Not bad news?'

'On the contrary, excellent news. Judy, will you stay to lunch?'

She looked at me, hesitating. 'Won't it seem rather a compromise on your part? When you ought to be rousing the city – '

'I don't intend to rouse the city,' I said.

'I have given you the chance.'

'Thank you,' I said, grimly, 'but the only real favour you can do me is to stay and lunch.' It was then just on one.

'I'll stay,' she said, 'if you will promise not to make any sort of effort. I shouldn't mind, but it would distress you.'

'I promise absolutely,' I said, and ironical joy rose up in me, and the telegram burned in my pocket.

She would talk of it, though I found it hard to let her go on, knowing and knowing and knowing as I did that for that day at least it could not be. There was very little about herself that she wanted to tell me; she was there confessed a woman whom joy had overcome; it was understood that we both accepted that situation. But in the details which she asked me to take charge of it was plain that she also kept a watchful eye upon fate – matters of business.

We were in the drawing-room. The little round clock in

its Amritsar case marked half-past three. Judy put down her coffee-cup and rose to go. As she glanced at the clock the light deepened in her eyes, and I, with her hand in mine, felt like an agent of the Destroyer – for it was half-past three – consumed myself with fear lest the blow had miscarried. Then as we stood, suddenly, the sound of hoofs at a gallop on the drive, and my husband threw himself off at the door and tore through the hall to his room; and in the certainty that overwhelmed me even Judy, for an instant, stood dim and remote.

'Major Jim seems to be in a hurry,' said Mrs Harbottle, lightly. 'I have always liked your husband. I wonder whether he will say tomorrow that he always liked me.'

'Dear Judy, I don't think he will be occupied with you to-morrow.'

'Oh, surely, just a little, if I go tonight.'

'You won't go tonight.'

She looked at me helplessly. I felt as if I were insisting upon her abasement instead of her salvation. 'I wish – '

'You're not going – you're not! You can't! Look!'

I pulled it out of my pocket and thrust it at her – the telegram. It came, against every regulation, from my good friend the Deputy Adjutant-General, in Simla, and it read, *'Row Khurram 12th probably ordered front three hours' time.'*

Her face changed – how my heart leaped to see it change! – and that took command there which will command trampling, even in the women of the camp, at news like this.

'What luck that Bob couldn't take his furlough!' she exclaimed, single-thoughted. 'But you have known this for hours' – there was even something of the Colonel's wife, authority, incisiveness. 'Why didn't you tell me? Ah – I see.'

I stood before her abashed, and that was ridiculous, while

she measured me as if I presented in myself the woman I took her to be. 'It wasn't like that,' she said. I had to defend myself. 'Judy,' I said, 'if you weren't in honour bound to Anna, how could I know that you would be in honour bound to the regiment? There was a train at three.'

'I beg to assure you that you have overcalculated,' said Mrs Harbottle. Her eyes were hard and proud. 'And I am not sure' – a deep red swept over her face, a man's blush – 'in the light of this I am not sure that I am not in honour bound to Anna.'

We had reached the verandah, and at her signal her coachman drove quickly up. 'You have kept me here three hours when there was the whole of Bob's kit to see to,' she said, as she flung herself in; 'you might have thought of that.'

It was a more than usually tedious campaign, and Colonel Robert Harbottle was ambushed and shot in a place where one must believe pure boredom induced him to take his men. The incident was relieved, the newspapers said – and they are seldom so clever in finding relief for such incidents – by the dash and courage shown by Lieutenant Chichele, who, in one of those feats which it has lately been the fashion to criticize, carried the mortally wounded body of his Colonel out of range at conspicuous risk of depriving the Queen of another officer.

I helped Judy with her silent packing; she had forgiven me long before that; and she settled almost at once into the flat in Chelsea which has since been credited with so delightful an atmosphere, went back straight into her own world. I have always kept her first letters about it, always shall. For months after, while the expedition still raged after snipers and rifle-thieves, I discussed with Lady Chichele the probable outcome of it all. I have sometimes felt ashamed of leaping as straight as I did with Anna to what we thought the inevitable. I based no calculation on all Mrs Harbottle had gone back to, just as I had based no calculation on her ten years' companionship in arms when I kept her from the three o'clock train. This last was a retrospection in which Anna naturally could not join me; she never knew, poor dear, how fortunate as to its moment was the campaign she deplored, and nothing to this day can have disturbed her conviction that the bond she was at such magnificent pains to strengthen, held against the strain, as long, happily, as the supreme need existed.

'How right you were!' she often said. 'She did, after all, love me best, dear, wonderful Judy!' Her distress about poor Robert Harbottle was genuine enough, but one could not be surprised at a certain ambiguity; one tear for Robert, so to speak, and two for her boy. It could hardly be, for him, a marriage after his mother's heart. And she laid down with some emphasis that Somers was brilliantly entitled to all he was likely to get – which was natural, too . . .

I had been from the beginning so much 'in it' that Anna showed me, a year later, though I don't believe she liked doing it, the letter in part of which Mrs Harbottle shall finally excuse herself.

'Somers will give you this,' I read, 'and with it take back your son. You will not find, I know, anything grotesque in the charming enthusiasm with which he has offered his life to me; you understand too well, you are too kind. And if you wonder that I can so render up a dear thing which I might keep and would once have taken, think how sweet in the desert is the pool, and how barren was the prospect from Balclutha.'

It was like her to abandon in pride a happiness that asked so much less humiliation; I don't know why, but it was like her. And of course, when one thought of it, she had consulted all sorts of high expediencies. But I sat silent with remembrance, quieting a pang in my heart, trying not to calculate how much it had cost Judy Harbottle to take her second chance.

ETHEL WINIFRED SAVI
The Interloper

There was an air of expectancy at Mungalbari, for the magistrate was returning from England with a bride.

This bride! What heartburnings were awakened in the breasts of the Sahib's servants at the thought of the woman who was coming to rule in the bungalow and curtail their liberties! For it was always so when a wife arrived like a queen to be worshipped by her husband, and his entire household made to do her homage. A great deal of pessimism prevailed, since it was understood that English memsahibs were meticulous in matters of housekeeping, and had ideas respecting hygiene greatly at variance with methods familiar to the East.

'What-like will she be?' was murmured among the domestics, anxiously. 'Will she be easy-going and indifferent, or prying, and with a nagging tongue?' The question was left to answer itself.

Allison's return from *Belait*, whither he had gone on short leave, would have been welcomed by his staff had he but remained single; but some evil Fate had brought him in contact with the love of his boyhood's days, and forthwith he had married, then cabled the news with orders to prepare on a large scale for her reception. He had cabled to his friend Mr Wigley of the police, whose wife immediately supervised operations, creating with her feminine talent revolutionary changes in the magistrate's abode.

Spotlessly clean the bungalow had to be, and refurbished throughout. The stern asceticism of the Sahib's bedroom, particularly, was metamorphosed into a dainty apartment with futile ornamentation and flimsy decorations that were designed to increase instead of diminish labour, while the dining-room acquired additions which could only mean periods of unspeakable harassment for their upkeep. *Khansama-jee* gazed in consternation on the brilliance of the electro-plate and new silver, the cutglass, and the china, and shook his hoary head doubtfully. The assistant bearer regarded the highly polished surface of the dining table and sideboard with dismay, thinking of the 'elbow grease' that would be entailed if beeswax and turpentine were the mediums necessary to preserve that mirror-like polish.

'Go to!' sneered the *khansama* contemptuously. 'Who, in these enlightened times, uses *momerogun*? A dry *jharan* is all that will be necessary, for it is a polish that preserves itself. Think of the trouble in store for *me* – the sacrifice of my leisure to keep so much silver bright with plate-powder, otherwise there will be much abuse and fault finding. *Ai Khoda!* it's the devil's business, this marriage of our Sahib.'

'Why despair so soon?' remarked the sweeper in passing. 'This one, peradventure, might be of the sort that is more concerned with her person than her home. Like many another, she might seek to make herself attractive in the eyes of her male friends and leave her husband and home to look after themselves. God grant that she be not too particular, for with these carpets and new mats, I shall be killed by overwork. In my last place in Calcutta, there was a device that worked from a plug in the wall, in a manner none can explain, and with such a machine was labour thus rendered amusement. Alas! but what can one do in a place like this, where there is naught but a broom of cocoanut-fibre with which to sweep?' And grumbling to himself, he passed on his way.

In the kitchen, which was situated apart from the bungalow after the manner of Indian kitchens and was little

The Interloper

better than a glorified hut, there was a conference of servants to discuss the subject of the approaching trouble, in all its bearings. The last word, however, remained with the head bearer – a faithful follower of the Prophet – who had been longest in the service of the Sahib and was privileged above his fellows because of his dignity and great self-esteem.

'You all set up a cawing like crows on the house-top,' he growled, lighting one of his master's cheroots imitatively and blowing a perfectly marvellous smoke-ring, to the admiration of his friends. 'Wait, first, and see for yourselves how it will be, and then talk! Who can tell what Fate has in store? Like as not, this woman he is bringing from across the Black Water will have no tolerance for this land of ours. Many have I seen come and go,' he shrugged, 'and it's generally fear that turns their livers to water, for such have no stomach for difficulties. She will hear this and that. She will tremble when a thunderstorm breaks overhead with deafening crashes. The sight of a snake will paralyse initiative. Insects will be as pins in her flesh. She will be afraid to eat or drink lest she be seized with the Bad Sickness, and naught will content her but to sojourn in the mountains the moment the weather gets hot and the sun blisters the skin. Then, when it is established beyond doubt that a child is on the way, of a truth, she will turn and flee. Our Sahib will escort her to the docks and breathe a sigh of satisfaction when the vessel departs, realizing that freedom and contentment are only for the unwed, and that cursed is the man who yields his neck to the yoke of marriage when he is of the race that has ceased to uphold the supremacy of the male.'

'You are unduly hopeful, Favoured One!' jeered the *khansama*.

'In my experience, I have found reason to doubt the

success of these marriages made in *Belait*. But, let be! I advise patience in dealing with this period of the Sahib's bewitchment. Be not *nimuk haram* [a traitor], and all will yet be well.'

But the cook eyed the array of shining aluminium pots and pans in dismay. If the Sahib should expect him to keep them like silver, he would have to look elsewhere for a cook. 'Just you wait, brother, when you learn that your day is finished and that no more authority is yours, what will be? Peradventure, you will retain your office by virtue of the fact that you will be useful as an interpreter! If so, be merciful when you interpret her insults, taking care to soften the edge of her disapproval.'

'There is naught to fear,' said Emamdin, expectorating into the sink which was built into a corner of the kitchen floor with a hole in the wall for drainage. 'She will herself hold us in anxious distrust, and be afraid to open her lips to find fault till she has acquainted herself of our customs and the caste-limitations of the Hindus. Allah is merciful, and if we use tact and gently fan the flames of apprehension, she will not long trouble us here.'

'Listen to him! he speaks true words!'

'Leave him to rid us of the interloper!' was chorused.

'Of us all, he will be the greatest loser, for no more will he handle the Sahib's money or speak with authority in the place. His position will be degradation, and his humiliation will be great.'

'Get rid of her quickly, O friend and deliverer!' sighed the cook, feelingly, taking a pull at a *hookah*.

'And on your head we'll invoke divine blessings.'

A mild suggestion of winter was in the air when Raymond Allison arrived at Mungalbari, with his bride, and drove through the shady lanes to his bungalow. The duranta hedges were in full flower, the Gloriosa superba on an arbour, was a shower of gold, the poinsettia blazed scarlet in gardens by the way, while the morning glory painted the landscape blue under a cerulean sky. Colour rioted everywhere, and it seemed that all nature shouted a welcome to the happy pair, with palms swaying in the gentle breeze, and the sunlight dancing for joy through the leaves of the trees on the road below.

Tactfully, Mrs Wigley refrained from calling immediately. The newly wedded couple had enough of society on the boat, coming out, and would appreciate a little privacy while the bride grew accustomed to the strange conditions of her home. Presently, all the district would rush to pay their respects, for Ray Allison was too great a favourite for his wife to escape an ovation.

Raymond Allison pointed out the features of the station as he drove his wife through the rural scene, and his heart failed as he thought of the contrast of the life he was giving her to that which she had left, in order to belong to him. It made him feel very humble and grateful and a great many other things he could not put into words, while he wondered how she would bear the inevitable dullness of her days with only a club as the centre of diversion and recreation. Would she grow homesick and weary of it all, and shrink from the inconveniences and hardships that were unavoidable so far from town and city? He was ready to sacrifice anything to make her contented – the lovely little creature, with her sunny nature and clinging ways! But India was a hard school for one brought up in the midst of modern conveniences and luxury and he had seen many fail.

However, his little Irma was a wonderful 'sport' – a 'game kid', and knew how to take hard knocks, be it at hockey or in the natural order of things; and for that he had loved and married her.

As they drove up to the bungalow steps, a file of apprehensive servants *salaamed* low and received an answering salute from the Sahib, who whispered encouragingly to his bride. Among them stood Emamdin, tall, inscrutable, with a turban a foot high, and a look in his eyes that was almost a challenge; which immediately inspired Irma with fear and distrust.

'They seem a big crowd,' said Ray, 'but you will find them very useful. Surely, you are not scared?' This, when they had passed on.

'I *am* – frightfully! That tall man with a bushy beard and smouldering eyes is truly alarming. He looks as if he'd like to stick a knife into me for intruding here.' And she laughed to make it seem nonsensical. 'Must there be so many to look after only you and me?'

'Well – they each have their special duties that don't clash, owing to caste restrictions. The man you noticed, however, is a Muhammadan and a topping good sort. He will interpret for you, and make housekeeping easy, so you mustn't imagine he's anything but helpful and trustworthy. How do you like your new home?' for she was looking eagerly about her and taking in the cool daintiness of her surroundings.

'I love it all! Why are you so anxious? Do you think I am fussy and hard to please? Any place that is good enough for you, is good enough for me. Remember that.' And she snuggled closer, which encouraged him to indulge sentimental inclinations.

'I am tortured with the fear that you will find it slow and get homesick!' said he, in passionate apology.

'"Home" will always be where you are,' said she, with a catch in her voice. 'I shall never want any other. Why,

Ray!' and she laughed to cover the tendency to an emotional breakdown, 'it is going to be a delightful picnic for us both till the time comes for us to retire home for good.'

'Years hence! You will, by that time, be dyeing your hair, and I shall be bald.'

'What matter, if we have a family of boys and girls to keep us young and optimistic?'

'But how you'll hate leaving them in England to come back here to me!' tentatively.

'I wonder!' she teased, then kissed him tenderly. 'Put me to the test!'

What a little sport she was!

It was truly delightful to unpack their wedding presents and share the joy of making discoveries, which the excitement of a wedding and immediate travel had delayed. Even the preponderance of cruets failed to damp their ardour; or the tragedy of splintered cut-glass to depress their high spirits.

To learn a new method of housekeeping was in itself a joke, for it required the services of an interpreter whenever she had a wish to express. And calculating in rupees, annas, and pies, necessitated the overhauling of her arithmetic, which was, at least, something to the good. Best of all, for Ray, was the discovery that she refused to be horrified by dung-beetles that flew booming into the room, to crash against an opposite wall and fall with a whack to the floor.

'Poor little thing! what a headache it will have, to be sure!' was a new point of view with which to sympathize.

A bat circling round the room did not send her with a shriek of panic to hide under a mosquito-net in the bedroom, but she enjoyed tackling the situation from a corner with a carpet beater, and lunged at the giddy creature, while her husband did the same, at the other end of the apartment, with a walking cane, each competing against the other for first blood; and when it flopped to the carpet, after an accurate hit from the cane, she was all remorse and pity, wanting to restore the poor little thing – 'The innocent, wee creature with a darling, foxy face!'

'Oh, Ray! how cruel we are! I never knew a bat was like a mouse with wings. Can't I do something to make it well?'

That was Irma. And Ray had to console her for his wanton deed.

Another time, she saw a snake killed in the pantry. It had climbed on to the *jhilmil*, and the *khansama* had escaped certain death by a miracle, for he had nearly touched it with his hand as he was about to close the window. He stood shaking like an aspen leaf, while Emamdin killed it and laid it on the tiles for inspection – a deadly *karait*! To Ray's surprise, his beloved girl did not turn even pale, but took a lively interest in the specimen, and, thereafter, was particularly cautious in dealing with shutters and places likely to harbour reptiles, while Emamdin was instructed to warn the sweeper that a daily search for snakes under every piece of furniture was, henceforth, to be one of his additional duties.

To her husband's eternal gratitude, she made no complaints. If she had troubles over housekeeping, she was equal to them, and, very soon, had the reins of government firmly in her little hands. His only distress was her attitude towards Emamdin, whom she failed to understand or like. It was her firm conviction that he resented her, and longed for a chance to do her an injury. 'You can see the sullen look in his eyes,' she confided to Ray. 'They can't help giving him away.'

'You are quite mistaken, darling. Emamdin is a tried servant, and I have reason to be really fond of him. I wish you would try to forget your prejudice.'

'He is jealous, for I have come in his way.'

'My dear, he is the most faithful blighter alive, and for my sake would be loyal to you. Once I nursed him through cholera, and ever since he has stuck to me like a burr. When I have been sick, he has slept across my threshold and done quite menial tasks, so long as no one has been at hand to see him defiled, proud devil that he is!'

'All the more reason why he hates *me*. You see, he has to play second fiddle in the house, and from being a confidential servant, is now just a medium through which I pass orders. I know he'd be glad if I got out, but I'm sorry for his hopes, as I have no intention of abandoning my post while I live. I do think I could get on much better if I hadn't the feeling of his antagonism always to contend against. Besides, I don't understand these people – they are so queer and silent and automatic. You never know what they are thinking of, and so many are treacherous. I remember hearing on the ship some truly awful stories of treachery among natives –'

'Don't you believe a word of it. I'd sooner trust my life to a staunch Muhammadan friend or a conscientious Hindu, than to many a European, I grieve to say.'

'But how can you tell what they are? Their faces are expressionless.'

Raymond laughed. 'A self-respecting Indian servant makes a mask of his face, so don't you worry about that. But, if it will make you happier, I'll give him his *jawab*, old thing.' Ray was ready to be unjust to all the world rather than leave a single wish of hers ungratified.

However, for the moment, there was too much distraction to allow of his putting his promise into effect, and Irma was so taken-up with callers and found Emamdin so useful, that nothing further was said on the subject of his dismissal. For several days she was thoroughly confused as to people and names, and without the friendly assistance of Mrs Wigley, would have been greatly embarrassed.

After a giddy round of dinners and luncheons, afternoon teas, and introduction to club evenings, Irma began to return the hospitality she had received, with shy enjoyment. Her first dinner party was a thrilling ordeal and her admiration for Ray increased a hundred-fold when she found that there was nothing concerning the giving of such an entertainment he did not know, even to the assortment of their numerous guests and the question of social precedence. It was all delightful, and Ray's servants showed themselves the most wonderful robots in creation, for, in spite of their undying resentment towards the interloper, it was the *khansama*'s pride that none should point the finger of scorn at his master and say that he had servants who did not know their jobs, while the cook's ambition was to challenge the neighbourhood to better his performance.

The winter months flew and, with them, the nip in the air and all of the best that nature provides in Bengal. Fresh complexions faded, energy flagged, and amusements began to slump. Irma found that she could not play so many sets of tennis of an afternoon, and that dancing to the gramophone at the Club made her feel sticky and tired. However, it was all in the day's expectations, and her husband rejoiced to see that her step was just as light, her laughter as ready as when she first made the acquaintance of Mungalbari. Presently, he meant to broach the subject of the hills. Indeed, already Mrs Wigley and other friends of the feminine persuasion were discussing forthcoming plans with reference to Darjeeling.

Somehow, Emamdin was still head bearer at the bungalow, to his master's secret relief, for Irma had neglected to press for his dismissal. It seemed that, by degrees, she was beginning to understand the ways of her domestics and profit by peeps into their tortuous psychology. There were unending discoveries that led to mutual interests. She made friends with naked babies that sprawled about the backyard, and she learned, incidentally, that her servants had hosts of needy relatives quartered on them to their everlasting poverty and indebtedness. She made the acquaintance of shy-eyed wives who walked with a list sideways, as one hip was always at the service of a fat infant, generally smeared from head to foot with mustard oil.

What did not appeal to her was the presence of innumerable pariah dogs that made a thoroughfare of the garden, and goats that stole every opportunity to nibble the rose leaves, to the total destruction of the plants.

'What can one do?' the *mali* remarked with resignation when reproached through the medium of the interpreter. 'These pests are starved by their owners, and let loose to devour costly herbage. Truly, they are possessed with the cunning of the devil to work their will. Alas! If the Sahib would but put the owners in gaol!'

'He can't do that, but I shall recommend him to keep a dog to chase the goats away. What about mending the gaps in the fence?'

'Gaps?' repeated the *mali*, helplessly, scratching the calf of one leg with the big toe of an expressive foot. Clearly, the idea was new to his imagination. 'There are many gaps always coming in the long drought. Without rain, how can the hedges flourish?'

'Get you gone, *suar ka batcha*!' growled Emamdin, abusively. 'Sharpen your wits, and the next time goats destroy aught in the Memsahib's garden, you will be fined a month's wages and feel the weight of the Sahib's stick.'

The *mali* gazed reproachfully at the autocrat and slunk away, to complain to his fellow servants in the kitchen of the conversion of Emamdin who was no longer on their side, but espousing the cause of the Memsahib because of the softness of her voice and beguilement of her looks.

The next time Emamdin showed himself in the servants' common meeting ground of the kitchen, he was charged as a renegade, since he had personally taken upon himself the task of seeing that his mistress's orders were obeyed, even to a campaign against encroaching cobwebs, and the matter of garbage in the kitchen sink.

'Say what you like,' said Emamdin, having the grace to blush under his natural pigmentation, 'the Memsahib must be humoured. What is she but a product of modern teachings with a passion for cleanliness? Let be. As a wife to our Sahib, she is unsurpassed.'

'This very day will I tender my resignation,' said the cook; nevertheless polishing with a final effort the bottom of an aluminium pan.

'I, also,' said the *khansama* loyally, 'for never have I been so hardworked in my life.'

'I will venture to say that neither of you will give notice, for only this very day she said to me – and her voice sounded like a *busli*, so sweet was its music – "Emamdin, I much appreciate my servants, who have shown themselves capable and honest. As good servants need encouragement, I have suggested to the Sahib that each gets a reasonable rise in wages, so that none will feel discontented." Now, to leave one so full of understanding and sympathy, would be madness and folly. Go, if you will, but I believe you will stay.'

'It is good to see that one so new to the country has an understanding of our circumstances,' put in a menial whose relations were devouring his resources.

'As for me,' Emamdin continued, 'I want no better service. My Sahib, at the risk of his life, looked after me in sickness. Emamdin never forgets an obligation. He is no *nimuk haram*! . . . This young creature being as the sun, moon, and stars to him, she must be allowed freedom to please herself.'

'Ho! listen to Emamdin! He is himself bewitched.'

The first real scare Mrs Allison had at Mungalbari, was over a mad dog. A mongrel bull-terrier belonging to one of the police boys went 'queer', and suddenly disappeared.

'I'm afraid it's rabies,' said the young man, when he rode round to all his friends with a warning. 'He was bitten by a pi-dog a month ago, and for the past two days has been off his feed. I had him chained up, but, this morning, he broke loose, bit all the dogs at the chummery, and vanished. The police constables and sundry others are out looking for the brute, and I hope will locate him and put an end quickly to the danger.'

'That's hydrophobia?' asked Irma, fearfully. She had heard terrible tales of hydrophobia.

'Yes. Horrible idea! Be on the look out, and keep all your back doors shut. The peons can patrol the front of the house, and I wouldn't venture out alone, if I were you, till you know he's been killed – poor beggar! I was very fond of him.'

The young man rode away and Irma sat down, immediately, to write a warning to her husband at the *kachari*, telling him to take care of himself and be on his guard. 'Don't worry for me, as I am taking all precautions,' she concluded.

Hardly had the note been despatched, prior to the precautions she intended to take, when a peculiar sound drew her attention to the doorway of her bedroom, and she was paralysed to see a large bull-terrier on the threshold, foaming at the mouth and snapping at imaginary objects, right and left. It had evidently entered the bungalow by a back door and had not yet sensed her presence.

Irma felt glued to her seat in front of the desk, incapable of making a movement or crying aloud for help. She could only pray that the mad dog would pass out of the room without seeing her.

The horror of those moments will live in her memory for ever. It was her first experience of hydrophobia, and being perfectly aware of the danger of a bite from a mad dog, she was nerveless with fear. This was one of the things she was told she might have to guard against in the East, though, with some luck, she might never be actually in personal danger. However, she was unlucky, and was now face to face with the horror of it, and powerless to defend herself. What could she do but remain motionless and pray?

Her fascinated gaze was fixed in deadly terror on the suffering brute as it stood uncertainly in the doorway, dripping saliva from its torn and bleeding mouth. Suddenly, two inflamed eyes met hers, wild with hallucinations; and as it bounded forward, Irma, with a piercing shriek, scrambled on to the top of the frail desk and, seizing a ruler, was battling the next moment with the infuriated creature.

Again and again, it leapt at her with deadly intent, and again and again it was repulsed with blows from the ruler, while the desk rocked beneath her on its Chippendale legs, threatening every minute to collapse under the onslaught. Indeed, nothing could have saved Irma from a bad mauling, had Emamdin not rushed in to her rescue. He was in an adjoining room, valeting his master's clothes when he heard the commotion and the urgent cries for help. There was no time to look for a stick, so he came empty-handed, bursting upon the scene to grasp, on the instant, its peril. Though he had a full appreciation of his own danger, he did not hesitate an instant, but seized the raving dog in his vigorous hands and held it back, struggling manfully, though the blood dripped from his torn and bleeding wrists.

'Run, Memsahib!' he cried. 'Save yourself!'

This Irma did, speedily, calling loudly for help as she fled, with the result that many servants responded armed with lethal weapons, so that the animal was speedily despatched.

But Emamdin? . . .

When Irma saw the tragic state of his hands and realized what it might possibly mean, she broke down and wept.

'Oh, Emamdin! You saved me, but at what a terrible cost to yourself!'

'Don't cry, Memsahib,' said the heroic fellow. 'Within me is a great uplifting. By this act I have proved my loyalty to my Sahib, and the thought will support me, whatever may befall. We die but once; what matter, sooner or later, so long as we acquire Merit? This is *kismet*.'

Emamdin, however, did not die, for Raymond sent him, without delay, to an Institute, where he was given the antitoxins necessary for the elimination of the poison of rabies from his blood.

When he returned as protected and no longer in danger, he became a very much indulged and pampered servant, which would have thoroughly spoiled his magnificent nature had he not truly loved his master and mistress with a devotion that was faithful unto death.

NB The final episode of this story is founded on fact. Unhappily, the heroic Indian died of hydrophobia, there being no Pasteur Institutes at that time, in India, to give him a chance, though everything else was done that was humanly possible.

ALICE PERRIN
Mary Jones

The doctor stopped his dog-cart in front of a little wooden gate in the roadside hedge.

'Here's the last of them,' he said, relief in his voice.

His companion, a short, spare man, browned by Eastern sun, descended from the trap and waited while the doctor tied the reins to the gate-post. All this afternoon the two had driven about the scattered parishes to clumps of cottages, to lonely farms, now and then to superior dwellings, and once through many acres of park to where, in a great old stone house, a servant lay ill. Tomorrow the doctor would start on his long-delayed holiday; the thin, brown man was his locum tenens, and today had been spent in explaining and introducing the cases that were to be left in the stranger's care.

The surrounding country was bleak and high, with distant railway communication, wide, sloping fields, dense hedges, thick stone walls, and steep hills; the habitations seemed to have been placed, purposely, as far apart as possible. But it was spring-time. Primroses clustered close about the roots of giant trees, bluebells wove a coloured carpet for the copses; the plaintive, exacting bleat of lambs quavered on the clean, fresh atmosphere, and across the azure brightness of the sky marched a great army of white clouds in triumphant procession.

The Anglo-Indian looked about him, and breathed the pure air with keen enjoyment. In his thoughts he contrasted his present surroundings with the sun-baked land he had left but a few weeks back – where human beings, both dark and white, might be perfectly well in the morning and dead before the day was out; where he had seen natives die by hundreds in the twenty-four hours; where he had treated, continuously, such terrible maladies as plague, smallpox, leprosy, cholera. Today he had seen teething ailments, whooping-cough, rheumatism, 'bad legs' and worn-out, bedridden peasants dying peacefully, readily, of old age – their approaching ends discussed in their presence with cheerful interest by their friends.

How different it was! The homely complaints, the old-world cottage interiors, the remote and monotonous lives, the English landscapes, the fresh, uncertain weather. And yet, in the midst of his appreciation and relief, the doctor from India was conscious reluctantly, of a curious little throb of nostalgia for the vast sun-soaked plains he had left; the seething bazaars, redolent of musk and spice, and Oriental humanity; the little villages flanked by clumsy mango-groves; and the great, silent spaces of the jungle.

Yet, how thankful he had been to get away. Tired, in indifferent health, weary of exile, but still having within him the incurable unrest of the seasoned Anglo-Indian, the unrest that had driven him to answer the advertisement of a country doctor and take this temporary work that he might have occupation for mind and time, the while he gained benefit from bracing air and comparative quiet.

'Old Jones had a stroke a couple of years ago,' said Dr Rowe, pausing at the gate. 'He's a very old man, nearer ninety than eighty. He may go out at any moment now, so I just keep an eye on him.'

He pushed open the gate and led the way up a narrow, flagged path, with cabbages on either side and clumps of daffodils and wallflowers at irregular intervals. A jackdaw swung in a wicker cage by the cottage door. It made Sayne, the man from India, remember captive mynas, quail, partridges, parrots, hanging outside the bungalows of departmental clerks and subordinates. He felt vaguely annoyed that he could not shake his memory free of India, even over the veriest trifle.

Bending his head, he followed his leader through a dangerously low entrance into the dimness of a cramped little dwelling-room. The usual stuffy cottage odour met his nostrils. He saw, against the opposite wall, an oak dresser covered with a miscellaneous collection of objects – japanned trays, wooden boxes, shells, china and glass ornaments; much modern rubbish mingled, ignorantly, with some genuinely 'old bits'. A deal table stood in the middle of the floor, and a shabby chair-bed was stretched beneath the window. A fire smouldered in the tiny range, and a kettle hissed drowsily. Over the high mantelshelf that bore china dogs and gaudy biscuit-boxes hung a crude, coloured picture. Sayne, glancing at it, recognized the Taj at Agra. Good heavens! India again. Then, seeing a white-bearded patriarch dozing in a cart-wheel chair, he wondered if Jones had been a soldier in his day, and had seen service in the East!

Behind the chair, in the shadow, stood an old woman, who curtsied in respectful welcome. Her straight white hair was crowned with a man's cloth cap, she wore a faded print gown, and a coarse apron; her shrivelled skin was the colour of tanned leather, and sunken dark eyes glinted deep in her head.

Sayne observed the old lady with interest while Dr Rowe explained to her the situation, and made inquiries concerning the health of her husband. There was something about the woman's wrinkled face that puzzled Sayne – something in the dull fire of the deep-set eyes and the outline of the head and shoulders that seemed to him different from the ordinary type of countrywoman. For all her evident years she retained traces of beauty in the modelling of her features, and of grace in her carriage. The snow-white hair beneath the discoloured cloth cap was abundant and of fine quality, the ears were small and well shaped, the wrists and hands slender.

Old Jones sat vacant, helpless. Mary, his wife, made respectful replies with a strong rustic accent to Dr Rowe's questions and remarks. The kettle sang, the spring sunshine penetrated between the flower-pots that blocked the window-sill, and shot in a golden shaft across the red-tiled floor. Close to suffocation was the atmosphere, and the two doctors were glad to escape from it as soon as possible.

'Is Mrs Jones of gipsy origin?' asked Sayne, as presently they drove down the narrow lane.

Rowe glanced at his companion in some surprise. 'Not that I know of – why? She's much the same as all the other old bodies about the countryside – white hair, a wrinkled skin, and a general air of stupidity!'

'She struck me as rather out of the common; but, of course, I haven't much experience of English village folk,' Sayne deprecated.

'Oh! they're a very ordinary old couple. Jones was a soldier in his youth – a very long time ago now! They sell poultry and eggs and such-like at the nearest market. The old lady walks there every week, pushing a sort of go-cart full of her wares four miles each way. So far as I can gather, her power of endurance is the only uncommon thing about her. Look!' – pointing over the edge with his whip – 'there goes a fine old cock-pheasant. The shooting hereabouts ought to be first-rate, but nobody can afford to preserve, so it's horribly neglected.'

The talk turned on sport; Mary Jones and her husband were forgotten.

It was not until Dr Rowe had been more than a week in

enjoyment of his holiday that Sayne had occasion to remember the old couple again.

The day had been boisterous and showery; he had driven far that afternoon, and was glad as the evening drew in, sharp and chilly, to rest in a comfortable arm-chair in front of a welcome fire. But presently he was disturbed by the rush and throb of a motor-car and a violent peal at the door bell. He went into the little hall and interrupted a parley between his servant and a leather-clad, begoggled figure on the door-step.

'What is it?' he asked. 'Won't you come in?'

'Very sorry – can't,' was the answer. 'In a desperate hurry – must get on without delay. I inquired for the doctor's house when we reached the village, because I'm sorry to say we knocked down an old woman about three miles back, just outside her cottage gate. She was a bit dazed at first, but she said she wasn't hurt, and I don't think she was, for she walked up to her door all right. I gave her a sovereign. Her name's Jones. I thought it was best to let the doctor know, and here's my card in case anything happens. Sorry about it, but we weren't going fast, and she came out of her gate without the least warning. Good night.'

The traveller stepped into his palpitating conveyance, and was out of sight and hearing before Sayne had returned to his fireside.

So poor old Mary Jones had been bowled over by a motor-car! But according to the motorist she was unhurt. Sayne thought rather wistfully of the well-cooked dinner that was just ready, and looked at the comfortable chair with a low table beside it, on which lay a particularly interesting book together with his tobacco-pouch and pipe. Mary Jones had declared herself unhurt, had walked unaided into her cottage, and had the sovereign to console her. All the same, she was an old woman – the shock might easily produce the most disastrous consequences, even without actual injury; she was alone but for the presence of her helpless old husband. Yes, he must go. After a few mouthfuls of food and a gulp of whisky-and-soda, he packed a bag with possible medical necessaries and set off on his bicycle.

A light twinkled feebly from the Jones's cottage. The door was not quite shut, and Sayne pushed it open without knocking. There sat old Jones in the cart-wheel chair before the range, the kettle shooting at him a thin arrow of steam. The doctor looked around the close little room. On the bed under the window lay Mary Jones in her print gown and coarse apron, the cloth cap still on her white head. Her eyes were wide open, and she was muttering rapidly to herself. Sayne saw that she was delirious, but, as he laid his hand upon her wrist, he felt as though a sudden blow had been dealt to his understanding, for the words that were coming fast from her lips, were Hindustani words – Hindustani, not English! He listened to the familiar tongue, and heard the old woman babble incoherently of scented garlands and attar of roses, of marriage feasts, of spangled gossamer, of jewels and rupees, and of the beat of the tom-tom.

With an effort he gave his medical attention to the case; and soon the painful, unnatural murmur ceased, and the strained, glittering eyes closed gently.

Sayne sat beside the motionless figure, conjecturing as to what strange secret could be hidden beneath the disguise of plain old Mary Jones, described by Dr Rowe as being 'much the same as all the other old bodies about the countryside'. He examined one of the wrinkled hands; it was brown and toil-worn, the nails were dirty and broken, the thin wedding-ring hung loose. Certainly the skin was dark, but not darker than that of many an old Englishwoman of sallow complexion who had suffered constant exposure to all weathers. He glanced at Jones, unheeding and tranquil in his chair, and then his gaze wandered upward to the crude picture of the Taj, all white, and blue, and green. What was the connection between this outwardly prosaic old country couple and that land of eternal mysteries – India?

The patient lay quiet, the old man snored gently; presently Sayne rose and went out into the cool twilight for a breath of air. India seemed very remote and unreal to him as he stood there in the wild spring night; the cherry-tree at the corner creaked and rustled, the smell of wet earth, and the scent of daffodils and wallflowers was blown about him. How different from the musky perfumes and scented garlands babbled of by Mary Jones in her delirium! He almost laughed at the fantastic comparison, and began to question whether the old woman had really spoken in Hindustani, or if he could by any possibility have imagined it.

A sound from within the cottage made him turn to re-enter the little room, but on the threshold he paused, aghast, for Mary Jones was standing upright in the narrow space between the couch and the table. The cloth cap had fallen from her head, her white locks straggled to her shoulders; the sunken black eyes gleamed and glittered, and she began, in a cracked nasal voice, to sing a curious minor melody that Sayne recognized instantly. He had heard it chanted so often in native processions, had caught its echo from bazaar house-tops on hot-weather nights; it had floated towards him from dusky entrances, and he had listened to it in rajahs' palaces – the song of the *nautch* girl!

Then he saw that Jones was awake – that the old man had moved in his chair, and with palsied head, quivering helplessly, he was pointing a gnarled forefinger at his wife. Now she twisted and turned her old body, her feet, in their clumsy boots, shuffled on the brick floor, the wrinkled, withered hands waved and gesticulated. Mind and memory had swept back over the wide space of many years to the time of her youth when, surely, she had been no Englishwoman, no Mary Jones in print gown and coarse apron, with rustic speech and yokel apathy; but *what*?

All in a moment she swayed and tottered; the song ceased abruptly in a shuddering gasp, and Sayne, stepping forward, caught a lifeless body in his arms. Gently he laid it on the narrow chair-bed, and, as he listened for the heartbeats that he knew instinctively were stilled for ever, he became aware that the old man was trying to speak.

Patiently the doctor waited as thin, quavering sounds issued from that toothless mouth, till a few indistinct words were shaped with painful effort. They sounded to Sayne like 'Sixty-year – little wench', and, was it 'Kashmere'? Then the head sank forward, the worn-out consciousness relapsed into senility.

For a few moments the doctor stood, seeing the little room with its eminently English contents – the ornaments, the hissing kettle, the rag mat in front of the range, the rough, solid furniture. He looked at the huddled figure in the arm-chair dozing away the feeble remnant of life, and at the still form on the bed. What curious little history had he so nearly surprised? Was Mary Jones a native woman? Was it possible that in her far-off youth she had been a *nautch* girl?

He considered the comparative fairness of her skin – perhaps she had been brought down from Kashmere and bartered in one of the great cities of the plains? Had Jones taken her from a bazaar, married her, and brought her home as little more than a child, according to English standards? Stranger things had happened, Sayne knew, in those bygone Indian days! And had she been severed for sixty years from the old life and language to return to it in spirit at the hour of her death?

The doctor roused himself. It was necessary to summon the parish nurse. And he went out from the fusty little dwelling into the boisterous night, his imagination aflame with questions that could never now be answered.

ALICE PERRIN
Caulfield's Crime

Caulfield was a sulky, bad-tempered individual who made no friends and was deservedly unpopular, but he had the reputation of being the finest shot in the Punjab, and of possessing a knowledge of sporting matters that was almost superhuman. He was an extremely jealous shot, and hardly ever invited a companion to join him on his shooting trips, so it may be understood that I was keenly alive to the honour conferred on me when he suddenly asked me to go out for three days' small game shooting with him.

'I know a string of *jheels*,' he said, 'about thirty miles from here, where the duck and snipe must swarm. I marked the place down when I was out last month, and I've made arrangements to go there next Friday morning. You can come, too, if you like.'

I readily accepted the ungracious invitation, though I could hardly account for it, knowing his solitary ways, except that he probably thought I was unlikely to assert myself, being but a youngster, and also he knew me better than he did most people, for our houses were next door, and I often strolled over to examine his enormous collection of skins and horns and other sporting trophies.

I bragged about the coming expedition in the Club that evening, and was well snubbed by two or three men who would have given anything to know the whereabouts of Caulfield's string of *jheels*, and who spitefully warned me to be careful that Caulfield did not end by shooting *me*.

'I believe he'd kill any chap who annoyed him,' said one of them, looking round to make sure that Caulfield was not at hand. 'I never met such a nasty-tempered fellow, I believe he's mad. But he can shoot, and what he doesn't know about game isn't worth knowing.'

Caulfield and I rode out the thirty miles early on the Friday morning, having sent our camp on ahead the previous night. We found our tents pitched in the scanty shade of some stunted *dâk* jungle trees with thick, dry bark, flat, shapeless leaves, that clattered together when stirred by the wind, and wicked-looking red blossoms. It was not a cheerful spot, and the soil was largely mixed with salt which had worked its way in white patches to the surface, and only encouraged the growth of the rankest of grass.

Before us stretched a dreary outlook of shallow lake and swampy ground, broken by dark patches of reeds and little bushy islands, while on the left a miserable mud village overlooked the water. The sun had barely cleared away the thick, heavy mist, which was still slowly rising here and there, and the *jheel* birds were wading majestically in search of their breakfast of small fish, and uttering harsh, discordant cries.

To my astonishment, Caulfield seemed a changed man. He was in excellent spirits, his eyes were bright, and the sullen frown had gone from his forehead.

'Isn't it a lovely spot?' he said, laughing and rubbing his hands. 'Beyond that village the snipe ought to rise in thousands from the rice fields. We shan't be able to shoot it all in three days, worse luck, but we'll keep it dark, and come again. Let's have breakfast. I don't want to lose any time.'

Half an hour later we started, our guns over our shoulders, and a couple of servants behind us carrying the luncheon and cartridge bags. My spirits rose with Caulfield's, for I felt we had the certainty of an excellent day's sport before us.

Caulfield's Crime

But the birds were unaccountably wild and few and far between, and luck seemed dead against us. 'Some brutes' had evidently been there before us and harried the birds, was Caulfield's opinion, delivered with disappointed rage, and after tramping and wading all day, we returned, weary and crestfallen, with only a few couple of snipe and half-a-dozen teal between us. Caulfield was so angry he could hardly eat any dinner, and afterwards sat cursing his luck and the culprits who had forestalled us, till we could neither of us keep awake any longer.

The next morning we took a different route from the previous day, but with no better result. On and on, and round and round we tramped, with only an occasional shot here and there, and at last, long after mid-day, we sat wearily down to eat our luncheon. I was ravenously hungry, and greedily devoured my share of the provisions, but Caulfield hardly touched a mouthful, and only sat moodily examining his gun, and taking long pulls from his whisky flask. We were seated on the roots of a large tamarind tree, close to the village, and the place had a dreary, depressing appearance. The yellow mud walls were ruined and crumbling, and the inhabitants seemed scanty and poverty-stricken. Two ragged old women were squatting a short distance off, watching us with dim, apathetic eyes, and a few naked children were playing near them, while some bigger boys were driving two or three lean buffaloes towards the water.

Presently another figure came in sight – a *fakir*, or mendicant priest, as was evident by the tawny masses of wool woven amongst his own black locks and hanging in ropes below his shoulders, the ashes smeared over the almost naked body, and the hollow gourd for alms which he held in his hand. The man's face was long and thin, and his pointed teeth glistened in the sunlight as he demanded money in a dismal monotone. Caulfield flung a pebble at him and told him roughly to be off, with the result that the man slowly disappeared behind a clump of tall, feathery grass.

'Did you notice that brute's face?' said Caulfield as we rose to start again. 'He must have been a pariah dog in a former existence. He was exactly like one!'

'Or a jackal perhaps,' I answered carelessly. 'He looked more like a wild beast.'

Then we walked on, skirting the village and plunging into the damp, soft rice fields. We put up a wisp of snipe, which we followed till we had shot them nearly all, and then, to our joy, we heard a rush of wings overhead, and a lot of duck went down into the corner of a *jheel* in front of us.

'We've got 'em!' said Caulfield, and we hurried on till we were almost within shot of the birds, and could hear them calling to each other in their fancied security. But suddenly they rose again in wild confusion, and with loud cries of alarm were out of range in a second. Caulfield swore, and so did I, and our rage was increased ten-fold when the disturber of the birds appeared in sight, and proved to be the *fakir* who had paid us a visit at luncheon-time. Caulfield shook his fist at the man and abused him freely in Hindustani, but without moving a muscle of his dog-like face the *fakir* passed us and continued on his way.

Words could not describe Caulfield's vexation.

'They were pintail, all of them,' he said, 'and the first decent chance we've had since we came out. To think of that beastly *fakir* spoiling the whole show, and I don't suppose he had the least idea what he had done.'

'Probably not,' I replied, 'unless there was some spite in it because you threw a stone at him that time.'

'Well, come along,' said Caulfield, with resignation, 'we

must make haste as it will be dark soon, and I want to try a place over by those palms before we knock off. We may as well let the servants go back as they've had a hard day. Have you got some cartridges in your pocket?'

'Yes, plenty,' I answered, and after despatching the two men back to the camp with what little game we had got, we walked on in silence.

The sun was sinking in a red ball and the air was heavy with damp, as the white mist stole slowly over the still, cold *jheels*. Far overhead came the first faint cackle of the wild geese returning home for the night, and presently as we approached the clump of palms we saw more water glistening between the rough stems, and on it, to our delight, a multitude of duck and teal.

But the next moment there was a whir-r-r of wings like the rumble of thunder, and a dense mass of birds flew straight into the air and wheeled bodily away, while the sharp, cold atmosphere resounded with their startled cries. Caulfield said nothing, but he set his jaw and walked rapidly forward, while I followed. We skirted the group of palms, and on the other side we came upon our friend the *fakir*, who had again succeeded in spoiling our sport. The long, lanky figure was drawn to its full height, and white eyeballs and jagged teeth caught the red glint of the setting sun, and he waved his hand triumphantly in the direction of the vanishing cloud of birds.

Then there came the loud report of a gun, and the next thing I saw was a quivering body on the ground, the wild eyes staring open in the agony of death. Caulfield had shot the *fakir*, and now he stood looking down at what he had done, while I knelt beside the body and tried hopelessly to persuade myself that life was not extinct. When I got up we gazed at each other for a moment in silence.

'What are we to do?' I asked presently.

'Well, you know what it means,' Caulfield said in a queer, hard voice. 'Killing a native is no joke in these days, and I should come out of it pretty badly.'

I glanced at the body in horror. The face was rigid, and seemed more beastlike than ever. I looked at Caulfield again before I spoke, hesitatingly.

'Of course the whole thing was unpremeditated – an accident.'

'No, it wasn't,' he said defiantly. 'I meant to shoot the brute, and it served him right. And you can't say anything else if it comes out. But I don't see why anyone should know about it but ourselves.'

'It's a nasty business,' I said, my heart sinking at the suggestion of concealment.

'It will be nastier still if we don't keep it dark, and you won't like having to give me away, you know. Either we must bury the thing here and say nothing about it, or else we must take it back to the station and stand the devil's own fuss. Probably I shall be kicked out of the service.'

'Of course I'll stand by you,' I said with an effort, 'but we can't do anything this minute. We'd better hide it in that long grass and come back after dinner. We must have something to dig with.'

Caulfield agreed sullenly, and between us we pushed the body in amongst the thick, coarse grass, which completely concealed it, and then made our way back to the camp. We ordered dinner and pretended to eat it, after which we sat for half an hour smoking, until the plates were cleared away and the servants had left the tent. Then I put my hunting-knife into my pocket, and Caulfield picked up a kitchen chopper that his bearer had left lying on the floor, after hammering a stiff joint of a camp chair, and we quitted the tent casually as though intending to have a stroll in the moonlight, which was almost as bright as day. We walked slowly at first, gradually increasing our pace as we left the camp behind us, and Caulfield never spoke a word until we came close to the tall grass that hid the *fakir*'s body. Then he suddenly clutched my arm.

'God in heaven!' he whispered, pointing ahead, 'what is that?'

I saw the grass moving, and heard a scraping sound that made my heart stand still. We moved forward in desperation and parted the grass with our hands. A large jackal was lying on the *fakir*'s body, grinning and snarling at being disturbed over his hideous meal.

'Drive it away,' said Caulfield, hoarsely. But the brute refused to move, and as it lay there showing its teeth, its face reminded me horribly of the wretched man dead beneath its feet. I turned sick and faint, so Caulfield shouted and shook the grass and threw clods of soil at the animal, which rose at last and slunk slowly away. It was an unusually large jackal, more like a wolf, and had lost one of its ears. The coat was rough and mangy and thickly sprinkled with grey.

For more than an hour we worked desperately with the chopper and hunting-knife, being greatly aided in our task by a rift in the ground where the soil had been softened by water running from the *jheel*, and finally we stood up with the sweat pouring from our faces, and stamped down the earth which now covered all traces of Caulfield's crime. We had filled the grave with some large stones that were lying about (remnants of some ancient temple, long ago deserted and forgotten), thus feeling secure that it could not easily be disturbed by animals.

The next morning we returned to the station and Caulfield shut himself up more than ever. He entirely dropped his shooting, which before had been his one pleasure, and the only person he ever spoke to, unofficially, was myself.

The end of April came with its plague of insects and scorching winds. The hours grew long and weary with the heat, and dust storms howled and swirled over the station, bringing perhaps a few tantalizing drops of rain, or more often leaving the air thick with a copper-coloured haze.

One night when it was too hot to sleep, Caulfield suddenly appeared in my verandah and asked me to let him stay the night in my bungalow.

'I know I'm an ass,' he said in awkward apology, 'but I can't stay by myself. I get all sorts of beastly ideas.'

I asked no questions, but gave him a cheroot and tried to cheer him up, telling him scraps of gossip, and encouraging him to talk, when a sound outside made us both start. It proved to be only the weird, plaintive cry of a jackal, but Caulfield sprang to his feet, shaking all over.

'There it is again!' he exclaimed. 'It has followed me over here. Listen!' turning his haggard, sleepless eyes on me. 'Every night that brute comes and howls round my house, and I tell you, on my oath, it's the same jackal we saw eating the poor devil I shot.'

'Nonsense, my dear chap,' I said, pushing him back into the chair, 'you must have got fever. Jackals come and howl round my house all night. That's nothing.'

'Look here,' said Caulfield, very calmly, 'I have no more fever than you have, and if you imagine I am delirious you are mistaken.' He lowered his voice. 'I looked out one night and saw the brute. It had only one ear!'

In spite of my own common sense and the certainty that Caulfield was not himself, my blood ran cold, and after I had succeeded in quieting him and he had dropped off to sleep on the couch, I sat in my long chair for hours, going over in my mind every detail of that horrible night in the jungle.

Several times after this Caulfield came to me and repeated

Caulfield's Crime

the same tale. He swore he was being haunted by the jackal we had driven away from the *fakir*'s body, and finally took it into his head that the spirit of the murdered man had entered the animal and was bent on obtaining vengeance.

Then he suddenly ceased coming over to me, and when I went to see him he would hardly speak, and only seemed anxious to get rid of me. I urged him to take leave or see a doctor, but he angrily refused to do either, and said he wished I would keep away from him altogether. So I left him alone for a couple of days, but on the third evening my conscience pricked me for having neglected him, and I was preparing to go over to his bungalow, when his bearer rushed in with a face of terror and besought me to come without delay. He said he feared his master was dying, and he had already sent for the doctor. The latter arrived in Caulfield's verandah simultaneously with myself, and together we entered the sick man's room. Caulfield was lying unconscious on his bed.

'He had a sort of fit, Sahib,' said the frightened bearer, and proceeded to explain how his master had behaved.

The doctor bent over the bed.

'Do you happen to know if he had been bitten by a dog lately?' he asked, looking up at me.

'Not to my knowledge,' I answered, while the faint wail of a jackal out across the plain struck a chill to my heart.

For twenty-four hours we stayed with Caulfield watching the terrible struggles we were powerless to relieve, and which lasted till the end came. He was never able to speak after the first paroxysm, which had occurred before we arrived, so we could not learn from him whether he had been bitten or not, neither could the doctor discover any scar on his body which might have been made by the teeth of an animal. Yet there was no shadow of doubt that Caulfield's death was due to hydrophobia.

As we stood in the next room when all was over, drinking the dead man's whisky and soda, which we badly needed, we questioned the bearer closely, but he could tell us little or nothing. His master, he said, did not keep dogs, nor had the bearer ever heard of his having been bitten by one; but there had been a mad jackal about the place nearly three weeks ago which his master had tried to shoot but failed.

'It couldn't have been that,' said the doctor; 'he would have come to me if he had been bitten by a jackal.'

'No,' I answered mechanically, 'it could not have been that.' And I went into the bedroom to take a last look at poor Caulfield's thin, white face with its ghastly, hunted expression, for there was now nothing more that I could do for him.

Then I picked up a lantern and stepped out into the dark verandah, intending to go home. As I did so, something came silently round the corner of the house and stood in my path. I raised my lantern and caught a glimpse of a mass of grey fur, two fiery yellow eyes, and bared, glistening teeth. It was only a stray jackal, and I struck at it with my stick, but instead of running away it slipped past me and entered Caulfield's room. The light fell on the animal's head, and I saw that it had only one ear.

In a frenzy I rushed back into the house calling for the doctor and servants.

'I saw a jackal come in here,' I said, searching round the bedroom, 'hunt it out at once.'

Every nook and corner was examined, but no jackal was found.

'Go home to bed, my boy, and keep quiet till I come and see you in the morning,' said the doctor, looking at me keenly. 'This business has shaken your nerves, and your imagination is beginning to play you tricks. Good-night.'

'Good-night,' I answered, and went slowly back to my bungalow, trying to persuade myself that he was right.

ALICE PERRIN
Ann White

The little English churchyard looked so peaceful, so cool, that I paused at the entrance; then made for a fine old yew tree to rest for a while in its shade on a flat tombstone that was age-worn, bespattered with lichen. I was tired and hot, having wandered farther than I had intended that sultry summer morning; people who have lived in the East feel the heat more severely than those who have never experienced months on end of stifling days and nights, pitiless metallic skies, the white glare of a death-dealing sun. It is a fact that is rarely recognized by untravelled folk; so I smile and say nothing when I am told that, of course, coming from India, I must revel in heat waves.

How pleasant I found it in this sacred green garden filled with the perfume of flowers, silent save for the humming of bees, the sweet, clear calling of birds! As I glanced about me I thought what a contrast to the arid cemeteries I had seen in India, with their neglected memorials to victims of exile, all the tragic inscriptions that told of untimely deaths; women and little children who in England might have recovered from sickness, men cut off in their youth, or when long-looked-for retirement was in sight; sometimes whole families swept away by cholera. Few white people die natural deaths in India; if they live they go home, and if they die there is seldom one of their kindred in the country to visit and attend to their graves.

Close to where I sat was a marble cross; at its base a wealth of blue flowers. I read that it was erected to the memory of Ann White, by her sorrowing grandchildren;

and of a sudden it brought to my recollection a plain stone slab, in an Indian cemetery, that marked the last resting place of another Ann White, also an old woman. Drowsed by the warm perfume and peace, I let the curious history of that other Ann White steal through my mind slowly, dreamily.

The first time I saw her was at the beginning of the hot weather, soon after I had arrived in India to keep house for my brother. She was seated, with an untidy-looking *ayah* squatting beside her, on the edge of the old concrete bandstand that still remained at one end of the deserted parade-ground. Before the mutiny Jutpore had been a military cantonment; now it was no more than a small civil station, remote from the railway, out of all proportion in size to the teeming native city, whose turbulent and fanatical population caused ceaseless anxiety to the few European officials and an inadequate staff of police. I remembered remarking to my brother as we rode past the bandstand, that it was surely unusual to see an Englishwoman of that age living in India – who was she? And Tom said, indifferently, he didn't know; he believed there was some legend about the old lady, but he couldn't remember. What did it matter?

Tom was an engineer, and mysteries connected with human beings held no interest for him. Had I made some inquiry concerning bridges or bricks, buildings or roads, I should no doubt have received voluble and animated information.

'But she looks so quaint!' I persisted; 'a sort of early Victorian sketch. Do try to recollect what you have heard about her.'

'No use, my dear. Whatever I might have heard went in at one ear and out at the other. You'd better apply to the missionaries. I think she lives with them, but whether they're CMS, or Baptists, or Papists, I can't say. There are samples of all kinds in the country, much to the mystification of the natives.'

Being of an imaginative, or, perhaps more truthfully, an inquisitive disposition, I felt a longing to ferret out the old lady's history. What was she doing in India at her time of life, and looking like a ghost from the past, dressed in a poke bonnet and a voluminous grey gown? She might almost have been wearing a crinoline. There must be some interesting story.

Consequently, next morning I started out alone, on foot, for the parade-ground, hoping to find her. Yes, she was there, seated on the bandstand, and with her the *ayah*, a stout, pocked-marked person chewing betel-nut, who regarded me apathetically as I approached.

The old lady was crooning softly to herself; she had a small crumpled-up face that reminded me of a peeled walnut; her eyes were a faded blue, the loops of hair, beneath the old-fashioned bonnet, like fleece. I was struck by a certain daintiness about her appearance, a lingering grace in the way she held herself; one would fancy her being described years long ago as 'a sweetly pretty young female'. She merely nodded and smiled when I greeted her with some polite remark, and continued her soft little song.

The *ayah* bestirred herself fussily, dragged her wrapper over her head, opened a large, white umbrella, and turned aside to spit forth red betel juice. Then, with the curious sort of respect that the lower classes all the world over seem to entertain towards mental affliction, she explained proudly that the old lady was *paghal*. I knew the word, for I was learning Hindustani; it meant crazy, mad.

I nodded sympathetically, inquired where they lived, and the *ayah* pointed to a solitary thatched bungalow that stood facing the parade-ground some distance from the residential quarter of the station.

'Missun,' she said, through her nose. 'Kristarn Missun-school.'

With that she bawled indulgently at her charge, helped her up, *salaamed* to me, and the pair started off across the bare plain. I watched their slow progress, the *ayah* clopping along in loose shoes, the old lady stepping feebly, supported by the native woman's arm, the white umbrella bobbing up and down – watched them till they passed between the two gateless white posts to disappear amongst plantain trees and shrubs.

That evening I shirked the usual visit to the Club, made some plausible excuse to Tom with secret satisfaction, since I played tennis and bridge badly; and also I was glad for once to escape the well-intentioned adjurations with which I was always deluged by the memsahibs regarding the correct management of servants and fowls, goats and cows, all the talk about charcoal and dusters and bazaar prices, the ordering of stores from Bombay, and so forth. Not that I was ungrateful for kindly advice, or undervalued the importance of good housekeeping, but beyond a point my interest in such matters failed; and I had never been good at games, mental or physical.

With a sense of adventure I drove to the white gate-posts I had noted that morning, boldly turned into the compound, and drew up before the thatched bungalow. As a newcomer to the station, it was quite in accordance with Anglo-Indian etiquette that I should make the first call on anyone I chose, a sensible custom among an ever-fluctuating official community.

One or two native children were playing in the verandah, who fled when I shouted the immemorial summons, '*Quai hai.*' Presently out came a neatly garbed little Englishwoman with a round, pleasant face and steady grey eyes, who proclaimed herself to be Miss Brownlow, assistant missionary to Padre Grigson and his wife; both, she said, were just now absent in the district 'itinerating'. Rather to my dismay, she took it for granted that my errand was not to make a formal call, but to give an order for mission needlework.

'Come in, do come in!' she cried civilly, 'and see all the lovely things made by our girls and women. What is it that you particularly require?'

I could hardly explain that I particularly required information about the *paghal* old lady! There was nothing for it but to pretend that I was anxious to buy something manufactured by the converts. As a result, I spent an hour, and a good deal of money, at the mission bungalow, allowing myself to be lured into purchasing mats and tidies, tray-cloths and handkerchiefs, none of which did I 'require'. All the same, Miss Brownlow contrived to excite my interest in the work she and the Grigsons were doing for India, and so engrossed did I become in our conversation that I completely forgot the real object of my visit until, just as I was leaving, I caught sight of my bandstand acquaintance, the fat *ayah*, crossing the compound.

'Why, there,' I exclaimed with cunning, 'is the *ayah* I have seen in the mornings on the parade-ground with an old lady!'

'Yes, our dear old Ann White, and Tulsi, who looks after her. It's their favourite little walk, across the parade-ground and back, with an interval of rest on the bandstand. Ann can't walk far nowadays, and there is no other place within easy reach where she can sit down. I am afraid soon she will not be able to leave the compound, she is failing very fast.'

'Was she a missionary?' I asked, dawdling purposely at the top of the verandah steps.

'Oh no, poor old thing! She has been imbecile since her childhood. In fact, no one knows who she is, and we shall never know unless, as Mr Grigson says happens sometimes in these cases, her memory should return in the hour of her death. She was named Ann White by the mission people who were here at the time of the Mutiny. It's a sad story. Are you in a hurry? Can you wait while I tell you?'

I felt that not even the most desperate need for haste would have prevented me from waiting to hear about old Ann White. And this was what I heard as I waited:

When in '57, the native regiment at Jutpore mutinied, murdering officers, women and children, the only Europeans to somehow escape death in the station, as far as was known at the time, were the members of the mission. But when, alas, too late, a British relief party arrived and were scouring the neighbourhood in search of the rebels, a little English girl of about ten years old was found in the jungle, starving, disguised as a native. What was her name, who had disguised her and hidden her away, could never be ascertained; she herself was too exhausted to speak when rescued, and though in time her bodily strength returned, both reason and memory had been lost beyond hope of recovery. The missionaries took charge of her, and a small grant was made by the Government for her support. There, ever since, she had lived, handed on with her pitiful story from one succeeding mission family to another, in the thatched bungalow, well cared for, no trouble, unless, as Miss Brownlow confided to me with a smile, anyone should attempt to dress her differently; then she would cry, refuse to eat, until the poke bonnet and full skirts were restored to her.

'So Mrs Grigson and I make new bonnets and gowns for

her when she needs them, copying the old patterns faithfully – the fashion she was accustomed to see in her childhood. It's the only thing she seems to remember at all. And doesn't she look an old darling!'

Cordially I agreed and departed, saddened by the pathetic history of Ann White, yet well pleased with my visit, because I felt I had gained a friend in the missionary lady, and that the embroideries were cheap at the price. (I sent them all home next mail to a relative whose mania was foreign missions.)

From that day I saw much of Emily Brownlow, also made friends with Padre Grigson and his wife when they returned from their tour in the district – an earnest, hard-working couple who yet were under no delusion as to the apparent hopelessness of their task in India. I grew to understand and appreciate their efforts, to share their conviction that though the work might seem but a scratch on the surface of idolatry, it was infinitely worth while, and must lead eventually to a deep undermining of ignorance and superstition among a people steeped in Nature worship, cruelly oppressed by higher castes, the priesthood, and indirectly by each other.

So far, the Grigsons admitted, the converts had been drawn principally from a class that had nothing to lose – indeed, everything to gain – by becoming Christians; but in the future the descendants of these converts would count, multiply into a strong community that sooner or later must rise to the top, triumphant. I found it all very interesting, though Tom chaffed and declared that I was fast going the way of our mission-mad kinswoman. The other ladies in the station assured me that when I had lived longer in India I should realize that the ardour of missionaries like Mr Grigson did more harm than good, interfering with ancient faiths that suited the people, forcing new wine into old bottles, often making trouble in the bazaars where already trouble enough was brewing. Here in Jutpore, for example, it was well known that a strong feeling existed against mission influence. Anything at any moment might lead to a riot, the missionaries would be the first to suffer if the mob got out of hand, and then probably we should all have our throats cut.

I remembered their sayings with a sick sense of foreboding one morning when Tom was away on inspection, and I had ridden over, before the sun got too hot, to spend the day with my friends at the mission bungalow. I found Mrs Grigson and Emily in a state of suspense and anxiety, for Mr Grigson was out preaching in the bazaar, and the native Bible teacher who accompanied him had just raced back, scared and breathless, with ill news. The city, he said, was in an uproar, it had been over something to do with rival religious processions that had clashed; the police had come; there was fighting. What had happened to the padre-sahib he was unable to say; they were separated in the crowd, he himself had been attacked, knocked down.

The man could tell us no more. Exhausted with fear and his flight, he collapsed.

We all knew that there was grave cause for alarm. Quite recently there had been a ghastly affair of the same kind in another part of the province, a riot during which the mob had turned on a missionary, beaten him to death in the street, and a general massacre of Europeans and natives had only been averted by the strongest measures. Mrs Grigson's behaviour was wonderful; not for a moment did she falter as she gave her orders. Emily Brownlow and I helped to collect the women and children from the outhouses and gather them into the bungalow, a chattering, frightened flock, for the bad news had spread in the compound. We kept them away from the side of the house where old Ann

White lay asleep. During the past few days she had been ailing, nothing very definite beyond a slight temperature, and loss of strength.

Mrs Grigson asked me to have a look at the old lady in case she had awakened. Tulsi was useless, she deserted her charge, wept, and declared her liver had turned to water, and resolutely joined the huddled throng in the living-room. I went and sat beside Ann White, who still slept undisturbed by the commotion, all the time straining my ears for sounds outside. Now and then above the ceaseless murmur of native voices within the bungalow I fancied I caught the echo of shots. What if the police should be overcome!

I looked at the peaceful, wrinkled old face on the pillow. When Ann was a child had her mother, possibly with other children about her too, gone through such an anxious period of waiting before the end came? I imagined the subsequent confusion, the cries, the horror, and shivered. Some faithful servant must have saved the little girl, fled with her, disguised her; but what actually had happened would never be known unless as Mr Grigson had said, Ann's memory should return before she died. For Ann's sake it was only to be hoped that it would not.

The heat became intolerable, for the *punkah* hung motionless. Presumably every coolie had fled, and the silence in the compound was sinister; no sound of the padre's return.

All the stories I had heard and read of the Mutiny crowded into my mind. Was history about to repeat itself at Jutpore? At last I could bear it no longer. Old Ann was all right, sound asleep, and I crept from the room, threaded my way through squatting groups of native women and children to seek Mrs Grigson. I found her standing in the verandah, regardless of the hot wind that was like the blast of a furnace. She was shading her eyes with her hands that she might gaze over the bare parade-ground in the direction of the city. How long we stood there together in silence I don't know – to me it seemed hours – until suddenly, above a line of mango-trees in the distance, a flame shot up, paled by the strong sunlight, then a column of smoke.

Mrs Grigson drew in her breath.

'They have begun burning, looting,' she whispered hoarsely. 'Oh, my husband, where are you?'

I passed my arm about her, fearing she might faint; indeed, I felt like fainting myself. But her courage held, bracing my spirit, too, even when there came to our ears the sound of a muffled roar, the roar of an angry multitude. The dull clamour grew louder, and a few moments later we saw a vast concourse of people pouring out from behind the trees, spreading over the opposite end of the plain.

Mrs Grigson pulled me back.

'They will come here,' she said, quietly. 'We must go in and shut the doors.'

The last thing I saw as we shut the long door-windows, bolting them top and bottom, was that mad, surging crowd making, as it seemed, direct for the mission bungalow. I had a dim recollection of hearing her voice, clear and strong. I think she was speaking to Emily Brownlow and me – telling us to be brave, to pray, asking us to help her to keep the knowledge of approaching danger and death from the little flock for as long as possible, and she started them singing a hymn. I tried to join in, but my throat felt dry, a mist swam before my eyes, my heart beat wildly with terror. I could see nothing, hear nothing, but that murderous crowd outside. The doors would be burst open, and then –

I know I called out 'Tom! Tom!' in a frenzy, but my own voice sounded far off; and after that, to my shame, I must have lost consciousness, for next I found myself on my knees in a corner, leaning against the wall. Slowly my senses began to clear. I dared to look up, and could hardly believe my eyes when I saw the padre! As I struggled to my feet the room seemed to spin round, and I should have fallen but that Emily Brownlow caught hold of me.

'We're all safe – *safe*!' she said loudly in my ear, half-laughing, half-crying.

I noticed that the 'flock' were streaming out into the compound, dancing and shouting like children released from school, and that Mrs Grigson was cutting away the coat-sleeve from her husband's right arm. I heard him say:

'It's only a flesh wound, no bones broken. Lucky it wasn't my head!'

It was not until later, when the injured arm had been bathed and bound up, and we were all refreshing ourselves with tea, that I learned what had happened. Just as the mob were overpowering the police, and the padre, his right arm rendered helpless by a savage blow, believed that his last hour had come, a British infantry regiment had suddenly made its appearance as if by magic. Not a shot was fired; the soldiers had simply marched through the streets, thumping the butt ends of their rifles on the toes of the petrified crowd, driving it before them, until it broke and fled, scattering over the parade-ground. A sergeant had helped the padre into his trap and seen him off safely; but where the regiment had come from, what was the explanation of its merciful arrival, Mr Grigson said he was too dazed at the time to inquire.

'We shall know all about it sooner or later,' he added.

And we did know, much sooner than we anticipated; for shortly afterwards we heard the sound of hoofs outside, and an officer rode up to the verandah steps. Of course, we all hurried out.

'The colonel wants to know if you are all right, padre!' he shouted. 'A near shave, wasn't it? A little longer and it would have been all U.P. with you, and probably everyone else in the station!'

No thanks! Very sorry, but he couldn't come in; hadn't time. The affair had delayed the regiment on the march; they must be getting on to the next camping ground. Anyway, these rascals in the city had learnt a lesson they wouldn't forget in a hurry!

He saluted and turned his horse's head.

'One moment!' called Mr Grigson. 'How did you hear of the row? The fellow who stopped the regiment ought to be rewarded.'

The officer drew rein, looked back over his shoulder.

'It was an old woman. She met us on the road; told the colonel we were wanted.'

'An old woman?' we chorused.

'Yes, an English woman, a queer-looking old dame in a poke bonnet. I don't know where she got to. By the time the order had been given to turn out of our line of march, she'd disappeared. We couldn't see her anywhere. But, knowing what these riots may mean, we took her word for it. Just as well we did, eh?'

Again he saluted, and this time galloped off.

We looked at each other in amazement.

'Old Ann!' Mrs Grigson exclaimed. 'We'd forgotten all about her. She must have got up and gone out!'

Then we flew to Ann's room, fearful as to what had become of her, expecting to see the bed empty. But there she lay, sleeping, just as I had left her, a serene smile on her old face. Nothing pointed to her having moved. The poke bonnet and grey dress hung from their pegs on the wall; her underclothing lay folded on a chair. Certainly the small pair of shoes beneath the chair were dusty, but as no housework had been attempted that morning, dust was thick everywhere.

Mrs Grigson bent over the pillow.

'Ann,' she said, gently, and again a little louder, 'Ann!'

There came no stir, no response from the quiet form on the bed as we listened in the hot silence; and when, presently, Mrs Grigson looked round, held up her hand, I knew from the expression on her face that Ann had gone to where memories cannot hurt, do not matter, where she would answer to her real name.

It is, and ever will be, my firm conviction, that Ann's spirit went forth that morning to save the lives of those who had loved and taken care of her on earth, and, in their secret hearts, I think both Mrs Grigson and Emily Brownlow were inclined to hold the same view. But, with the curious prejudice against belief in the supernatural shared by many truly pious people, the padre was entirely opposed to such an idea. Whenever we touched on the subject, he would repeat obstinately that the dying often displayed remarkable vitality shortly before the end came – the proverbial flash in the pan. He always maintained that Ann had risen and wandered out on to the Grand Trunk Road, which wasn't far off; that having met the regiment on the march, the sight of English soldiers had just for the moment awakened her recollection of that day in '57, when the relief party found her as a little girl in the jungle, when her one overwhelming desire, could she have uttered it, must have been to bid them go on to the rescue of her people. There was plenty of time, he would argue, for her to return. She had come back to die quietly in her bed; as a proof, were not her shoes covered with dust?

To my mind, this explanation seemed far more unlikely, even more miraculous than my own; but I never could get the padre to agree with me.

And now, as I sat beneath the yew tree in an English churchyard, the green mounds, the flowers, the tombstones faded from my sight. I only visioned the corner of a desolate cemetery, rank with coarse yellow grass, bounded by a mud wall. I saw an old monument, the inscription on it almost obliterated – 'mortal remains . . . Ensign . . . of sunstroke . . .' – and close beside it a newly laid slab that marked the grave of one whose true name was not Ann White.

ALICE PERRIN
The Fakirs' Island

On the ramparts of a red sandstone fort, built by Akbar, the great Moghul Emperor, in the days when Elizabeth was our Queen, stood a fair, fresh English girl. She was looking down on a scene that had been enacted year after year for some twenty centuries, with but little variation, save that comparative law and order now reigned where formerly riot, murder, theft and treachery were accepted as a mere matter of course.

Behind the dainty little figure in white towered the rugged red battlements, so indicative of the mighty character of the man who had raised them. Over her head blazed the electric blue of the Eastern sky, and below her surged nearly two millions of human beings, who had gathered from all quarters of India to bathe in the holy Ganges River and wash away their sins.

It was the time of the Khoom Mela, or great religious Hindu fair, and the noise that rose on the dry air was deafening; everyone shouted, everyone expostulated, gongs were being banged, bells rung, hymns chanted, and trumpets and conches blown furiously by the priests as they marched in long, fantastic processions towards the river's edge.

The clear blue of the Ganges' water was dulled and soiled for nearly a mile in the direction of the huge iron bridge that crossed her, and over which special trains had been labouring for the last three days, bearing densely packed crowds of enthusiastic pilgrims.

'What a sight!' said the girl, gazing down at the sea of

humanity. 'I believe one could walk on their heads with the greatest ease.'

The man who stood at her side was looking at her, and not at the seething throng below, and the beauty and perfection of her face and figure struck him with a thrill, as it had struck him again and again since she had arrived fresh from England, two months ago, to keep house for her bachelor uncle, who commanded the fort.

George Robertson had fallen deeply in love with Mona Selwyn the moment he had seen her, and he was a man of whose love a girl might have been very proud. A steadfast, honest, self-reliant soldier, older than his thirty years in mind and character, well-born, well-bred, and with a straight, resolute face.

'Aren't they horrid?' continued the girl, pointing downwards with her white parasol. 'They make such a noise, and kick up such a dust, and smell so nasty. I hate natives.'

'But they are a wonderfully interesting people,' said Robertson, dreamily, thinking of the great civilization that had been firmly established when Britons were yet barbarians, and that had, nevertheless, practically stood still for hundreds of years.

'I can't say I see anything the least bit interesting in them. Look at them down there like a disturbed ants' nest, making the most awful fuss about bathing in an ordinary river!'

'It's anything but an ordinary river to them, and, after all, it is much the same theory as our baptism.'

'But we don't make such a row about it.'

'No.'

'Why do you say "no" like that? Do you think we ought to shout and scream, and crowd and push, and go quite out of our minds over a religious ceremony?'

Captain Robertson laughed.

The Fakirs' Island

'Of course not. But, at the same time, I believe that this people's religion is far more real to them than is ours to us. Some say that is what has kept them at a standstill; but, at any rate, it is extraordinary what they will voluntarily suffer in its cause. Look over the river at that island. That is where the *fakirs*, or priests, are quartered during the fair time. I went there this morning and saw a man hanging by his heels to a sort of gallows, swinging his head to and fro through a fire he had lit below him. Another was buried up to his chin in the ground, and had been there for four days. I saw other men lying on beds of long, sharp nails, and one old fellow arrived from Peshawur while I was there, having measured his length the whole way along the ground for hundreds of miles. It is mortification of the flesh with a vengeance. They all believe that such doings will ensure them bliss in after-life, and our own old saints had much the same ideas.'

'Oh! How I should like to go over to the island and see them all! Will you take me there, Captain Robertson, to-morrow morning?'

The man's brown cheek flushed.

'I would rather not,' he said gently. 'I shouldn't like you to go there.'

'What rubbish!' she uttered pettishly. 'Why did you excite my curiosity about things that would interest me, and then calmly say you won't take me to see them? Why shouldn't I go, pray?'

'You wouldn't like it. You would probably see some very unpleasant sights, and it is dreadfully dirty and smells abominably.'

He thought of the fierce, fanatical faces, the hideous deformities, the lack of clothing on most of the holy men, and the evil attention that the presence of a young English girl would attract in such a crowd.

'You wouldn't like it,' he repeated.

'Yes, I should. And I have set my heart on going. Besides, I know Mrs Calcraft went, so why shouldn't I?'

'Mrs Calcraft is an elderly woman, and writes for the papers.'

'All right, if you won't take me I shall ask someone else.'

'I certainly won't take you,' he replied, with a touch of temper.

She was charmed to have made him angry; now she would make him jealous. It gave her an exquisite pleasure to know that she had the power to rouse this man's feelings. It was worth more to her than all the adoring demonstrations of her other slaves. She beckoned to a young man with a fair moustache, who made one of the group near them, and he instantly flew to her side.

'Mr Kerr, will you take me to see the *Fakirs*' Island tomorrow morning? It would be an object for a ride.'

'Of course I will! What a lark to see all those old Johnnies burning themselves alive and chopping off each other's heads! Isn't that what they do, Robertson?'

But Captain Robertson had moved off with a sore heart and a set jaw, and though Miss Selwyn laughed and joked with the fair-haired subaltern, there was a little cloud in her blue eyes, and a droop at the corner of her red mouth for the rest of the afternoon.

However, the following morning, when the sun was drawing the mist from 'Mother Ganga's' silver bosom, she rode with young Kerr over the bridge of boats leading to the *Fakirs*' Island in the gayest of spirits. The long rows of temporary sheds were astir with life; prayers were being chanted, and praises sung to every god and goddess in the Hindu mythology. Holy water was being freely sprinkled over shrines erected for the time being; already gay with

The Fakirs' Island

offerings of flowers and tinsel decorations. Morning ablutions were being performed, hair clipped, heads shaved, and sacred face-marks applied. Mona Selwyn and young Kerr got off their horses and walked down the little street, looking about them with lively curiosity.

'There's a man on a nail bed!' she cried, pointing with her whip. 'How hard his back must be. I should have expected *him* to be an early riser at any rate!'

'By Jove!' said her companion, putting up his eyeglass. 'I never believed it was true before. He must have a hide like a rhinoceros.'

'Captain Robertson told me he saw a man roasting his head over a fire.'

The delicate colour in her cheeks deepened as she mentioned George's name, and the next moment, with a guilty feeling of shame, she recognized the reasonableness of his objection to her expedition, for a group of almost nude priests passed close by, on their way to the river to bathe, staring boldly at the girl with fierce, blood-shot eyes. One of them whose body was smeared with ashes, and whose hair, matted with tow, hung down to his feet, walked backwards as he gazed at Mona, muttering to himself. She turned away frightened and impatient, and vexed with herself for having come at all.

'He was quite right,' she thought; 'he is always right. I ought to have listened to him.'

'Oh! Look! Look!' cried Kerr, pulling her sleeve and pointing excitedly.

Coming towards them was an ancient *fakir*, with one arm held high in the air, withered to a stick, and fixed in that position. As he approached, it became apparent that the nails had grown through the palm of the hand, and were protruding at the back. Following him like a dog came a small humped cow; from its shoulder grew an extra leg, and from its forehead dangled another tail, both having been grafted into the little creature's flesh soon after its birth, – a very sacred animal, rendered still more holy by the cruel deformities that had been practised on it. The old man himself was a loathsome sight. His arm rigid, his long white hair caked with mud, his wrinkled body grey with ashes and hung with filthy rags. Chains clanked on his bony ankles, and he moaned dismally for alms as he proffered his copper begging-bowl to every passer-by. Behind him crawled a crowd of squalid, diseased, half-naked people – professional beggars. Some huge with elephantiasis; others literally dropping to pieces with leprosy, a few sightless from smallpox, and all covered with sores, and clamouring for alms. The old *fakir* thrust his begging-bowl in front of Mona and gibbered.

'Oh! what does he want?' she said, shrinking back in horror.

'He wants the stick!' said Kerr, angrily. 'And he shall have it if he doesn't clear off. Git! You old brute,' he added menacingly to the old man, who only raised his voice and wailed a still more discordant demand for money.

The crowd of beggars gathered round, whining, cringing, crawling, stretching out claw-like hands and fingerless stumps towards the English people, while the little cow stood on the outskirts of the group and lowed plaintively. One woman, her face a mass of corruption, caught Mona's skirt, and dragged herself blindly towards the girl, who shrieked aloud in fear and disgust. Kerr raised his cane and struck the begging-bowl from the *fakir*'s hand. It clattered to the ground, and the pressing, whining crowd of beggars shrank back. The old priest's tawny eyes blazed with rage. He raised his living arm aloft until it matched the dead one, standing a weird, grotesque figure before the angry man and frightened girl. Then he cursed them loudly and venomously – 'and thou,' he concluded, glaring at Mona's white face, 'before ten suns have set thy beauty will be gone – thou wilt be as those – ' pointing to the mumbling mass of maimed, halt and blind that had withdrawn to a safe distance from the Englishman's cane.

'Oh! come away quickly!' cried Mona, gathering up her habit skirt and seizing her companion's arm. 'I wish I had never come. Why did you bring me? Make haste – ' and they half ran up the path between the two rows of huts, from which horrible faces seemed to peer at them on every side.

They rode back to the fort in silence. Kerr with his mind misgiving him for having taken the girl to such a place, Mona with a white, troubled face, haunted by the voice and manner of the old *fakir*, for she had understood that he was threatening her, though his actual words had been unintelligible. They were a depressed couple as they dismounted in front of the officers' quarters, and Mona did not recover her spirits all day, in spite of the prospect of a ball in the evening. The said ball was also a failure as far as her enjoyment was concerned, for when she arrived at it she was greeted with the unwelcome information, imparted by a casual acquaintance, that Captain Robertson had gone away on a month's leave.

'Very sudden, isn't it?' she asked, with a sinking heart.

'Oh, Robertson often goes off like that. He had a letter from a pal in the Dhoon, asking him to go up there at once for some "para" shooting, so he got his leave and started. He never can resist the chance of a shoot.'

Mona felt hopeless. She wondered if she had been the cause in any way of his departure, – or was it that he was quite indifferent and preferred shooting to herself? She contemplated the coming month with a sensation of utter dismay, as she realized what a blank it would be to her. She wished she had been nicer to him, that she had taken his advice about the *Fakirs'* Island, that she could do something to show her penitence. Perhaps if she rigidly abstained from accepting the attentions of any of her other admirers from this time forward, he might, on his return, notice the change, and understand. But, probably, if he thought about her at all, he was thoroughly disgusted with her. Oh! why had she been such an utterly silly, vain, frivolous little fool? Mona cried herself to sleep that night, and the next day, instead of going to a picnic, she stayed at home and studied Emerson's essays, because George Robertson had once told her she ought to read them.

Captain Robertson's leave extended itself to two months before he returned to the station. Work was slack, camps of exercise were over, the hot weather was coming on, and he had been easily spared. Therefore, as his shooting instincts had led him into regions where letters could not follow him, he arrived in blissful unconsciousness that during his absence Mona Selwyn had been at death's door. He heard it while breakfasting at mess on the morning of his return.

'Awful hard luck on the girl,' remarked a subaltern helping himself to fried bacon, and addressing Robertson. 'Smallpox, you know, and they say she's badly marked. Supposed to have caught it at that beastly fair.'

'How is she now?' faltered Robertson, with a dry tongue and a queer feeling in his throat. He had been making heroic efforts to stifle his love for Mona Selwyn during these two months, but he knew very well he had not succeeded.

'She's practically all right again, and, I believe, out of quarantine; but she won't go anywhere, she's so cut up about the havoc played with her looks. She goes out on the fort walls in the evening, and the Colonel said he hoped fellows would keep out of her way a bit, as she hates to be seen. Beastly hard lines – and such a pretty girl as she was!'

Robertson rose abruptly, letting his knife and fork fall into his plate. He could stand the other's chatter no longer – he must go to his room and be alone to think.

The outcome of his cogitations was that in the cool of the afternoon, when the water-carts were laying the dust on the broad, white roads, and the scent of reviving flowers was stealing on to the freshened air, he drove rapidly down to the fort, and, leaving his dog-cart outside, made his way to the ramparts.

In the back verandah of the Colonel's quarters he could see a long couch, with a figure reclining on it. He stood still for a few moments, gazing at the figure, and shading his eyes with his hand, for the evening sun was powerful. Then he walked quickly forwards, down a flight of stone steps, across a yard, up more steps, and finally into the verandah. The girl started, and turned her face towards him. She was greatly disfigured, but the marks were yet fresh, and would lessen with time. The fair, curly hair had been cropped short, and the blue eyes were full of a sadness that cut Robertson to the heart. His love and pity went out to her. Thank God, she was alive, and if she would take his life's devotion it was hers. She gave a distressed little cry, and covered her face with her hands. Robertson knelt down by the couch and drew her hands gently away.

'Mona,' he said.

Tears of weakness, disappointment, misery, ran from her eyes, and she sobbed helplessly.

'Darling, I never knew till this morning, and now I have come to ask you if you will forgive me for going away, and love me a little? I have loved you ever since I first saw you;

but I thought I had no chance. Will you let me comfort you, and take care of you, always – for ever?'

'I can't,' she sobbed. 'I am so ugly. Look at me!' She shut her eyes, and resolutely turned her face towards him. He kissed her mouth.

'It is you I want, dear,' he said gently, and reverently, and then he took her, unresisting, into his arms.

There was a hushed silence in the air, broken only by the monotonous cry of a plover and the splash of oars in the river below. Their thoughts flew back to the day when they had last stood on the fort walls together, and looked down on the restless, seething, excited multitude below and the stained, turbid waters. Now the Ganges flowed softly blue, clear, still. Nothing marked the banks but a few fishermen and the green patches of water-melon. The sky was flushed crimson with the setting sun, and peace reigned where but a short time before all had been confusion, clamour, dust and strife.

MAUD DIVER
Sunia: A Himalayan Idyll

I

O very woman – god at once and child!

The pearly glimmer of dawn was over the mountains; the far-off snows looked indescribably pale and pure against the dove-like tones of the sky. Away, across the valley, Kálatope ridge, serrated and majestic, made an incident of massive shadow amid the tenderer tints around.

A Himalayan dawn is brief as it is beautiful: and now, sudden and swift as magic, the full splendour of morning flashed along the sky. Rapier-like shafts of light pierced the purple lengths of shadow which lay along the deeper ravines and engulfed the still slumbering valley. They threaded their golden way through the sombre, level pine-boughs of Kálatope forest, and stretched out their radiant length along the narrow verandah of a low wooden bungalow that stood alone in the heart of this silent, smiling mountain world.

In that verandah, a solitary Englishman sat, peeling plantains and drinking tea, in full view of the valley and the brightening east. From time to time his eyes rested on the magnificent scene before him with the quiet satisfaction of one who looks on the familiar face of a friend; for, under the high-sounding title of Deputy Conservator of Government Forests, Phil Brodie reigned sole monarch of this his paradise – a peaceful and eminently satisfactory form of kingship.

Having eaten his last banana, he rose and sauntered to

the low wooden railing, hat in hand. He was a long, lean man of sportsmanlike build, though the face – sallow, serious, and self-contained, with a suspicion of cynicism about the mouth – suggested possibilities of cultured thought and feeling.

Anon, as he stood thus, his keen eyes brightened curiously – and not without good reason.

From out the black mass of pine and deodar to his right the figure of a young girl emerged, and neared the hut with swift, elastic step. Dress, face, and carriage proclaimed her a child of the Himalayas – a child-woman, such as the East alone can beget.

When a Hill girl is beautiful, you will scarce find her match in the five continents; and Sunia was beautiful past question. For eighteen months, morning after morning, Brodie had watched her approach him thus, bearing on her head his daily tribute of fruit and flowers; yet did her beauty still take him by surprise and demand a reiterated recognition of its quality. There were evil moments, of course, when he realized with a pang that in five years' time she would be coarse and commonplace, and in ten a wrinkled hag. But at the present moment she was incomparable – and she did not know it! Therein lay the miracle.

The face was a pure oval, with flower-like curves of cheek and chin, and eyes of that rare pale brown which is only found among true Hill folk, and that none too frequently. A flower-like silver ornament in one of her delicate nostrils seemed set there with coquettish intent to accentuate its exquisitely tender curves. The soft fullness of her lips suggested passionate possibilities, and the scarlet of betelnut upon them made an enchanting incident of colour amid the dusky tints of her face and dress. This last was of woollen homespun, a few shades darker than her skin. The graceless, close-fitting *pyjamas* were atoned for and partially concealed by a rough brown tunic, bound about the waist with smooth black coils of twisted goat's hair and fastened loosely across her breast with a silver pin. Around her brown throat she wore a narrow necklet of goat's hair strung with quaintly fashioned lumps of raw turquoise, onyx, and amber; and from the midst of these hung a grotesquely patterned plaque of hammered silver. Her small ears drooped with tinkling silver trinkets, and bangles and anklets of glass and silver clinked musically as she walked.

A round, flat basket, piled conically with garden produce, rested without support upon her close-fitting cap of yellow cotton, from beneath which her hair fell in one long braid, almost to her knees. The Eternal Feminine is one and the same the wide world over; and it is humiliating to reflect that two-thirds of this same braid – its wearer's dearest bit of vanity – had been borrowed from the back of a mountain goat.

With a gracious sweep of her arms, Sunia uncrowned herself and laid her *dáli* at Brodie's feet, then lowered her forehead thrice to the ground.

'Live for ever, Lord of my Life!' she murmured. The conventional greeting was uttered with passionate fervour.

Brodie stooped and lightly touched the quaint assortment of almonds, walnuts, and early vegetables, around which were set, with scrupulous symmetry, alternate clumps of blood-red rhododendron blossoms and the first wild white roses of the year. One of these last he chose, and put into his coat with quiet deliberation.

'Roses, Sunia?' he said, speaking the soft Hill dialect as musically as the girl herself. 'Thou hast been far afoot to procure so fine a sheaf of blossoms?'

She stood before him now slim and upright as the young pines all about her, and a sudden flush showed dimly beneath her olive skin.

'What matter how far, so my lord be well pleased?' she made answer with veiled eyes. 'Away there, down in the valley, they were scattered abroad like stars of silver; and I said within my heart, their shining will make beautiful the *Hazúr*'s house; and what should this slave live for save to give pleasure to my lord? Were it not well that I should bear them now to Dhunnu, that they faint not for lack of water?'

Brodie gave silent assent. Then, with eyes averted, and a smile half quizzical, half tender, he noted how she hastily plucked two roses from the same bunch as his own and set them, Hill-fashion, just above her small pink ear. That done, she abased herself once more, took up her burden, and departed with much delicate jingling of anklet and armlet.

Brodie watched her reflectively till she passed out of sight. 'She's a queer child,' he mused. 'Shows her gratitude, though, in the prettiest fashion.'

He raised the lapel of his coat and glanced down at the wild white blossom, whose fragrance filled his nostrils, with a curious softening of his eyes.

'She must have tramped for miles to get all those,' was the thought in his mind. 'And for eighteen months she has slaved for me, of her own free will, without payment of any sort. The puzzle is – what does it all mean? One can call it gratitude, of course. It is more seemly; and saves analysis. But sometimes – I begin to be afraid – Bah! I'm a conceited ass, making a mountain of tragedy out of a very prosaic molehill!'

Nevertheless, a vision of Sunia selecting the two blossoms nearest his own, and of the tell-tale blush which had accompanied the act, forced itself again and yet again on Brodie's mind that morning and set him puzzling anew. For, without being unduly hampered by the shackles of

Sunia: A Himalayan Idyll 219

conventional morality, Brodie favoured 'fair play', even when the other factor in the game had the misfortune to be a woman. It irked him to think that, by some inadvertent overflow of kindliness on his part, he might have sown in Sunia's passionate Oriental heart the seedling of a hope that could bear only bitter fruit.

Briefly, this somewhat perplexing relationship between Pure Passion and Cultured Cynicism had come to pass in this wise.

Eighteen months previously, Brodie, whilst 'shikarring' bear among the lower Chamba hills, had been flung into the arms, as it were, of a pitiful little domestic tragedy wherein he had found himself cast for the part of the warrior-prince who arrives in the nick of time.

The scene was vividly imprinted upon his memory; still more vividly, perhaps, on hers. A small, tawny figure at the roadside, crouching beneath a beetling granite boulder; and, not fifty yards off, the huge shaggy form of a bear, which came on with shuffling, swaying gait, and a low snarling sound, gruesome to hear. Brodie had deliberately covered the brute's heart and fired . . . with fatal effect. Then, whilst his men made haste to secure the prize, he had found himself brought to a standstill by two brown arms, that clung about his boots, whilst a voice from the earth blessed him fervently and fulsomely after the fashion of the East. Stooping, he had raised the girl to her feet, with reassuring words, and, in so doing, had looked upon Sunia's face for the first time – a sensation no man would ever be likely to forget.

From that day forward the girl had attached herself to his establishment; steadily refusing to give any information as to the whereabouts of her native village; working vigorously and zealously, as only a Hill woman can work; and scoffing at the notion of payment in any form.

In course of time it transpired that her mother had been out with her cutting wood at the time; but, in her abject terror at sight of the bear, had lost her foothold on the narrow path and been hurled to instantaneous death in the boulder-strewn gorge below. Further personal history Sunia had none to relate; or, rather, none that she chose to relate. With a captivating mixture of dignity and obstinacy she merely reiterated her intention of remaining with her 'Heaven-born', the 'Preserver of her life', and of serving him so long as her fingers could bind a faggot or wield an axe.

Dhunnu, *máli*, a one-eyed, ape-like old gentleman of irreproachable lineage, had been induced, by the prospect of a monthly *backshish*, to receive the new-comer under his own roof, as one of his household. A small patch of garden-ground had been handed over to her care, and its tillage had become for her almost a religious rite. Every flower and vegetable reared thereon had been laid in her *dáli* – a self-imposed tribute of gratitude – at Brodie's feet. The man had not failed to note these dumb expressions of devotion; at first with a tolerant amusement, which had gradually given place to a lurking tenderness, duly tempered by cynicism, and a characteristic reluctance to take his own, or anyone else's, emotions too seriously. But when an Englishman chances to encounter Oriental passion, in all its pristine simplicity and strength, he is fairly compelled to take it seriously, whether he will or no. Brodie was just beginning to be aware of this fact, and the discovery made him feel not a little anxious and uncomfortable.

There were others also who were growing daily more anxious on Sunia's account. These were the one-eyed *máli*, and *Mai* Râdha, his gaunt and grizzled wife; for they had knowledge of which Brodie dreamed not.

They knew of a treasured box of withered flowers, to

which one or two were added daily. The box had once held a hundred Havanas, and had lived on Brodie's office table. They knew of long night-watches spent in stringing scented wreaths of golden marigolds, and white, waxen 'champa' blossoms; of secret flittings, in the first pale glimmer of morning, to the tiny hamlet that clung to the steep hillside some two hundred feet below. They knew, moreover, that Sunia's wreaths – yea, and even fruit and flowers from her own cherished garden – were destined for the 'Mundar', or shrine of Kála Dévi, the dread goddess of whom every pious Hindu stands in holy awe; and *Mai* Râdha's soul waxed wrathful within her at the knowledge.

'Truly it is fool's talk and shameful,' said she to her less aggressive spouse, 'that a maid, young and good to look upon, should do this thing. Are there not men without number of our own *ját*, who would give rupees in plenty for so fair a chattel? A true Rajpoot, with a face radiant as the morning! And we are old, thou and I, and I had hoped that from this girl's dower we should purchase rest in our old age. Lo, this two years have I been to her as a mother, and the ingrate rewards me thus! Were it not meet thou shouldst speak to the Sahib of this foolishness?'

But Dhunnu was a chicken-hearted little man, and at this startling proposition he turned his two hands about in expressive native fashion.

'*Ná, Ná,* valiant one, I love not to thrust my head betwixt a lion's teeth. Speak thou, if thou art minded to.'

And *Mai* Râdha did speak, fluently and to the point, not to Brodie, for even she dared scarce go such a length, but to the delinquent herself.

She reaped small reward for her labour. Sunia – her wonderful eyes ablaze, her small hands clenched so that the knuckles stood out sharp and white – gave her back eloquence for eloquence, good measure, well pressed down.

'What sayest thou of the shame that a maid should live unwed? Nay, I tell thee it is thou, grey-haired though thou be, that talkest shameful talk, and I will not hear it, for I am none of thine!'

'*Ai tobah!* but these be brave words, insolent, from one who hath eaten of my salt these many months,' the elder woman retorted in shrill wrath.

'Nay, not one grain of thine have I eaten, O *Mai* Râdha. Thou hast forgotten surely whence came the rupees. What! And should *I* take to myself a man? I, who own but one lord of my life, and my body, and my heart! I, who would even now be dust as is my mother, but for the strength of his arm! And yet thou canst prate to me of men-folk! Betrothed was I, long since, to a son of mine own people; but now am I my lord's slave, and none other's, till I die – till I die!'

Her soft lips quivered a little over the last words, and two gleaming tear-drops hung upon her thick lashes.

But *Mai* Râdha had eyes for none of these things. She was a woman, and old, and this girl stood between her and the money her lean fingers itched to hold. Wherefore she spoke harshly, as before.

'Oh fool, and blind! This thy lord whom thou worshippest hath no thought of thee in his mind. It is ever so with these English. They are stonehearts all. For, as the wind blows, and the water flows, so kind calls to kind, and he will assuredly take to wife some bold white "Miss", with hair like the sunshine and eyes like the noonday sky, and what will be thy portion then, O thriftless one?'

A dull grey pallor creeping slowly over the girl's clear skin told how the thrust had gone home. But her lips were steady now, and the eyes dry and bright.

'There is always – Death,' she made answer slowly. '*Mai*

Káli must needs accept my life at my hands, if none other offering availeth.'

Phil Brodie, seated within at his office table, his mind deep in the intricacies of an official report, had no knowledge either of *Mai* Râdha's vicious prophecies, or of Sunia's secret prayers. Only at his side, in a wineglass of water, bloomed the wild white rose of the morning, fresh and fragrant still. He could scarcely tell what had prompted his desire to preserve it; nor did he trouble himself to search out the reason for so unwonted a freak of sentiment.

Sunia, on the other hand, had no knowledge of the rose on Brodie's table; so that she went heavily for many days, a haunting fear at her heart, a ceaseless prayer upon her lips. Also she redoubled her offerings at the 'Mundar' of Kála Dévi, who, being herself a woman, must surely understand, and hear.

II

> Love, that keeps all the choir of lives in chime;
> Love, that is blood within the veins of time!

But prayers and votive offerings failed to avert the decree of Fate. *Mai* Káli was deaf, or hard of heart in those days; or, maybe, she was busy with the affairs of wealthier folk. For lo, as June was drawing to a close, and the patient pines were sighing for the summer rain, there came to the hut on the hill-top the 'white Miss' of *Mai* Râdha's prophecy, 'with hair like the sunshine and eyes like the noonday sky'. And Sunia's heart within her dried up like an autumn leaf; for she knew that her hour had come.

In prosaic Western terms the fateful event may be set down as follows:

Edith Lindon, escorted by her brother and by a certain Colonel Polden of Brodie's acquaintance, had been riding Dalhousie-ward one sultry afternoon, on their return from the yearly race-meeting at Kajiar. They were hot and thirsty; for they had ridden eight miles, and the air, even at that height, was heavy with the coming monsoon. Colonel Polden suggested a raid on Brodie's hut, with a view to obtaining rest and refreshment – a proposition to which his companions assented cheerfully. On the road thither the Colonel, by way of entertaining Miss Lindon, indulged in a rhapsodical word-picture, half quizzical, half sincere, of Brodie's 'bewitching little Hill Beauty'.

'Saved her from the embraces of an amorous bear, winter before last,' he wound up. 'And she's served him for love ever since. A very pretty little woodland romance, isn't it?'

'Charming! But you must be sure and persuade your friend to let us see the girl. Perhaps he might let me make a sketch of her. I should like that above all things. I'm making a collection of Indian figure sketches to take home, and the Hill costume is so very picturesque.' If Sunia could but have heard her!

She saw her, however, which was more than enough in the way of anguish. Crouching in the warm odorous shade of a group of deodars, she saw Brodie lift the fair girl from her saddle; saw her yellow hair flash in the level stream of sunlight; saw the blue eyes, clear and shadowless – the magic pink and white of the soft round face. Then she glanced down at her own brown, shapely hands, and shuddered. '*Mai* Râdha spoke true talk,' she whispered. 'I have been a fool, and blind – blind!'

But, though the sight hurt her straining eyes, though the tinkling laughter from the verandah made her wince and shiver, she stirred neither hand nor foot, but continued to look and listen with feverish eagerness.

Tea was served in the verandah. A typical *Khansamah*'s tea. Rockingham tea-pot, with damaged spout; plush tea-cosy; hideous slabs of cake, and a plate of *meta biscoot*, which signifies 'mixed biscuits'! The 'bold white Miss' presided over the tea-pot with as much ease and freedom as though she were mistress of the house; which, indeed, she already was, in Sunia's excited fancy. The Sahib had sent money, doubtless, to his own land far over seas, and the grey-head, her father, had brought him this his bride.

Such was her Oriental rendering of a chance tea-drinking between comparative strangers.

But a more potent factor than chance seemed to be at work on Kálatope ridge that June day.

A grey cloud swept suddenly across the face of the sun, and the parched pine-boughs over Sunia's head stirred and whispered mysteriously. She knew the sound and its meaning well. Two minutes later a snaky streak of lightning flashed past her, and a sound as of the rattle of musketry rent the sky. Then, one after one, like liquid bullets, fell the first rain-drops of the Great Monsoon.

In less than five minutes' time the clouds were emptying themselves, in a solid sheet of water, upon the thirsty hills, whilst the southwest wind battled lustily with creaking boughs. Sunia fled, dripping, to her smoke-grimed hovel; and endured, in silence, *Mai* Rádha's drastic comments upon the new turn of affairs.

In Brodie's hut a council of war was in progress.

'No question of your going back tonight,' he said to young Lindon, as they looked out upon the drenched landscape. 'It'll be a little awkward for your sister, I'm afraid. But if she doesn't mind using my room, she is more than welcome to it, such as it is; and I think my little grass-cut girl could manage to act as *ayah* for once in a way. You two fellows can have the second room; and I shall sleep like a top on the lounge in here. I only hope your sister won't be abominably uncomfortable.'

'Oh, rather not. Awfully good of you to give up your room. She'll be as right as a trivet, thanks,' responded the other, with brotherly unconcern. 'She's not a faddy sort at all.'

And it appeared that he spoke truth.

'It will be quite a lark!' the fair Edith declared with a naïve frankness which did not ill become her, but which jarred a little on Brodie's unaccustomed ear. 'And I shall see the little Himalayan beauty after all! Will she *really* consent to do *ayah* for me?' This, with a pretty laugh, and an arch look at Brodie, which missed its mark altogether.

'She will obey my orders,' he returned with grave politeness.

But his assurance on this point proved a trifle premature. For once in her life, Sunia was disposed to be rebellious. When the order reached her that she should cleanse herself to the best of her ability, and carry hot water and a lamp to the Miss-sahib's room, she sent answer flatly: 'Tell the Sahib that I cannot do this thing.' But the courage of despair is too often the effervescence of conscious weakness; and, even as she spoke, Sunia knew that love and long habit would, in the end, compel her to eat her own brave words.

At the first sound of Brodie's voice calling her from the back verandah, she dashed, headlong across the rain-lashed 'compound', and flung herself, dripping, at his feet.

'O my lord, forgive thy slave that she spoke unseemly words in the bitterness of her heart. Let the Sahib command what he will. It shall be done.'

Then she rose and faced him, in the fullness of her

Sunia: A Himalayan Idyll

wonderful beauty; her hands clasped, her small frame a-quiver with emotion held bravely in check.

Brodie was not a little mystified by her evident reluctance to wait on Miss Lindon. But her words and manner stirred him strangely, and he would willingly have annulled his order, were it not that he shrank from encountering Edith Lindon's arch comments and Colonel Polden's quizzical asides. As it was he spoke soothingly.

'I make no command, Sunia. I ask only that thou shouldst do this thing because that it would be shameful talk that a Miss-sahib should be alone in my house having no woman to wait on her – and that thou knowest.'

'It is enough, Sahib. I go. What pleasure hath this slave in life, save to do the *Hazúr*'s will?'

And she departed, fulfilled with righteous resolve, but very sore at heart.

Edith Lindon was not more light-minded than others of her sex and age; but she was young, and attractive; and – perhaps not without reason – very well satisfied with herself and with the world at large. She was just now engaged, pleasantly enough, in 'doing' India; because it is the correct thing to 'do' India in these days – to roll Bombay, Delhi, a native state or two, and scraps of the Himalayas, into one great dust-coated pill, and swallow it whole, to be reproduced – with harmless necessary embellishments – at Western dinner-tables, for the benefit of the Great Uninitiated.

She regarded her present predicament chiefly in the light of an excellent anecdote, for addition to a well-stocked list. To complete it there was but one thing needful – a sketch of Sunia herself. But on that point Brodie had proved politely obdurate; and Edith was fain to content herself with taking a mental photograph of the girl's appearance, to be committed to paper as soon as opportunity should offer. The process entailed a good deal of frank British staring on Miss Lindon's part, when at length Sunia presented herself with the necessary hot water and towels. It did not, however, occur to the Western girl that the 'wild little Hill creature' could possibly resent being inspected. Wherefore she inspected her carefully, and not without evident admiration.

But – for all her barbaric dress, and her peculiar prejudices in the matter of cleanliness – Sunia was human. A dull, hot flush burnt through her brown skin, making her look more enchanting than ever; but she preserved her Sphinx-like gravity of expression.

The goat's hair necklace, with its rough gems and silver pendant, caught Miss Lindon's fancy. It would look charming on her 'curio' table at home. Happy thought! Perhaps the girl would sell it.

With the frank assurance of a spoilt child, she stepped up to Sunia, and laid a light, irreverent finger upon a mottled blue lump of turquoise.

'*Burra accha chēse. Hum mangta*' (Very good thing. I want it), she remarked smilingly. Her Hindustani, though limited, was terse and to the point. '*Kitna dām? Panch rupee?*' (What price? Five rupees?).

Sunia recoiled from her touch as though she had been struck, and a fierce light leaped into her clear eyes. 'These be mine own jewels, Miss-sahib. I am not of the *Bunnia-lôg*, that I should bargain with white folk for rupees.'

For a moment Miss Lindon was taken aback. But, being gifted with more business capacity than sentiment, she concluded that her offer had not been large enough.

'*Dus rupeea déga. Bus – aur nahin*' (I will give ten rupees. That is all – no more). And she held out an expectant hand.

Sunia, with one glance of speechless scorn, turned and fled through the blustering night.

This, then, was the bride-elect of her Sahib, her hero, her demi-god among men – this smiling, insolent, pink-faced Miss! The strong rush and roar of the storm through the forest mercifully drowned the passionate sobs which racked her body half through the night.

The sun rose on a green, babbling world next morning. Prismatic hues flashed from swaying boughs; birds, brooks, and cicadas waxed garrulous exceedingly, and, from out moist fissures of rock, the little brown *krait* (viper), with others of his slimy kindred, sled stealthily, only to vanish at once amid the moist verdure of the flower-beds. Away over the plains, a white, billowy mass of cloud gave promise of the triple tyranny of mist, mildew, and mackintoshes.

Brodie and his guests were early astir, and the latter were in their saddles by eight o'clock.

As her host lifted Edith Lindon to her Arab she reminded him laughingly of some English violets he had promised her overnight.

'Please don't trouble about them now, though,' she added sweetly; 'I'll forgive you for forgetting them!'

But Brodie was already in the verandah.

'Won't take me two minutes to pick them,' he called back as he went.

He had made a hobby of his little garden; and there were certain flowers kept sacred even from Dhunnu's zealous fingers. Now, therefore, Brodie knelt down bareheaded in the sunlight, and plunged his hands among the dripping violet leaves. The violet beds being at the back of the house, and the horses in front, he was alone – or apparently so. At all events, he was unconscious of eager eyes that devoured his face from within the sheltering shadow of two deodar trunks.

But those eyes, in spite of their absorption and of the tears that were in them, saw what his did not – a slimy, living streak of brown, within half a foot of his left hand. In a flash Sunia was at his side, and her hand was laid on his – not one second too soon.

Brodie sprang to his feet with a startled cry, and made a futile lunge at the vanishing snakeling, whose name is Death.

Then he turned to Sunia.

'How didst see the reptile? Great God!' – look at thy hand! Did he bite thee, child?'

'Aye, *Hazúr*, he bit me – and – I die. But what matters it, so that the Sahib lives – to make marriage with the – the white Miss? And I – I pay my debt.'

She swayed where she stood, and a little quiver convulsed her frame. Quick as thought Brodie's arm went round her, and a sharp little sob escaped her as she leaned all her light weight upon its strength.

'*Kohi hai!* Nizam Din!' he shouted. 'Take these flowers to the Miss-sahib, and tell the Sahibs to go forward. I cannot come. I will send a letter. And see, bring me at once coffee at the blackest, and the flask of brandy from my dressing-case. Run!'

Then with voice and face all tenderness, he turned to the dying girl.

'Walk, child, walk – for the love of God! The brandy may be here in time.'

But she resisted his effort to hurry her forward.

'Nay, Sahib, I have chosen, and – I die. When my lord taketh to him a Memsahib, and goeth hence, then what shall come to this slave? Death is easy, and I – I pay my debt.'

A sudden suspicion flashed into Brodie's mind. Sunia's

whole loving soul was in her eyes, and he read it like an open book.

'There stands no debt betwixt us, Sunia; and what meaneth this talk of Memsahibs? I take no Miss-sahib to wife.'

'But the white "Miss", who came – who spoke – '

Her voice broke, and she shuddered again.

'Poor child, poor child,' Brodie muttered under his breath. Then aloud: 'But, Sunia child, the white "Miss" was naught to me – naught. Lo, she is gone, and I shall not see her more. See, here is the brandy. Drink. Thy Sahib commands thee – drink!'

He forced the glass between her lips. She took one sip; then shook her head wearily. 'It is *Kismet*, Sahib. I take no brandy. Let – him go – I die.'

Further argument was useless. The poison was working swiftly; for the *krait* knows no half measures.

With a stern, '*Kohi mut aou*' (Let no one come), Brodie waved Nizam Din away, and drew the girl's lagging feet toward the verandah.

He laid her tenderly in his own long chair, and bent close down to her as he spoke. A strange new light illumined all his face.

'Sunia, thou art dying, speak truth. What right hadst thou to do this thing?'

The glazing eyes lightened for an instant, and the lips parted in a radiant smile.

'The only right that belongs to women-folk, *Hazúr*. I – loved.'

'And I? What thinkest thou?'

In the emotion of the moment he did not stay to weigh his words.

'I think naught, Sahib. I love – it is enough.'

Her voice was a mere whisper now. But her wide eyes clung desperately to his face. Impelled by an irresistible impulse, Brodie stooped and kissed her fervently upon the lips and brow.

'Live for ever, Lord of my Life,' came the familiar greeting. But he saw the words rather than heard them.

Then *Mai* Râdha came, and smote the hill-sides with vociferous grief; for she claimed her right to mourn as foster-mother to the child.

Brodie retreated to his office, and sat there for two full hours, staring blankly at a half-written letter, and considering the strange thing that had come to pass.

He was a lonely man – sisterless, motherless – but until this moment he had not been aware of the fact. Slowly it dawned on him that he was not, and would never be again, quite as he had been; for a hitherto unacknowledged element had been added to his conception of life. He had seen with his own eyes the love that is strong as death; and to see that once in a lifetime is a wholesome thing for a man.

When, at length, he rose, and shook himself back into his official shell, he realized that he had narrowly escaped committing an act of sentimental folly, which would probably have ruined his career. For which mercy he was scarcely as grateful as he ought to have been.

But the best of us are three-parts human after all.

KATHERINE MAYO
The Old Grey Cow

> Hinduism believes in the oneness not of merely all human life, but in the oneness of all that lives. Its worship of the cow is, in my opinion, its unique contribution to the evolution of humanitarianism.
>
> GANDHI. *Young India*, 20 October 1927

An old grey cow – mouse-grey – pale. Eyes narrow and long, their lids, at the outer corners, subtly upcurving in secret and brooding beauty. Eyes like the eyes of a princess of Egypt carved in stone.

Around her neck a string of sky-blue beads. And her life reckoned holy – so holy that he who should take it must suffer the pains of hell, to be escaped only through forfeits and heavy penances.

But her bones almost cut through her skin, the edge of each one slashed sharp against gaunt shadows sunk in the hollows beneath. In her prime, she had scarcely given two quarts of milk a day; for she was an ordinary cow of India. And now it was years since she had ceased production.

But the prosperous farmer, her owner, still doled out to her an occasional handful of husk-diluted seeds or a little dry straw, dealing with her piously as with all his cattle. Also, daily, she and they wandered forth with the herd of the village, out into the jungle to graze.

'Jungle', they called it, yet meant no forest, no luxuriant greenness, but rather, waste stretches, where, in the long dry season, the bare earth cracked and gasped with thirst – a dead, grim desert of clay heaved into small, sharp ragged hillocks like seadunes half devoured by surf.

Here and there over the waste, far apart, faint dark stains appeared – bits of herbage perhaps the breadth of a man's two hands; and here and there on the peak of a hillock clung a scrawny, twisted shrub, scantly tufted with harsh, dry, mould-green leaves. These were the plums of the grazing.

Taking all together a square mile's surface would scarcely produce a bushel of nourishing fodder – and the herd of the village numbered over a hundred head.

Once and again the old grey cow, searching with the rest, would secure a nibble of ground growth. But to climb the hillocks required more strength than she possessed.

Otherwise, like her mates, she scavenged the streets of the village, in sheer necessity devouring things beneath a vulture's notice – stuff whose presence in the streets was one of the reasons why the villagers so liberally died.

Now it was mid dry season. These many days the old grey cow had scarcely eaten at all. Clearer eyes had discovered each morsel before she saw it. Or swifter limbs had distanced her feeble gait. Or heavier shoulders had thrust her aside, if by rare luck she chanced on substance of any sort that famine could call food.

Therefore, this morning when her owner turned her forth, her head swung low and her knees wavered, though habit and the herd still carried her on, out into the 'jungle' waste. But in the push for sustenance the old grey cow to-day stood no chance. And when at last the herd headed back toward home she could not keep its pace, but lagged ever farther behind – a pitiful sight enough had there been one to see who cared for dumb beasts' misery.

Farther and farther they distanced her, until, near dusk, though the village walls were already in view, she could strive no more. So still she stood, wistfully watching the cloud of dust that enveloped them, as it drifted away and away through the twilight into the mud-grey town.

Was it before, in her weakness she fell, that the dogs found her? Did they leap and pull her down, seeing their hour was come?

Gaunt-jawed, fierce-eyed, with staring ribs and hip bones, pink with sores and wounds, deformed with unheard-of-diseases, in their scores they gathered. Gasping, choking, snarling in their need, they flung themselves upon her, and tore at her where she lay.

Tore so eagerly that, when Dennis O'Sullivan approached the spot, never did they perceive him till, on his horse, he loomed above them. Then with bared teeth, they drew back, half threatening, half afraid.

All but one thrice-desperate bitch, whose long flat teats told of the litter that somewhere dragged on her life; she, with the courage of motherhood leaping forth as the others faltered, sunk her fangs deep into the throat of the old grey cow.

Deep into her throat, so that, as life fled, the necklace broke and the sky-blue beads spilled abroad, rolling hither and yon in the trampled dust.

Dennis O'Sullivan, District Officer, could not sleep that night. His men had pitched his tent in a decent place; his cot was easy enough; the work of the day had certainly earned him an honest rest, and the work of the morrow would begin with dawn. But somehow Dennis O'Sullivan could not sleep.

Instead, over and over again, he saw the old grey cow, saw the starved bitch's piteous fury; saw the eyes of the pack ablaze with hate and fear. And facts and obstinate figures and helpless compassions, each and all as futile as familiar, churned around and around in his weary brain.

One hundred and forty-seven million head of cattle in British India, half of them useless. Great cattle-owning areas where no fodder at all is planted. Little children in myriads withering for lack of milk. Cows in myriads milkless from starvation. Cows and children daily multiplying, multiplying, multiplying. Cows, unlike children, sacrosanct to the Hindu world, so that to kill one useless, suffering, moribund skeleton were a desperate crime – an incitement to holy war. Yet cows left without compunction to perish slowly, since even the holy cow, as a re-incarnate soul, but pays, in any present pain, the price of sin committed in an earlier life.

What use, then, labouring to get these people to plant more fodder? How long could an ocean of fodder sustain such crazy demands? Why struggle about that or anything? Why . . .

'O-oh! o-oh! *o-oh!* – O-oh! yip-yip! *o-oh!* O-OH!' The cry of the jackals a-hunting – that echoing, shivering cry in which some hear the wail of babes in torment and others the shrieks of sub-human souls adrift in space. 'O-oh! *o-oh!* O-OH!' – jackal packs on the run, scouring the village streets, chanting, chanting the old, old song of the Indian night.

With a sigh, O'Sullivan shifted in his bed, once again to seek escape from the treadmill of semi-consciousness.

Yet morning found his mind still heavy – his inner vision still haunted.

So that when, soon after dawn, he sat down with the rulers of the village to discuss vital statistics, he had no will to keep his oppression from his tongue. He told them of the killing of the old grey cow.

'It was her fate,' they said, without sentiment. 'She did but pay a debt of bygone sin.'

'And the dogs,' continued O'Sullivan, 'all the stray, sick, starving dogs, that you kick and stone but never feed?'

'It is a sin to feed stray dogs,' one replied for the rest.

'Yet you will neither stop their breeding nor put them out of their pain.' Even as he spoke, O'Sullivan knew that his fatigue, not his intelligence, pronounced the useless words.

'It is a sin to break the stream of life,' said he who before had spoken.

'Yet, truly, Sahib,' another put in, 'the dogs have done us much harm of late. There is madness amongst the jackals. Mad jackals have bitten the dogs, which, being themselves stricken with madness, have bitten men. And these men have died miserably. Out of this village nine have gone since the last full moon.'

But O'Sullivan, at the words, felt, as it were, a sudden breeze let into a stifling room.

'How if I, myself, undertake to rid you of these multitudes of dogs that, whilst they starve, threaten you all with madness? For me,' he said, 'it is no sin to take their lives.'

His audience exchanged glances – hesitated. Then, 'The Sahib's reckoning is with his own gods' – it was the youngest of the lot who spoke. 'What the Sahib does can be no guilt of ours.'

O'Sullivan swept the circle with his eyes. None ventured nearer either 'yes' or 'no'. 'I need not drive them to the length of speech,' he thought, and aloud added: 'Be my acts upon my own head.'

Within the hour, accordingly, he had despatched an order to the local dispensary. Within two hours four outcaste men, who, having no purity to lose, might do such work, had set out at his command to spread food before the dogs. And when, in mid-afternoon, having finished all business and broken camp, he was about to ride farther on his tour, O'Sullivan sent for the outcaste four, to inquire of their performance.

'What about the dogs?' he asked.

'May it please the Sahib, the dogs are quite as before,' they answered.

'What! Did you neglect, then, to put the powder into the food, according to the order? Did the dogs refuse the food?'

'Nay, Sahib, not so. We did as the Sahib commanded. And the dogs ate, each and all. But other men followed close behind us, and where we fed, there they fed too, promptly. And it appears that the food they gave contained also a medicine. Which medicine caused each dog instantly to cast up all our food that he had eaten. Therefore it is that the dogs remain exactly as before.'

Ill though he could now spare time from the road, O'Sullivan sent for the headman of the village.

'What,' he asked, 'is the meaning of this utter, utter folly concerning the dogs? The responsibility was mine. You knew. You agreed. Why did you cause the work to be undone?'

'Nay, Sahib, Upholder of the World, be not displeased. For after the council, we, considering together, perceived two things. We perceived that if the dogs died as planned, the Brahmans, for all our innocence, would declare us guilty, and would force us all to pay them a heavy fine, to give them a great feast, and to go a pilgrimage at much cost and pains to bathe in Holy Ganges. We also remembered that a dog, like a man, dies only in his appointed hour. If, when the Sahib gave poisoned food, we had done nothing, the Brahmans might have cursed us to hell unless we dearly bought their absolution. But if, when the Sahib gave poisoned food, we quickly gave powerful emetics, the dogs would none the less have died if it lay in their Fate then to die, and we should escape the screws of the Brahmans.'

As O'Sullivan rode away from the village he passed the skeleton of the old grey cow – such as remained of it. A few blue beads still lay in the dust amongst the bones.

CHRISTINE WESTON
The Mud Horse

When I was twelve years old and my brother was ten, we lived in a brick house near a level crossing of the East Indian Railway, in a place called Aligarh. One of our favourite pastimes was to escape from surveillance and go for long walks or bicycle rides unescorted. It was not much fun when any of our native servants came with us, for they got in our way and, although unable to prevent our doing as we pleased, they were not above carrying tales and getting us into hot water with our parents.

My brother was very fond of drawing and, because I was quite without talent, I admired his greatly and liked to watch him while he made pictures of men and animals or what he called 'land-escapes'. One day just before the beginning of the hot weather, we gave our household the slip and walked off across the fields which bordered on the compound and on down a dusty white road toward the level crossing. My brother wanted to draw a picture of a train coming, as he described it, 'straight at us'. I remembered some perfectly awful photographs of people who had been caught by trains which came straight at them. The children of the station-master had once shown us the official railway album of horrors, which had made my brother deathly sick. But today he merely shrugged and said, 'We can always get out of the way.'

'The old woman in the photograph didn't,' I reminded him. 'Nor did the man whose stomach – '

My brother interrupted. 'I want to get that look of a train

– you know, the funny feeling it gives you when you see it coming awfully fast down the tracks.'

'But,' I objected, 'you can't do a picture of a *feeling*!'

'You probably couldn't, but I can,' he replied.

My brother was an exceedingly stubborn boy and had all his life been frustrated in his attempts to draw pictures of a train coming straight at him. So I said no more and we walked along, dust collecting on our sandals and the sun beating on our white topees. The level crossing was protected by two low white gates which were let down when trains passed, and on our side of it lived the Hindu who tended the gates, and his family, whom we knew by sight. Today the gate-tender, wearing the faded-blue coat, broad leather belt, and red turban customary with most government subordinates, squatted in his door, smoking his morning pipe between trains. His wife was inside, preparing their midday meal, and as we walked behind the house and turned left to follow the railway embankment we saw their little son sitting against a whitewashed wall near a refuse heap, playing with mud. We had seen him before, but always at a distance. Now something in his appearance made us pause to look at him. He was about six years old and wore nothing except a yard of white cloth round his loins, and he sat in the wonderful posture which comes naturally to children and to Orientals – one leg folded under him, the other bent at the knee with the foot resting squarely on the ground. What arrested us was his air of concentration, a serene, absolute forgetfulness of the world around him.

'What are you doing?' I asked in Hindustani. He looked up and, instead of running away or retreating into agonized shyness, like many native children, just sat and gazed at us with large, dark, shining eyes. His face was a perfect oval, his mouth a bright coral, his head shaved except for the traditional topknot. He answered my question in a grave little voice: 'I am making a palace for my horse.'

'Your horse?' we echoed. He picked up a small mud object and set it upright on his palm.

'Why,' demanded my brother, 'is your horse so fat and why have you made one of his legs longer than the others?'

The child answered calmly, 'It is fat because it is a she horse and is going to have a little one.'

We laughed, and my brother declared that he, for one, would be ashamed to make a horse which looked like that.

'Would you?' asked the boy wonderingly. 'Why?'

'*Why?* Have you ever *seen* a horse with one leg longer than the others?'

'Yes,' said the gate-tender's son, and went coolly back to his task of kneading dirt and water into a thick paste.

'Well,' my brother said after a brief pause, '*when* did you ever see a horse with one leg longer than the others?'

'Here it is, in my hand.' He held it up. 'And you too have seen it.'

'That! And besides, who ever heard of a mud horse having a young one, I'd like to know?'

The child replied, without looking up, 'In the fullness of her time she will have a little one.'

'Owl!' said my brother disdainfully, and we walked on, following a footpath along the embankment on our side of the tracks. Below ran the two double lines of rail, for this was the broad gauge which connected the cities of the United Provinces with those of Bihar and Orissa. The tracks glittered in the sun and from the embankments stretched fields of pulse and millet. The level expanse was dotted with mango trees and beyond the farther embankment three camels were grazing near an acacia while their owners slept in the shade.

* * *

The Mud Horse

We had not gone far when, glancing back, I saw the gate-tender's son running after us along the path. When he caught up with us, we saw that he carried his mud horse tenderly in one hand. 'What do you want?' we demanded, in the belligerent accents we saved for people younger than ourselves. He gazed at us with shining eyes.

'May I come with you?'

'Certainly not,' my brother said. 'You're too little.'

'Nay, I am old enough.'

'About three, I suppose,' I suggested condescendingly.

He shook his head and said, 'I am thirty-four.'

This made us laugh and we decided that if everything else failed we might amuse ourselves by teasing him for a while. 'Very well,' I said, 'you may stay and watch the *Chota* Sahib draw a picture of the train. But you're not to interrupt or we'll beat you.'

He smiled and nodded toward the tracks. 'Here is a good place to wait for the train. You can see it coming from a long way off.'

He had, strangely, taken us under his diminutive wing and we allowed ourselves to be advised by him. A stunted acacia grew out of the embankment and we sat under it to wait for the train, while our new friend explained to us that his name was Kulloo and that he was his parents' only child.

'They must have been surprised,' I said, 'when you were born and they found that you were thirty-four years old!'

He shrugged his small brown shoulders. 'Oh, no, they were not in the least surprised.'

There was no reasoning with him. He settled down beside my brother, who had begun to make a drawing of the tracks, the telegraph poles, and the horizon. 'Why,' demanded Kulloo at last, 'why do you make all those thin and crooked lines?'

'Because, silly, they are the outlines of things.'

'But when I make something of mud it hath a middle also. See, for instance, my horse. And at home I have cows, goats, and men which I have made. All have middles.'

We preserved an exasperated silence and presently Kulloo left us and wandered down the embankment toward the tracks, saying, 'I am going to give my poor horse a drink from that river.'

'There is no river and your horse is only a mud horse and can't drink anyway, and you'll get run over,' I called after him.

But he ignored me and continued down the embankment. We watched him squat down on a sleeper, setting his mud horse beside him. Above us the telegraph wires hummed and great painted grasshoppers fed on the poison milkweeds near our feet. The smell of acacia flowers hovered in the air. Then we heard a sound and saw a train far, far away, up the glittering railway tracks.

'Kulloo!' I cried. 'Kulloo, here comes the train.'

'There's heaps of time,' said my brother, drawing like mad.

The train grew before my eyes; a plume of smoke lay in the sky behind it. I shouted again, 'Kulloo! Come away, you little owl!'

He answered without moving. 'Fear not. There is time.'

But this was the Calcutta mail, advancing at a fearful speed. The sun flashed on its metal body. It bellowed, and the sound boomed out across the sunlit plain. 'Kulloo!' I shouted, jumping to my feet.

He rose and stood, shading his eyes, staring up the track. There was an enormous rushing sensation in the air, a sensation which obliterated everything else. A moment before, the train had seemed many miles away, but the next second it loomed as a monster which bore down upon us –

glittering, black, fantastic, its ferocious throat emitting bellows which made us flinch.

'Kulloo!' I screamed. He turned and came scrambling up the bank towards us. Then, like a fool, I added, 'Your horse! You've forgotten your horse!'

Kulloo turned and plunged back down the bank, and we saw him stoop to pick up the mud horse. Then the train was there; we smelled its frightful breath and recoiled before the crashing force of its passage. Our eyes were convulsed by a vision of gleaming pistons and sparkling convolutions and the sound of its voice almost beat us to the ground, but not before we heard a thin, high scream and lost sight of Kulloo under the savage wheels.

Rooted, we stood glaring at a long regiment of carriages which rocked past. People leaned from the windows and some of them waved to us, but we made no response. I felt the ground swaying and the sky pressing upon my head. I dared not look, for I knew what I would see. I had seen such things before, in pictures and in my imagination. But this, this was my fault, all my fault.

With the disappearance of the train, a great silence had fallen, and upon this silence I opened my eyes at last. My brother crouched beside me, his face quite colourless. Across the tracks stood Kulloo, laughing at us. 'Ayee!' he cried jubilantly. 'Ayee! Did you make a picture of the train?' He came scampering down the farther embankment, across the hot rails, up the near bank, and stood before us, shining with merriment. 'Show me the picture!'

My brother had risen, his face twitching. 'We thought you'd been run over.'

'Run over?' Kulloo looked astonished.

'I heard you scream.'

'But I didn't scream.'

'You did!' My brother's voice was charged with hysteria. 'You did scream! We both heard you.'

'Nay, that was not I. That was my horse. She was frightened by the train.' He looked from one to the other of us and his eyes filled with a grave and tender concern. 'Were you frightened? So was my poor horse. Only I was not.'

This was too much for my brother. He snatched the mud horse from Kulloo's hand and flung it on the ground, where it broke in four pieces. We stood for a moment, motionless, silent. Kulloo made no protest. Quietly he pointed to the fragments which lay at our feet. 'See,' he murmured. 'The little one.'

Reclining among the fragments was another, much smaller horse, made of mud, like the one which had contained it, but perfect, each of its legs uniform in length and shape. Kulloo picked it up and set it on his palm. 'I told you,' said he in his serene voice, 'I told you that my horse was going to have a little one.'

Shortly after this adventure the hot weather shut down and our family went away to live in the hills, so we did not see Kulloo again. There are almost four hundred million people in India, but I often wonder what became of him.

CHRISTINE WESTON
The Mangoes Are Gone

One winter evening in 1914, we sat, my parents, my brother, and myself, under the *pipal* tree watching the garden dim and fade in the swift Indian night. For us children it was a favourite time, the hour before we were banished into the house and to bed. We were English. Indian children are luckier; they go to bed when they want to.

None of us could have said when or how the old man arrived; perhaps he drifted down from the silent leaves above us, perhaps some pore of the earth gave him up to our unprepared vision. There he was, standing near our semicircle of chairs, a figure like a twisted branch, naked except for his loincloth.

'It is a beggar,' declared Abdul the bearer, emerging from the house behind us. 'I warned him not to intrude, but he moves like a shadow.' Abdul turned his august white beard toward the stranger. 'We have nothing for you. Begone!'

But the old man stayed motionless and my father addressed him. 'Who are you, old one? What is it you want?'

The answer came in a voice like a cracked reed pipe. 'Protector of the Poor, my name is Mahala. I have walked a great distance and for two days I have not eaten.'

'All of which is your affair, not ours,' said Abdul, for, like all old and privileged servants, he was aware of his masters' sentimental weaknesses.

'God has guided my feet to this house. You cannot send me away empty.'

'Depart, depart!' Abdul took a threatening step forward.

For a moment the old man stood like a wraith, then, without warning, he collapsed in the dust and sent up a prolonged wail full of reproach, entreaty, and despair.

'A child's trick,' said Abdul disgustedly. 'It means nothing.'

My mother interposed. 'Give him a rupee, Abdul.'

'A rupee! O Allah!' Grudgingly Abdul produced the coin and flung it into the dust beside the prostrate figure. As mysteriously as he had appeared, the old man gathered himself together and vanished.

Next morning my brother and I were taking our usual exploratory stroll through the garden and the mango grove. We had forgotten our ancient visitor of the night before, but now we suddenly came on him as he squatted under a tree, engaged in weaving a sling from a piece of rope. When he saw us he rose and made a deep, trembling obeisance. 'I have eaten. Now I would make a sling to drive away the parrots and vermin from my lords' mangoes. I am too old to be of much use, but that I *can* do. See!'

He placed a stone in the sling, whirled it round his head, and let fly. The stone plopped down two yards away and he beamed with heartbreaking delight. 'Yes, I shall be the death of those thieving birds. Thus, thus I shall repay my debt.'

There was nothing to be done about it; we could not drive him away nor could we let him work without a wage. He was, of course, quite useless, with scarcely enough strength to draw a *lotah* of water from the garden well or to whirl his absurd sling. The parrots ignored him, the squirrels hardly troubled to get out of his way, and the other servants sneered. They had, after the manner of their kind, banded together in their jealousy, fearful lest the perquisites which might otherwise come their way be diverted to this pitiable creature. Partly to spite them, we set to work to make old Mahala feel at home. We persuaded our parents to buy him a quilted jacket against the cool nights; we forced the gardener to contribute an old string bed from his own quarters and the gardener's assistant to erect a straw shelter under the mango trees, where Mahala had taken up residence. My brother and I smuggled out one of our own blankets and other gifts for the sheer pleasure of seeing the old man's eyes light up. His gratitude was touching. Whenever he saw us he would rouse himself to a short-lived frenzy, giving little shrieks of warning to the parrots, whirling his sling, and dancing like some brittle old dust devil.

He never left the mango grove except to go to the well, a few hundred yards away; there he lowered his brass *lotah* at the end of its rope while the gardener watched and muttered vindictively from a distance. Once, when he was watching, the gardener said to my brother and me, 'The mangoes have always been *my* responsibility. Now word will get round and the presence of this old fool will be a direct invitation to thieves and trespassers.'

Mahala seemed quite unconscious of the diverse effects which his arrival inspired within our household. He lived a strange, aloof existence under his trees, among birds and squirrels and butterflies and big black ants. In a little while a queer friendship grew up between the three of us – Mahala, my brother, and myself. It was, I think, based on the inarticulate, unconscious affinity which sometimes exists between youth and old age. We stood on separate thresholds, on the brink of separate mysteries, yet our minds were curiously akin. We children never hesitated to laugh when he missed the insolent parrots and uttered bloodcurdling threats against any harmless stranger who entered the premises, but he never resented our laughter; in fact, he liked to make us laugh. And when we did what was forbidden us, when we climbed the laden branches and ate the unripe fruit and were secretly ill, Mahala said nothing. When we tormented the gardener and threw stones at the well bullocks to make them kick, Mahala's eyes shone with a childish glee.

We never found out anything about his past, and as a matter of fact we did not dare ask him questions about it, for we had acquired an almost superstitious feeling toward him. In our eyes he stood as unique, far removed from the dull category of ordinary adults. We were convinced that he must be five hundred years old, and the thought made us breathless and dreamy. Occasionally, stirred by interest, he would give us a peculiarly intimate and loving glance, and we knew that he understood us as no one else could ever understand.

One day when we went out to the mango grove we found Mahala standing alone beside the well. He turned dejectedly and held out a length of rope. 'It broke as I was drawing it up, and now my *lotah* lies at the bottom!'

We examined the rope, which was a new one; it was obvious that it had been partially cut by a sharp knife and that someone had cut it intentionally. Our suspicions centred at once on the gardener, but there was little use in voicing them, since the accusations of children or of beggarly old parasites would carry small weight. However, we wrought a slight revenge by filling the gardener's shoes with marmalade stolen from the dining-room cupboard and by promising Mahala a new *lotah* at the earliest opportunity.

A few days later we noticed that he no longer wore his black quilted jacket. 'It is gone,' he confessed, and made a despairing glance. 'While I slept, it disappeared.'

Abdul the bearer clicked his teeth impatiently. 'The old man is deaf and almost blind. Thieves could come and take the shoes off his feet and he would never know it.'

'Besides,' said the *ayah*, jingling her glass bracelets, 'he gets paid for doing nothing. Let him buy himself another jacket.'

In spite of stern threats from our parents to the other servants, neither the *lotah* nor the jacket was ever retrieved. My brother and I tied knots in Abdul's turban while he took his afternoon nap and we seized every opportunity of discussing, in public, the *ayah*'s intrigue with the *syce*. But Mahala made no complaint. Crouched under the mango trees, he slept as the very old sleep, in fits and starts; by day he moved from tree to tree, berating the birds who hid their green bodies among the green fruit, or else he crept up with awful intent on native boys who occasionally trespassed too close to his beloved grove.

In the meantime the mangoes were ripening, and when, hot from the sun, one fell at our feet, my brother and I ate it and washed the flat white seed, combing it clean so its white hairs stood up like the hackles of a wild boar. Then we pencilled eyes on it, and nostrils, and gave it to Mahala to console him. By way of return he made us each a little sling, with which we took pot shots at the other servants, in no way adding to their love for us or our protégé.

The days became blazing hot and we were not allowed to go out except in the early morning or when the sun had subsided; then the parrots fled in green tides to their distant roost and regiments of flying foxes took their place. Two months after Mahala's first appearance, Abdul and the gardener presented themselves just as we were sitting down to breakfast. In his most profound voice, Abdul exclaimed, 'The mangoes are gone!'

'Yes,' said the gardener. 'And with them – Mahala!'

We stared in stupefaction. 'The mangoes are gone? Mahala gone? You must be mad!'

'Then come and see for yourselves. It was a put-up job. His friends came in the night and footprints in the dust show that there were several, all of them as agile as monkeys. They must have brought baskets and sacks and they have carried off every mango in the grove.'

The entire household streamed out to the grove. Mahala was gone, but the straw mat which had kept dew and showers off our old friend was still there; so were the blanket and a few odds and ends. Everyone was talking at once and there was a general, jubilant air of I told you so.

'This is what comes of trusting strangers,' said the *ayah*, jingling the bracelets which the *syce* had given her.

'True,' agreed the *syce*, who regularly stole the horses' grain and sold it in order to pay for the bracelets. 'No question but that the old man was ringleader of a hardened band of *budmashes*.'

We gazed desperately at our parents and my brother inquired, 'If Mahala was a thief, why did he leave the blanket?'

'Something in that,' said my father, frowning.

I ventured, 'He must have been asleep when the thieves came. Then, when he woke up and found the mangoes gone, he went away because he was ashamed and frightened and he wouldn't have known what to say to us.' I had not thought of this until I started to speak, but suddenly I knew it to be the truth.

'Bah!' said Abdul. 'You argue like children! There is nothing for it but to summon the police. Mahala is too old to have gone far. The police will soon find him.'

'No!' cried my brother. He stood rigid, his face crimson. 'No!'

The Mangoes Are Gone

'Now listen,' begged my mother appeasingly.

'No!' My brother flung himself on the ground and began to writhe and bite his clothes. Already trembling, I caught the contagion and began to scream too, at the top of my lungs. The servants drew away in a frightened bunch as our hysterics drove every bird and squirrel into hiding. My father finally succeeded in making his voice heard above the din. 'Stop it! Stop it at once!'

We went on screaming. 'No no no no no!'

'*Aré!*' wailed the *ayah*. 'Do not let them cry. They always make themselves sick.'

'Stop it, stop it, stop it!' yelled my father furiously.

'*No no no no no!*'

My mother put one arm round me and shrieked to make herself heard. 'No one is going to hurt Mahala. We know it was not he that stole the mangoes.'

'Then promise!' raved my brother, with further demented squirmings.

'Good God!' said Abdul. 'Are the mangoes gone or are they not gone?'

My brother's voice and mine rose excruciatingly. 'Promise! Promise! Promise!'

'I promise, we promise. No one will touch Mahala. Now for heaven's sake, stop this noise!'

Hot, sobbing, and breathless, we were led back to the house. The mangoes were gone; next year there would be another crop, but as for Mahala, we never saw or heard of him again.

CHRISTINE WESTON
Mimosa

This story was told me years ago by my mother, when we were revisiting the place where it all happened.

In the year 1900, my father, at that time an official in the British Indian Police, was stationed at a place called Basti, in the United Provinces. My mother was with him, and their first child, my brother, was soon to be born. Basti was an unimportant civil station. Social life centred in the Club, where the English contingent gathered to play tennis and billiards, to exchange news and read the months-old magazines. They talked of home, of English gardens, of vanished friends and other days, recapturing the past, just as later – in another time and still another place – they would talk of Basti and of each other with a similar sense of loss, for memory is sometimes a kind of regret to which there is no end.

For my mother this was a tedious interlude because of her condition and because my father's duties took him far afield and sometimes days and weeks would pass before she saw him again. She whiled away the time by reading, by exchanging visits with the other English wives, and by taking long drives along the dusty Indian roads. The landscape was not especially interesting; sunbaked plain cut by an occasional *nullah*, or watercourse, and dotted with *babul*, the native mimosa, on whose feathery leaves the herd boys feed their goats. There were mud-walled villages set off the highway and reached by rough cart tracks; it was to these villages, and to others more distant that my father's work took him in pursuit of bandits and other criminals, and he usually had an exciting story to tell when he came home. About ten miles from Basti stood the jungle, famous in earlier times for panthers and tigers and wolves, but generations of hunters had killed them off or driven them away, and forest life had become almost as tame as social life at the Club.

As the weeks passed, my mother went less often to the Club, preferring long drives in the trap, drawn by her favourite horse, a lively chestnut. With her maid, the *ayah*, for company and a groom perched behind, she drove for miles, and as she drove she thought of England, of her parents, and of summers spent by the sea when she was a little girl. Sometimes a tremendous homesickness came over her and her sensibilities were so quickened that she could recapture voices, incidents, tastes, and perfumes long forgotten. Her favourite drive took her beyond the cantonment, into the open country. After a few minutes' brisk driving, she was in the middle of a vast plain dotted with trees. The road became the channel for her meditations and interior soliloquies, so that afterward, when she recalled a thought she'd had, the recollection brought with it every detail of the surrounding country. The horse, said my mother, soon learned to head for this road, and they would ride until they reached a particular landmark once casually selected by her – a mimosa tree, black and twisted, its fanglike thorns hidden amid the delicate foliage and clusters of yellow flowers.

When my mother had driven as far as this tree, she would pull the horse to a stop and they'd turn and start back at an exciting clip, the horse knowing that its stable and supper waited at the end of the ride. They came here so often that the horse soon got to know the mimosa and, at first glimpse of it, would slow down and attempt to turn about. This amused my mother, who would engage in a tussle to keep him headed toward the tree. The *ayah* and the groom were equally amused by the game, and whenever they sighted the tree and the horse began to jib, they'd exclaim, 'Ah, the lazy good-for-nothing!' 'Give him a taste of the whip, Memsahib!' Occasionally, in order to drive the lesson home, my mother would halt the trap beside the tree and force the impatient animal to wait while she gazed around her at the plain and smelt the warm breath of the mimosa as it drifted against her face. She remarked that this sudden, wild, furred scent reminded her of a fox barking at night, and decided that scent and sound must have something in common.

One afternoon during my father's absence, my mother went for one of her drives, and as they came abreast of the mimosa tree, the horse gave a snort and shied violently. My mother pulled him up and disciplined him with a cut from the whip, then looked to see what had excited him. Something moved under the tree and a very small child stepped forward. He was dressed in the usual half-yard of rag, with a tiny trinket on a string round his neck; he might have been five or six, though age is difficult to gauge in Indian children. When he saw my mother, he said something in Hindustani, and the *ayah* exclaimed, 'Impertinence!'

'What does he want?' asked my mother, who understood the language but had not heard what he said.

The child addressed her in a low voice: 'Take me with you.'

'Where do you live?' she asked, and without removing his gaze from her he answered. 'Over there, across the field and beyond the *nullah*.' My mother looked beyond the watercourse and saw, about two miles away, the mud roofs of a little village.

'But that is not far,' she told him, 'and there is no road for me to drive you there. Why don't you go back as you came?'

'Because I am afraid.'

'Afraid of what?'

He hesitated, and now she saw that he was shivering, although the air was very warm. The *ayah* interposed sharply, 'Pay no attention, Memsahib. He just wants a ride so that he can go home and boast of it to his friends.'

'No,' whispered the child. He seemed unable to speak out, nor would he glance in any direction except toward my mother.

She said, 'Tell us what it is you fear.'

'For three days it has followed me.'

'What has followed you?'

'The thing.'

'What thing?'

'The *bagh*.'

In that part of India, *bagh* means tiger, and my mother joined the servants in their laughter. 'Silly child,' said the *ayah*. 'There has been no *bagh* here for years before you were born. The *sahib-log* have killed them all. Someone has been telling you stories.'

My mother added, 'It is silly to listen to such tales. Now run along home. We'll wait here until you're out of sight.'

He stared sadly, fixedly into her face. 'Take me with you,' he repeated.

At this point the horse, restless from the long delay, whirled suddenly and set its face toward home. My mother had a vision of the child as something very small, inarticulate, and helpless; then the horse put its head down and tried to bolt and she had her mind and her hands fully occupied until she reached home. But that night the memory of the child kept recurring to her and she could not sleep.

Next afternoon she drove out as usual, hoping to get a glimpse of him, but he was not under the tree, or anywhere in sight. The plain lay brown and peaceful under her gaze, and a weight lifted from her spirit, a weight which must have been heavier than she had acknowledged to herself, and when, on the ride home, a great mangy dog peered at her from a ditch and sent her temperamental horse into a gallop, she let him have his head, laughing at the servants' frightened protests.

The following day my father returned. He had been held up an entire evening, he said, by something that occurred at a village on his way home. The villagers had greeted him with the news that one of their children, a boy of six, had just been killed by a wolf. The distraught parents explained how the child had come to them and insisted that he was being stalked by something, but when they asked him what it looked like, he said it was a tiger. They laughed and told him that there were no tigers within several hundred miles, and sent him away, telling him to go tend to his duties with the goats. Then last evening, when he and the other herd boys were driving their goats home, a pair of wolves suddenly appeared among them; one seized this child, and both vanished with him down a dry *nullah*.

The brutes must have wandered down from the jungle and selected the outskirts of this village for their stalking ground. No one had seen them before that evening, but two or three goats had disappeared mysteriously and the village dogs had seemed more than usually restless. The child, who had never seen a tiger or a wolf in his life, had no way of making his story believed. They would probably have paid even less attention if he had said wolf instead of tiger. He felt that he was being relentlessly dogged, and he was right. With the instinct of their breed for selecting a particular victim and waiting for the chance to make their kill, the wolves had singled him out from all the other children of the village.

Whenever my mother told me this story she ended on a wistful note: 'Even if I had saved him that first time, wouldn't *they* have got him sooner or later? But if only I had known, if only I had believed him!'

Biographical Notes

FLORA ANNIE STEEL, *née* Webster (1847–1927): Born at Harrow-on-the-Hill, she married a member of the Indian Civil Service and left for India in 1868. During the next twenty-two years she served India in various capacities and, unlike most of the Anglo-Indian ladies of the time, managed to establish relations with Indians of all classes. She returned to England in 1889 and wrote numerous novels: the finest of these being *The Potter's Thumb* (1894) and *On the Face of the Waters* (1896) – the latter a fine study of the Indian Mutiny. She is equally well known for her collection of short stories *From the Five Rivers* (1893), *The Flower of Forgiveness* (1894), *In the Permanent Way and Other Stories* (1898) and *In the Guardianship of God* (1903).

BITHIA MARY CROKER (c. 1850–1920): Little is known about her. She was the daughter of a rector in County Roscommon, Ireland, and wife of Lieutenant-Colonel John Croker of the Royal Scots and the Royal Munster Fusiliers. She spent fourteen years in India and Burma and wrote some twenty romances set in India. Among these are *Proper Pride* (1882), *Mr Jervis: a Romance of the Indian Hills* (1894), and *Cat's Paw* (1902) – dealing with club life in South India. Her short story in this collection is from *In the Kingdom of Kerry and Other Stories* (1896).

SARA JEANNETTE DUNCAN (1862–1922): Born in Brantford, Ontario, Canada, and educated there and in Toronto, she turned to journalism after a brief spell at teaching. She wrote for the Toronto *Globe* and the Montreal *Star*, using the pseudonym 'Garth Grafton'. In 1891 she married Charles Everard Cotes and went to live in India where her husband was the curator of the Indian Museum in Calcutta. Although she was not primarily interested in portraying the Indians, her novels give a brilliant insight into the lives of the British in India. Among these are *The Simple Adventures of a Memsahib* (1893), *His Honour and a Lady* (1896) and *The Burnt Offering* (1909). She wrote only four short stories, published under the title *The Pool in the Desert* (1903).

ETHEL WINIFRED SAVI, *née* Bryning (1865–1954): Born in Calcutta of British and American parents, she was educated privately at home. Married at eighteen, she spent the first twelve years of her married life in rural Bengal on the Ganges. While in India she wrote short stories for English and Indian journals, but on retiring to England in 1909 she took to writing full-length novels, averaging some two per year to a grand total of over ninety books. Her story, 'The Interloper', is from the volume *Mixed Cargo* (1932), which also has stories (though not about India) by Charles Barry.

ALICE PERRIN (1867–1934): Born in India, she belonged to the Old John Stock Company, her father being General John Innes Robinson of the Bengal Cavalry. She married a medical officer of the Indian Civil Service in 1886, and with him spent twenty-five years in India. Almost all her novels are about India, but she is at her best in the short story. Her most successful collections, *East of Suez* (1901), *Red Records* (1906) and *Rough Passages* (1926), reveal a gentle irony and humour rarely found in Anglo-Indian literature. After her return from India she lived in Switzerland until her death.

MAUD DIVER, *née* Marshall (1867–1945): Born at Murree, a hill-station in the Himalayas, and sent by her parents to England for schooling, she returned to India at the age of sixteen. She married a subaltern in the Royal Warwickshire Regiment and soon after left for England again. It was in England that she began writing her many novels of Anglo-India and of the British heroism in India. Her first novel, *Captain Desmond VC*, was an immediate success, but she is equally well known for *The Englishwoman in India* (1909) – a balanced defence of the rôle played by the memsahib in India.

KATHERINE MAYO (1868–1940): Born of American parents in Ridgeway, Pennsylvania, she was educated at private schools in Boston and Cambridge, Massachusetts. She made her mark in the United States with *Justice to All* (1917), but it was *Mother India* (1927), a sensational study of child marriage in India, with which her name is chiefly associated. Several rebuttals were published by indignant Indians, and *Volume Two* (1931) was Miss Mayo's documented defence of her statements. Her collection of stories *Slaves of the Gods* (1929) was, she claimed, 'not fiction, although cast in fiction form'.

CHRISTINE WESTON (1904–   ): Born in Unao in the United Provinces, the daughter of a naturalized Englishman in the Indian Imperial Police, she was educated at a convent school in the hills, and lived in India until her marriage to an American in 1923. She started publishing in the early forties, and her novel *Indigo* (1944) has been compared to E. M. Forster's *A Passage to India* for its authenticity and understanding of the complexity of the Indian problem. She has also published some of the best stories on the Raj in a collection entitled *There and Then* (1947).

Glossary of Indian Words and Phrases

Ai Khoda: oh, God!
Ai tobah: oh shame!
Allah: name of God among Muhammadans
Aré, Ari: oh!
Ayah: Indian nanny; lady's maid

Baba: respectful address for an old man or a father
Baba-logue: children
Baboo-jee, Babu-jee: a learned man; term of respect
Backshish: a gift; present
Badmash, Budmash: rogue
Badshah: King
Belait: England
Brahman, Brahmin: member of the highest caste among Hindus
Bullah: an exclamation
Bunnia-lôg: shopkeeper; member of the merchant class
Busli: a kind of musical instrument

Chota: young, small
Competition-wallah: a member of the Indian Civil Service selected through competition as opposed to appointment by favour

Dâk: the palässa tree
Dáli: wicker basket
Dhatura: a narcotic plant
Dhoby: washerman
Dhooli: a covered litter carried by people
Durbari: courtier (from *Durbar* – a royal court)

Fakir: Muslim religious mendicant. Used equally for Hindu religious mendicant as in 'The Fakirs' Island'
Farâsh: medium-size tree found in northern India

Hazúr, Huzoor: Sire; also, abstractedly, the Government
Hindustani: language spoken in north India
Hookah: hubble-bubble
Hut: move off

Imâm: Muslim high priest

Jai Káli Ma: hail, black goddess
Jât: people widely distributed in northwest India, mostly Hindus, and given to cultivation
Ját: caste
Jawab: dismissal

Jee: often used as a suffix denoting respect
Jharan: cloth for dusting
Jheel: swamp; a sheet of shallow water
Jhilmil: window shutter; venetian blind

Kachari: law courts; Government offices
Kaiser-i-Hind: Imperial title assumed by Queen Victoria in 1877
Káli: malevolent black goddess requiring propitiation through sacrifice
Karait, krait: a highly poisonous snake
Khânjee: term of respect for a Muslim
Khansama, khansamah: cook
Kismet: fate
Koi hai: is anyone there?

Lât-sahib: a high official, a governor or Viceroy
Lotah: tumbler, usually of brass or copper

Mahratta: a once numerous and dominant race in Maharashtra
Mai: mother
Máli: gardener
Momerogun: wax polish

Ná: no
Nautch: dancing girl
Nimuk haram: false to one's salt, a traitor
Nullah: river-bed

Pipal: large Indian fig-tree allied to banyan, bo-tree
Poggle, Pagul, Paghal: mad
Punkah: fan, properly one suspended from the ceiling
Purdah: veil or curtain used to shelter women from male gaze
Purmêshwar: the Great God
Pyjamas: loose-fitting trousers

Quai hai: is anyone there?

Rajah: title of a Hindu prince
Ram: Hindu god
Ram! Ram!: a Hindu salutation
Râm rukkhi: thread tied by a Hindu woman on a man's wrist giving him the status of brother

Sahiban: plural for sahib
Sahib-log, sahib-logue: sahib people
Salaam: Indian salutation with bow of head and right palm raised to forehead
Seer: Indian unit of weight – about a kilogram
Sirkâr: Government: also a high government official
Sitar: a string musical instrument
Suar ka batcha: son of a pig
Subadar-major: chief Indian officer of company of sepoys
Syce: a stable groom

Vishnu: name of a major Hindu god
Vizier: high state official

Wah! exclamation of
appreciation or surprise
Wallah: signifies occupation;
person

Fiction by Women Writers in Stories from the Raj *(1983) and* More Stories from the Raj and After *(1986)*

FLORA ANNIE STEEL
Mussumât Kirpo's Doll
The Fakeer's Drum
The Reformer's Wife
Lâl
Heera Nund

BITHIA MARY CROKER
The Proud Girl

SARA JEANNETTE DUNCAN
A Mother in India

ALICE PERRIN
The Centipede
The Rise of Ram Din
The White Tiger
Justice

MAUD DIVER
The Gods of the East

KATHERINE MAYO
The Widow

CHRISTINE WESTON
A Game of Halma
The Devil Has the Moon